HE
THAT
IS
DOWN
NEED
FEAR
NO
FALL

He That Is Down Need Fear No Fall

BRUCE ARNOLD

ashfield PRESS

DUBLIN 2008

Published in 2008 by
ASHFIELD PRESS • DUBLIN • IRELAND

© Bruce Arnold, 2008

ISBN: 978-1-901658-70-5 HARDBACK
ISBN: 978-1-901658-71-2 SOFTBACK

A catalogue record for this book is available from the British Library.
All rights reserved. No part of this publication may be reproduced, stored in a
retrieval system or transmitted in any form or by any means, electronic,
mechanical, photocopying, recording or otherwise, without the prior,
written permission of the publisher.

This book is sold subject to the condition that it shall not, by way of trade
or otherwise, be lent, resold, hired out, or otherwise circulated without
the publisher's prior consent in any form of binding or cover other than that in
which it is published and without a similar condition, including this condition,
being imposed on the subsequent purchaser.

This book is typeset by Ashfield Press
in 11.5 on 14 point Adobe Garamond and Zapfino
Designed by SUSAN WAINE
Printed in Ireland by BETAPRINT LIMITED, DUBLIN

Contents

PROLOGUE
Page 7

PART ONE
Till Voices Break
Page 13

PART TWO
Learning to Love
Page 109

PART THREE
A Time of Crisis
Page 179

PART FOUR
An End to Affairs
Page 239

What a lot of things I have to tell you, some of them happy and others sad. My letters are a faithful history of my life, more or less. It would need a lot of courage to reveal everything.

DENIS DIDEROT to SOPHIE VOLLAND
Paris, 14 July 1762

And he shall turn the heart of the fathers to the children, and the heart of the children to their fathers, lest I come and smite the earth with a curse.

MALACHI, Chapter IV, Verse 6

PROLOGUE

A Box of Letters

A box of letters lies before me. All are love letters written by my father, George Arnold, to one person, Barbara Young. The earliest of them dates from well over half a century ago. The last of them was written in 1975, shortly before his death. The nature of his love was to adore and the strength of it is at times palpable. George yearned for Barbara and depended on her. They never married; yet in the time of these letters he married two other women, had affairs, 'lost' her, in the sense that she went away from him; found her again. And when he first met her he was still married to his first wife, Connie, with whom he had had two children, followed by five other children, with Margaret, my mother, who had died in 1943. The break-up of his first marriage was in part due to his drinking; his failure to hold his family together after my mother's death was also due largely to drink. He carried with him, from the start, a damaged reputation. The pitch of his affection, the intensity of it, was a reassuring discovery – when the letters came to me – of a kind of constancy not really characteristic of him and therefore surprising. It was a constancy of such bizarre character, such funny, sad episodes and so woeful a narrative, as to leave me now, years on, with laughter on my lips and tears in my eyes. When Barbara died in 2003, her nephew and one of her nieces went through her possessions and found that she had kept all the letters, cards and notes she had received from George. She threw nothing of his away. They considered what to do with them and in the end took the trouble to contact me and to offer to return them. I bless them for this thoughtful and kind decision. At first I dipped into them, very tentatively, expecting to find painful endorsement of my memories of them, which were all about the fact that they never found lasting happiness together. And I did find such an endorsement, extensively spread over all those years. I rediscovered the sad uncertainty of his life. I read enough to see that the story was a painful one, and that much of his life during the period covered was unhappy. After that I left them for many months untouched. The early letters were uncertain. He had gone through many difficulties from the time of my mother's death in 1943 and they reminded me of my own unhappiness during that period, up to the beginning of the 1950s. The envelopes, the paper, the stamps – with George VI's still youthful profile persisting well after his sad death, and then being succeeded by that of his daughter, Queen Elizabeth II – are redolent of the period. The odour of time rises from them. Beyond that I realised the further truth; within this box lay a new interpretation of my life from childhood up to the point when I had established myself as a writer. Much of my own growth and development was there in casual references, proud comments, comparisons of me with other siblings, and his recollection of experiences from many years before. By the time I came back and engaged on the fuller journey through the past, using the letters as signposts, and travelling through three lives – his, mine and Barbara's – I had become charged with the energy emanating from his words. He was a passionate man, full of vitality and energy. In different ways these qualities are constant throughout the correspondence. She was rather different; hesitant, puzzled and uncertain. I corresponded with her towards the end of his life and she wrote to me of her love for him. Still later, after his death, we exchanged occasional letters and cards and I visited her. She would invariably speak of him, and always with love, though her affection and her recollections were all the time tinged with laughter. Why this was so will appear in these pages. In part that view of him seemed to be provoked by the image she had of his impossible, irredeemable character. He loomed before her, as he did before me, a giant among men. And whatever her mixed and puzzled feelings, they were strong enough for her to keep every missive he sent her, every fragment of paper, scribbled with orders, exhortations, messages of love. She never told me of the letters nor showed them to me. I wonder did she look at them herself from time to time? I rather think not. It makes me wonder as well why people keep such things. They are like shreds of our own tissue, parts of us that cannot be thrown away. Yet few enough people preserve such material, and those who come after often fail to recognise what it is they find, how much letters can matter and what they should do with them.

Happily for me, this was not the case with Barbara's letters. They begin with drama. As the second letter indicates, George's entire future was at stake. He was floundering, and he was reaching out to her. I was a close witness of that, a close witness of all that followed. I was indeed his closest witness, over a number of years; and the beginning of these events came at a time for me of youthful vulnerability and uncertainty. The events took place throughout my childhood and youth. The force and strength of my father's personality, the intensity of his passion and the tenderness of his love, leave me feeling now as I felt then: that I was the witness of a great movement forward in his feelings and his affections, and in his life, though it was a movement towards nowhere in particular. George had great strength of purpose, but never grasped what the purpose really was.

All George's hopes and fears were wrapped up in his many declarations of love for Barbara. There were brief exceptions to this, but in the flow of the story, which he wanted to write to her even when there was little enough to tell her, there is a compulsive love underpinning his actions. He was the human, vulnerable manifestation of the philosophic concept of solipsism. He bullied and harassed my eldest brother, failed my sisters and criticised them for their mistakes. There were terrible lurches and blunders in what he did. In his final years he was surrounded by a situation little short of absurd.

Yet I loved him all this time. Barbara loved him as well. I knew of the love in the early years of these letters. I was by his side much of the time, but even I knew only in part and only for the early years. I had no sense of it at all later. Thus it is that receiving the letters has meant so much and has proved so much as well: that the love meant a great deal to both George and Barbara, that she gave happiness and purpose to his life and that their passion for each other lasted through quarter of a century.

The letters are uncertain at first. He was unsure of himself, lacking in confidence. The early phrases and sentences offer a picture of this, combined with the strong determination to make something of his life. He never did. That part of the story ends in failure. But the rage for it within him is like the rumbling of distant thunder presaging storms, or the gathering of dark grey clouds and the first heavy drops of rainfall in one's face that shorten the warning and then end it.

Three of us made the journey. Others were involved. There

PROLOGUE

were other women. But I shared in my father's life, and he shared his life with Barbara, and Barbara and I loved him and cared for each other's fate. There were letters because we were all in different places. I was in England, Germany, finally Ireland. Barbara was in London, France, Cyprus, Egypt. Jobs took George all over England. The whole period of that epistolary life lasted for twenty-five years, the letters coming to an end with his death in 1975. But the story did not close until much later and though the first of his letters to her was written and sent in 1951, the story itself, for various reasons, stretches back more or less to the beginning of that century, to his days at King's School, Canterbury, to the time before the Great War, his career in the Royal Navy, and then the wasted years after he had left the Service.

I was fourteen when George first wrote to Barbara. I was in love with her because he was. Whenever I think of that time, I think of it through the prism of adolescent love. I shared with him a strange, itinerant life. My childhood was made up at times of criss-crossing England with him from place to place, following him wherever he went, finding my home wherever he was. For a time, early on with Barbara, there was the promise of stability. Then that ended. As I grew up, my father's wanderings went on. He lived and worked here and there in England, writing letters, yearning to be settled, longing for the jobs that he took to last, to work out, and they never did. They left him poor, vulnerable, and then on the move again. I was part of this during some of the years, as I was part of the correspondence. In it I discover myself, going here and there. I do things at school or with my friends which are commented on by him to her, and brought back to me, often from an entirely forgotten sequence of events. Certainly, in the early years, the comments are full of love for me and are accepted warmly as such by her; later, he became more critical. I am drawn into the story and I am able to add to it.

My father did not have friends. In one letter, from a job he had in a country club, he wrote to Barbara saying, 'Have met quite a lot of people but none I would call a friend – in fact I am not a friendly type.' And that indeed was the case. It was not in his nature. Too self-obsessed, he did not have the patience or the forbearance. He was without the art or skill of friendship, and always in too much of a hurry.

The speed of his judgement about events, and then of his execution of the necessary acts, is evident throughout the correspondence. He came to conclusions – about himself, about Barbara, about me – and then wanted to turn these conclusions immediately into new paths in our lives. Often it did not suit us. At times this was comical. At other times, unhappily, it was tragic.

Living with him formed me. It shaped my mind. It was a close relationship, made exclusive by his attitude to his other children and also by his failure with them. I saw at close quarters all the relationships he had. I was under his guard, closer than anyone, even the women. At the outset of this story it placed me in a position of privilege that has never really changed. I hope the letters, and what I draw from them, confirm this.

PART ONE

Till Voices Break

I

George wrote to Barbara from Sanderstead, in Surrey, on 9 February 1951:

Dear Barbara,
I won't be up tomorrow, Saturday, and on Sunday I think I will go to the concert which makes it rather late for coming up in the evening – so let's leave it till next week sometime – I'll try and get the ballet tickets one lunchtime next week. Will any day suit you? You have the programme. Also, my dear Barbara, I am beginning to agree with you that it is not good to see each other too often – I'm afraid it's like flogging a dead horse from my point of view and not pleasant for you.
Goodbye now,
Yours, George

It was his first letter to her. The tone could not be described as auspicious for a love affair. Whatever he was doing at that time, it was not going well. I had come home from school to spend the Christmas of 1950 with him. We were in lodgings in Sanderstead, and I remember the time, if not in a negative way exactly, as being without any real excitement or joy. I suspect that he was working in a school, possibly as a caretaker or odd-job man, which was one of his favoured options at that time. I think he chose such jobs in part because of me. I was too young to be able to look after myself, or to work independently of him, which became normal during later holidays. And in that setting, a suburb of London, I was probably something of a burden. What he chose to do was designed to give him free time during my holidays, though no doubt at some financial cost.

I remember the cramped little suburban house, the self-effacing and nervous landlady. She was respectful in her way of the faded gentility that I imagine surrounded the two of us. She had no other lodgers; the house was too small. She agreed to my practising on my violin, and I can see myself, sitting on the bed, the violin under my chin, the music propped up in some way, as I worked at one of Carse's studies. I'm sure I played Bach's 'Air on a G String'. I like to think of the mournful but attractive – even haunting – tune, perpetually part of the musical memory of anyone who plays the violin, echoing through the otherwise empty house and reaching the woman in the kitchen. It would have pleased my father on his return to find me, bow in hand, cradling the instrument. Yet the picture it gives me now is unconvincing, even slightly false. I was no child prodigy. I was a lonely, puzzled fourteen-year-old. I had come home from the frugal and austere life at Kingham Hill School, in the Cotswolds. I don't know what I had hoped for, but it was not there in his present circumstance. I remember the Christmas in Sanderstead and the bleakness of things there. Even the name makes me think of it in those terms. It was neither country nor town. The place had no shape, no purpose to it. It is, in my memory, lost territory. It is one of the places to which I have never returned, notwithstanding my curiosity about my own past.

And yet it was only a very short distance from the Waldrons, the tear-shaped double crescent of houses in

PART ONE

Croydon where I was born and where I lived until the death of my mother in 1943. It is quite possible my father and I walked to the Waldrons and revisited the house, number 21, and other places of my early childhood. My father suffered seriously from nostalgia all his life; never so much as during this period, as his letters will indicate. And the names of the places around Mayfield Road, in Sanderstead, are still to me reminiscent of the walks we made as a family, on Sunday afternoons, in the parkland off Purley Way or over towards Shirley and Lloyd Park.

Irene was there, somewhere in the background. She had been part of the previous Christmas of 1950, as she had of the two earlier Christmases. Irene Spindlo had been an attendant figure upon George for just over three years, but not significantly so just at that time. I think this may have had something to do with Barbara, though I cannot be sure. Uncertainty about Irene on his part would have added to my sense of the bleakness of things. My father never loved Irene Spindlo; yet, even more than Barbara, she was part of his story then and later, and she remained an important part of almost everything he did until his death. In respect of Barbara, Irene was the alternative woman in his life, soon to be partially displaced, but never disappearing completely. She is very much part of the more precise story contained within the letters. She is there at the beginning; she was to be there at the very end. Displaced she may have been; eclipsed, never.

Irene was born in Crawford, Nebraska in 1905 and was seven years younger than my father. She was the only child of a Chicago-trained dentist who had come out to the great dental school in that city – perhaps the greatest in the world at the time – and had then taken up practice in Nebraska. There he met and married Jessie Rowland, a schoolteacher.

He returned to work in Germany with his wife and daughter when Irene was still a child and then came back to England where he practised quite successfully for the rest of his life. Irene, who trained to be a secretary before World War II, had worked in various places, eventually taking a job at Kingham Hill School, working for the warden, in 1946. She met my father when he came for Prize Day in the summer of 1947. She fell hopelessly in love with him. I say hopelessly because the love was never reciprocated; yet she was always there to help him until the end of his life, and he almost always needed help.

At the time of their meeting, George was in charge of a Polish Military Camp containing some sixty Polish soldiers who had fought in Europe. The soldiers had been brought back to Britain and were awaiting repatriation, a life in some part of Britain, or a new life in America elsewhere.

Irene followed him wherever he went. After the job in the Polish camp, he went to London. She went too and worked for a London stockbroker. They lived together 'as husband and wife', separating when I came home on holiday but with Irene still very much present, trying to make Christmas into a festive event. She was not very good at it. One memory I have is of a treasure hunt in the impersonal surroundings of the double bed-sitting room in which they had lived before the holiday, and which my father and I now occupied. I still remember feeling that the attempts at entertainment were somewhat banal.

From the start I knew the relationship to be a difficult, unevenly balanced one; he slightly bored with her, polite and even attentive, both for my sake and for his own material well-being, but restless and impatient in his inner spirit. She was doting and yet very correct. She wanted to be a mother to me, but I was troubled by my father's uncertainty and by what he

PART ONE

would say about her when we were not with her. Part of the privileged position I enjoyed was to hear from him his views about all the people we knew, but particularly about Irene. I think he was vexed, even ashamed, of using her but not loving her and felt he needed to clarify this for me. I think he longed for an unforeseen circumstance that would change his life, and settled in the meanwhile for this half-hearted liaison. Barbara was to become the unforeseen circumstance.

His relationship with Irene was probably at its happiest in the autumn and winter of 1948. This was the time when they lived together in Clanricarde Gardens in London. Though this is a story concerned with another correspondence, there is one letter to Irene that has survived from that time. She kept it all her life until her death in her nineties. She told me about it in 1976, the year after his death. I had gone on a journey through parts of England, visiting the places he had worked in, calling on various people who had played a part in his life. On that occasion I said to her – and recorded the exact words – 'But tell me, would you have had it – the twenty-nine years – without him, if you could?' And of course the answer was 'No'. I have the letter and treasure it as a sad moment of near-possession in their life and love together. He says in it he is 'quite lonely' without her and he sends her love. This particular Christmas, two years before Sanderstead, saw the three of us together. I was twelve years old. Irene bought tickets for Covent Garden, a Christmas treat. We went on the Saturday evening of 8 January 1949, and saw Violetta Elvin dance the part of Cinderella in Prokofieff's ballet, Frederick Ashton and Robert Helpmann persecuting her as the Ugly Sisters.

In the summer of that year he went back to the Cotswolds and worked in a nursery that raised and marketed Alpine plants in Snowshill, a pretty village high in the Cotswold Hills above the small town of Broadway. The village was not far from my school and I spent a glorious summer holiday there. Again, Irene followed him and took a job as secretary to a building firm in Evesham. She lived in Broadway in order to be near him.

In March 1950 she returned to a job in London as private secretary to the banker Ernest Kleinwort, and that remained her job until she retired around 1965 with a generous pension. Her father had died about 1950 and for a time then she lived with her mother in East Sheen. My father gravitated back from the Cotswolds to London and the liaison with her went on. He did various jobs; I was towed along.

During that year, 1950, on my two holidays from school, at Easter and in the summer, we went to further performances at Covent Garden, and I mention it because of the reference in the Sanderstead letter – his first to Barbara – where he refers to tickets for the ballet. He formed a taste for what was undoubtedly lavish entertainment, always paid for by Irene and always involving stall seats in the Royal Opera House at Covent Garden, seats that cost the extravagant amount of 17s 6d. In April we saw the Sadler's Wells Ballet in *Swan Lake*, with Violetta Elvin as Odette and John Field as Siegfried, and in August of that year we saw the New York City Ballet dancing to music by Tchaikovsky, Stravinsky and Chabrier. George Balanchine was responsible for the choreography in all three ballets. Yet no programme remains in my possession for the Christmas of 1950 and it makes me wonder what went wrong.

I am also persuaded by this to think of my father's strange mixture of enthusiasms about music, theatre and entertainment. He had a keen and critical eye. He had a good ear. He also had a good voice. All this of course was part of an essentially amateur approach to entertainment, whether he was enjoying it or giving it. On these occasions of ballet I watched his keen attention and listened to his comments. As to the giving of entertainment, my memory is only of his soft, lilting baritone voice singing scraps of the songs he loved, often because they were hauntingly nostalgic, or quoting from some kind of set-piece poem like J. Milton Hayes's 'The Green Eye of the Yellow God'.

For some reason this evoked for him memories of his childhood in Calcutta – a long way from Kathmandu, it must be said – and he would deliver the picture of the broken-hearted woman tending the grave of Mad Carew with near-perfect recall of the emotional and dramatic story. At a time when the whole world seemed to gyrate to the best period of popular song and dance music in its history, my father's interest lay with songs like 'The Lily of Laguna' or Stoddard King's 'There's a Long, Long Trail A-Winding'. I can only remember him singing the chorus; indeed it is all that is memorable about the song, first sung in England when he was training on *HMS Worcester*. 'There's a long, long night of waiting until my dreams all come true; till the day when I'll be going down that long, long trail with you.' It breathed, on those occasions, of his heart's desire, about a land of dreams where nightingales sing and where the white moon beams. I became imbued with, and inspired by, the romantic yearning, not realising at the time, perhaps not realising until I read the letters so many years later, how poignant and how real the sentiments were for him. He wanted his dreams to come true; they didn't. He wanted finality in his union with the woman he loved; it never happened.

Whatever did happen at the end of 1950 – and I have no real understanding of what it was – created what was undoubtedly an unsatisfactory situation. I present it as the necessary though rather dull tapestry against which the coming drama would be played out. Real life began for me with the arrival of Barbara. Understanding why requires some sense of what went before. There was a predictability in Irene's slavish affection and in George's ultimate indifference towards her, which may have provoked some kind of crisis that Christmas.

Such a crisis was never the case with Barbara. It is this difference, in the way he looked upon these two women, which affected me so deeply and taught me so much. It made of this time a significant watershed, not so much in terms of events but in the understanding of how love transforms life. Many of the events were hidden from me. I was back at school when that first letter was written, on 9 February 1951. I knew nothing of the tantalising circumstances that provoked in my father the suggestion that they should not see each other too often. I would have recognised him using a phrase like 'flogging a dead horse'. It would have suited his view of Irene and himself. And all this must have been going on during that unmemorable Sanderstead Christmas as I sat on the bed playing my violin.

Life was being transformed and the coming richness of it was revealed to me, at the beginning, in small snatches of his prospective happiness as Barbara became the love of his life.

I knew he thought of Irene as boring. I knew he did not love her. I knew she adored him and that her love would go on, come what may, not just until the end of his life but until the end of hers as well. And so it turned out. I knew he would use her, as he did then. I suppose he was too vulnerable a person just to walk away and end it; end the relationship in all its emotional feebleness and have done with her forever. It would have been better for both of us. But it did not happen that

PART ONE

way, and Irene, introduced at the start of this narrative because she was the unsuitable and unloved alternative to Barbara, remained in the story throughout the next twenty-five years, playing at times a major role in the drama.

Unaware, then, of the true events at that time, as the Christmas of 1950 gave way to the coming year, I returned to school in the Cotswolds. Kingham Hill School is roughly equidistant between Chipping Norton and Stow-on-the-Wold. From the top of the hill on which the main school building stands, which is about 600 feet above sea level, both towns can be seen. Chipping Norton, which itself is on a hillside, is laid out on the slope facing the school and is more clearly visible, dominated by the great chimney stack above the Bliss Woollen Mills, once a main source of wealth and employment in the town. Stow in those days was quaint and old-fashioned, a relic of Cotswold market-town life; 'Chippy', as we called it, was bustling and busy, had two cinemas and modern shops like the Co-operative Store. My father had even worked there, in 1946, when he had been in charge of a German prisoner of war camp. I had been at the school since 1944. I went there six months after my mother's death.

I am able to recall readily enough my circumstances on my return there, late in January 1951, when the events of this story were really about to begin. The details are in my school reports; these I still have. They tell me that I had made 'a good start' on the violin. That had been in 1948, when I was in my twelfth year, and that I had made good progress thereafter. It is all recorded. My music master also wrote in that year: 'Musically he is very valuable to the school, but I have been a little disappointed this term.' What could that have been? Whatever it was, the air cleared and I went on doing well, not just in music but in all subjects.

By Easter 1951, when I came home again on holiday, my father had moved from Surrey into London. He was working at the London Bedding Centre in Knightsbridge and was living in Notting Hill Gate, in Pembridge Villas. His was not a nature to contemplate defeat. Though he had said, at the beginning of the year, that he and Barbara should part if the love were not there to bind them together, nevertheless he went on seeing her and expressing his love. He was determined to change her mind and make her love him. He drew me into this quest and soon I loved her too.

I must first have met her that Easter of 1951 when I was living with him in Notting Hill Gate, a place I came to know so well. I remember the evening journeys we took after he came home from Knightsbridge. The routine involved Irene, not Barbara. Irene was then living in or near Sloane Gardens. She took conscientious charge of my holiday, booking tickets to see the Ballet Rambert at the Wimbledon Theatre on 1 April and, further ahead, a gala occasion when we went to Ravel's *Daphnis and Chloe* at Covent Garden. It was the only occasion on which I saw Margot Fonteyn dance. When people present the conventional wisdom about how she changed after Nureyev, I think of the haunting magic of her performance then, transforming my understanding of the wonder of dance. As the captive shepherdess in the pirate den, expressing her longing for freedom and her love for Daphnis, she made the previous occasions with other dancers, in 1949 and 1950, seem events of a different genre. There was a pitiful, poignant sadness in her dancing, a physical liquidity I still remember. I was by way of being a connoisseur of ballet at the age of fourteen and this event was the high point of my experience.

Then one evening George announced to me that we would be visiting Barbara. Barbara? I was surprised at the suddenness of the announcement. What could it mean? He was not a man to explain in advance. I think he must have thought through his position, which was by no means as certain with Barbara as it was with Irene, and decided on a course of action. It was only a puzzle for a short time, a bus ride to Chelsea, and then that first meeting.

Immediately, I was captivated. It was instantly clear to me that this was an entirely different situation, one that was suffused with love. The first touch between them, the kiss and then my being introduced, all of it created waves of affection and warmth. Barbara declared that she had heard much about me, knew of my school, my interest in music and how well I was doing. She marvelled at the likeness between myself and my father, laughed in a gentle way, and was very welcoming. Shy of me, she seemed to be testing out the new emotional relationship. I looked round the room; saw the pictures on the wall, the soft light, the fading into darkness outside the windows where the curtains were not drawn.

He had obviously rung her and prepared her for this. She had supper more or less ready for us, and when she went into the kitchen to complete the preparations, she invited me to follow her and went on questioning me about what I planned to do with myself during the remaining days of my holiday.

Everything fell into place. The encounter was entirely free from the clumsiness I had generally experienced with Irene, who made obvious her view that I was not long out of childhood. Barbara was more subtle. Where Irene was boring, essentially and without much remission, Barbara was interesting, exciting, challenging and undeniably compassionate towards my awkward, youthful responses. She engaged my heart as she had engaged my father's heart, and there was no comparison to that, no challenge to it, from Irene. I felt twinges of guilt about it, then and later. I felt it on his behalf and on my own. But I realised a great change had happened and that I was directed towards a new life, still largely based on aspiration, but with fulfilment implicit in the warmth of that first encounter.

It turns out, in the light of the letters, that nothing, at that stage, had been resolved between them. They went on seeing each other. I went back to school. When I returned for the summer holidays that year, the encounters, just as happy, resumed. Not only that, I also met Barbara's sister Roberta and her three children and went away to stay with them for a weekend. It was the first encounter, the first broadening out of Barbara, into a family including children who, though younger than me, were natural holiday companions.

It therefore came as a surprise, when I read the second letter from George to Barbara, to see on how cold a note it began. Despite what I had witnessed, it seemed that little progress had been made in their love affair in the six months between the two letters. This second one was dated in the postmark 12 August 1951:

> 8 Pembridge Villas, London W11
> Saturday 9.30 p.m.
>
> Dear Barbara
> I am afraid it is so, but as you have no inclination of falling in love with me and as philandering is not really in my line, I think it would be better if we did not see each other.
>
> You know all the arguments and answers, So I won't repeat them except that I just worship you – but this would go on and on and on and we'd get nowhere and definitely I want to make some sort of show of the rest of my life without the eternal worry of hoping against hope – life together

PART ONE

would of course be grand for me and I should think fairly successful – if you can suggest anything constructive or hopeful, let's have – otherwise ...

Bruce is having a good time at Folkestone but he really enjoyed his weekend with you – I am going down tomorrow for the day and shall have a good chinwag with Peggy [his sister] and come back by the 8 something train – I am glad the children liked Bruce and perhaps he'll see them again sometime.

Business has been good this week and today I took over £300, making £600 for the week, but I still want more and am gradually building my clientele up – I saw a Jew last night about his garden and may go and work for him in my spare time to get extra money free of tax if he pays me the amount I want – big house in Avenue Road, Regent's Park – The more work and occupation I get the better I shall feel (+ the money), especially as it is certainly going to be hard for the next week or so until my thoughts tone down a bit – I hope you enjoyed the day with your friends, although it rained.

And now goodbye.

You have every ounce of love I have,

George

The 'business' he referred to was the London Bedding Centre in Knightsbridge where he was a salesman. He was good at selling, but I suspect his pay and the commission on sales were modest and, as the letter indicates, he needed to supplement them with his work as a jobbing gardener. Looking back, I realise, despite 'every ounce of love', that the love affair itself could have ended there. He was a decisive man. It is clear from the earlier letter, in February, that the trial period between them had already gone on for some time – the flogging of the dead horse – and was getting nowhere. How long this was so will remain always a matter for conjecture.

Instead of signing off, however, he began to lay before

He That Is Down Need Fear No Fall

Barbara a strange enticement; that she should become a witness of all that he did. He did not do it obviously, or at that time as far as I knew, but he set in motion a new departure or direction to their exchanges. He linked the appeal of his love for her – so far unrequited – with what sounded like a last desperate throw at life itself. He was, after all, fifty-three years old, with a chequered pattern of work behind him. No one would even call what he did a career as such. There were no great prospects ahead. He was effectively penniless, had no savings and no reserves. He relied simply on the power of his hands and arms, and perhaps as well on the appeal of his charm.

George was a man of great charm. He had good looks; rugged, it must be said – those of a warrior. There was the battered evidence in his face of struggle and uncertainty, but he spoke beautifully and had a soft and gentle tone to his voice. Supple, of average height, not overweight, he moved with an easy, fluid step, springy, as though balanced against the moving deck of a remembered vessel from his years as a Royal Navy officer.

George was telling Barbara, in those early letters, what Denis Diderot told Sophie Volland when he said to her, 'There is nothing which brings me closer to you than to tell you everything and by my words to make you a spectator of my life.' What he was doing to her, then, was what he had done to me all along. By choosing me, the one child he thought he could manage as a remnant of his dismembered family, he had made me so inescapably the spectator of his life. And it was not a life that would ever be easy to survey or witness. Countless others have been placed in similar positions. Witnessing each other's lives is the condition of all life. The desire for it is a mainspring of the operating mechanism by which we love each other. It is evident from his letters that he wanted that. It is evident from my testimony that it inspired so much of his feeling towards me and so much of his conversation – remembered still over so many years now distant and cut off by his death – and reinforced now, in that memory, by what I have written.

The setting down of events that became the material for my first novel, *A Singer at the Wedding*, the rearranging of their order and importance, inevitably involving the creation of imagined situations and imagined people to help forward the main story, always came back to him and Barbara as a primary inspiration. By the time this relationship was established, throwing into sharp relief the place of Irene in his and therefore in my life, the details of the fictional 'story' were in place. It would be years before I recognised the fact. A particular trigger was needed, an event that would release the floodgate of telling. And in due course it was delivered. But by 1951, what I came to need twenty-five years later was all more or less experienced and stored up in my memory. I cannot otherwise understand it as a human phenomenon. In similar circumstances people seek to forget and successfully do forget. Why or how I did the opposite, and did it so relentlessly, remains a puzzle to me.

Perhaps part of the answer is that I so wanted to be the witness he had made me. It was a demand that I willingly obeyed. I wanted to keep my eye on him and be with him during these perpetual vicissitudes through which he struggled, heaving himself up out of one set of complicated circumstances only to plunge on into another. Inescapably, it was the main activity of my life, whether I was with him or away at school. And nothing else that I did was as compelling or as magnetic.

This would change and I would move on. Another life did beckon. Other horizons were being shaped for me, notably by events at school and by the swift passage of time, altering options and ambitions. But during the time in which he met Barbara Young, and at first felt that the relationship was going nowhere, and then changed her mind and changed his own life, I was single-minded in my observation of all that happened and stored it up for an unknown future use.

George was no Diderot. At best he survived, unnoticed by the wider world, yet intensely watched by those closest to him. And to these he wanted to recruit her. I suppose in this he was already making the moves that in due course would win her over, confessing to her the inner thoughts about his own life, about myself, and about my impact on her sister's children. Telling her that they liked me and saying he was glad must have reflected my yearning as well as his own. Thus I find myself part of their story, drawn in no doubt by his concern for my welfare and therefore my inclusion in that strange triangle. He had decided on this and I have given a remembered account of the way he presented me to her. Our life together, his and mine, was a precarious assortment of ups and downs; but it *was* together. That was the important thing. And though precarious, it had gone on with an engaging and loving certainty through those bleak and difficult years, the late 1940s. From the end of the war until the time of which I write, we had been true and close witnesses of each other's endeavour, he of my life at school and I of the events that have now been coloured and changed by these letters.

Barbara was a perfect spectator. She came out of the shadowy, uncertain time that I associate with Sanderstead. And she was so right for both of us; so sweetly elusive. I thought her, from that first meeting, the exact and proper person to be drawn into a loving relationship with my father. This would then extend and enrich my life, along with his. The fact that I felt this to be the case began to emerge that summer. It was not obvious. Now that I know more of what happened, it was obviously not immediate. The tone of that August letter was still tentative and uncertain. And I think that the hidden realms of his mind, which were dark with foreboding about the 'show' he might make of the rest of his life, were kept from me. To me the outward appearances belied the shadows.

I went on that brief holiday, just a weekend, with Barbara, her nieces Georgiana and Charmian, and her nephew Ulick. We went to Steyning in west Sussex, inland from Shoreham-by-Sea. We stayed in Penfold Lodge and travelled down to the sea to bathe at Shoreham. At fourteen I was the eldest of the group. Because of the meticulous detail recorded less than a month before in my school report, I can describe myself exactly. Monitoring our physique was part of post-war security of good health and physical growth in austere times. It reflected the impact of Beveridge, whose report shaped social policy at the time, and of a new State approach to health and social welfare. I weighed just eight stone and was five feet four inches tall; my chest, when expanded, measured thirty-one inches. I wore wire-framed National Health glasses. I feel I can reconstruct myself now when I touch my chest and consider the ravages of time upon the human frame. There was I, that little puny person, voice still unbroken, able to thrill the air itself with clear treble music. I can unfold him, too, recreate him, feel compassion for him as he watched and waited for something to happen. That was how we were. Events were to unfold that would change my own and my father's life.

I did not know that he, my father, was feeling the same and

feeling it with great intensity. There was within him an anxiety that was at times frantic with the force of his eternal worry, 'hoping against hope' to resolve his life, his work and his love for Barbara. What did he mean and how did he think that she could prevail upon his life, her own life, their possible life together, and make it better? Yet that is the expectation of the August 1951 letter, with its ravelling up together of his work, his hopes, his worshipping of her and his embracing of me within that wild clutch of the components of his solitary existence.

I came back from Steyning and went on my own to Folkestone to stay with my wonderful Aunt Peg and her pretty daughter, Pan, some four years older than me. She was the most familiar of my aunts; the most loved. Unlike Aunt Jess, who was the eldest in the family, Aunt Peg was easy-going, full of laughter. She was my father's favourite, close to him at that time and to become even closer with the developing events. I remember the kitchen in her apartment, and the comforting smell of food wafted into the house by the warm sea breeze off the Channel blowing through the open window. A sailor's town, Folkestone had been the place chosen by my grandfather as the family home when he came back from Calcutta. From the house there he had sent my father to King's School, Canterbury.

The refrigerator stood in a corner of the kitchen and had a compartment in the back of it into which a man in overalls wearing a peaked cap and a blue-striped apron deposited a large block of ice, touching that cap and promising a replacement, and he named a day; I remember it happening perhaps twice a week. In the evenings, after supper, the three of us sat together round a small polished table. We divined our own futures and those of the ones we loved with the use of an upturned glass and the encircling letters of the alphabet. From

PART ONE

these we spelt out our future destiny in halting, uncertain sweeps across the table surface. I still remember the way the glass tipped, an almost human reaction to our collective determination to keep it spelling our way forward as we ignored the fact that it was possibly being pushed beyond its chosen, preordained order of revelation. It told me the name of the girl I would marry and provided for my cousin a parallel service. And we laughed together, the three of us, in carefree exultation. I asked no questions about my father. What was happening to him was still too private for me to share with others, even his sister.

Aunt Peg's husband, the writer Reginald Campbell, had died some years before. In 1935 he published *Teak Wallah*. I read it as a child with such pleasure and went on to read other books by him, not just about the teak forests of northern Siam, but about the wonderful life of the elephant and about Royal Navy life as well. He wrote exactly what I wanted to read at the time, the adventures among elephants in the Far East, a series of books, very special, haunting stories that satisfied my yearnings for the magic of travel.

Aunt Peg suffered his loss I think every day of her life and that loss was tragically deepened later. *Teak Wallah* is dedicated to Pan, their only child. She was a beautiful young woman when I first met her, and she was trying to become a writer herself. She died of cancer when still quite young. The blow was a terrible one to her mother. Peg survived it, of course, but lived on under its shadow, the resignation to the incomparably powerful tragedy leavened by her sweet nature and her courageous spirit.

I do not remember the distinction my father made in that August 1951 letter between the 'good time' in Folkestone and the declared fact that I 'really enjoyed' being with Barbara and her nephew and two nieces in Steyning, but I am sure he was right. Folkestone was 'family'; but the other event was as new and exciting as being a 'teak wallah' in Burma or Siam.

The mixture of events, during that long summer holiday, was rich and varied. Contact with Irene fell by the wayside. There were awkward moments; explaining the weekend in Steyning was one of them. Was my father there as well? Irene asked. What else had I done? she wanted to know. When would I be free for an outing with her?

My father and I went on with visits to Irene. He told her about his work. She yearned for more attention; he failed to give it. We had visits to Barbara and there were encounters in London with her sister's children. My father was in a confident mood. He was not contemplating defeat. He was able, energetic and ambitious in the modest terms under which he worked. And he loved Barbara.

Whenever I go into the bedding section of a department store, or, more rarely these days, a bedding shop *tout court*, and smell the mixture of fresh new cloth and ticking, the faint resin smell of timber, I am taken back in time. I am in that smart and successful shop in Knightsbridge where my father exercised his charm on the willing and the rich who were engaged in the business of furnishing their houses and apartments. Even the name of the shop, the 'London Bedding Centre', can invoke the freshness of smell, the clean, clear lines of its contents, the patterns of ticking and stitching. What tiny commission did he get on those large sums he made in sales? I know that he was good at it. My father had great charm at his disposal and the theatrical ability to deliver it freely to anyone who engaged with him. He spoke well and with authority, part of it the natural heritage of a naval officer, that firm flatness of stance, ready, it seemed, in case the floor itself

PART ONE

of the Bedding Centre might take the crew of salesmen and their cargo by surprise, and lift and tilt them in the strong tide of inexorable commerce. I remember him leaning down and pressing his large, strong, capable hands into the surface of a sprung mattress, indicating by gesture that its merits were really beyond words, and then exacting an order from a willing client. All clients buying beds are willing. Beds are a necessity of life as well as being a pleasure. One does not choose between a bed and an armchair.

At the same time he was building clients in the evening as a jobbing gardener. 'I saw a Jew last night about his garden' has a familiar ring to it. He chose his clients well.

I think of Barbara as I knew her in those early days and realise that her obvious reluctance, which clearly encouraged his passionate declarations of worship and of her having every ounce of his love, was in part because she was so right for him. She was weighing up the enormity of what was on offer. Here was a man who expressed himself passionately, who had lived a rich life. Granted, he was still married and there were the children of that union, together with a family from another liaison where the woman – my mother in fact – had been dead eight years. Yet he carried the complexity of this lightly.

There was a strange pattern to his work and his life. It demanded service and attention. It did, in fact, require her comment and reaction all the time. Is it any wonder that in those early months, as we might consider them, she should have given him the impression that she had no inclination of falling in love with him? *She was afraid.* It made her an even better spectator than she naturally was. She was good anyway. I think she was perfect for him, just at that time. Barbara was gentle, receptive and undemonstrative, but she was quite clear in her mind about what was confronting her.

In those hot, still days during the second half of August, well before my return to school, Barbara and I spent time together while George engaged the rapt attention of wealthy women buying interior sprung mattresses on large divan bases. I learned about her. She was shy at first, talking about herself in a very dismissive way, as though she did not matter. Her father had been an engineer and was descended from other engineers, his grandfather being the railway pioneer Timothy Hackworth, about whom Barbara's father wrote a memoir. He went to work abroad, first in India and then in Malaya. He was a civil engineer in Penang and became quite important in colonial Malayan society. He married Edith Lees, from Chester, in 1895 at St George's Church in Georgetown, Penang. They had six daughters; Barbara was the second youngest. Two of them died. Her father retired to St Leonards-on-Sea and died there in 1932 when Barbara was in her teens. The family stayed on in the town and in due course I came to know them all.

I knew little of this family history at that time, but enough to realise how much it represented in stability and security. Barbara gave the essence of it, though much more was to follow as one by one I met her sisters, the husbands of two of them, and, in the case of one, the three children.

What more can I tell of her? She was a games teacher and took classes in physical exercise or training. She had taught in an institute of gymnastics and dance in Antwerp between 1934 and 1936, made a success of it, and returned to regular teaching in England. During World War II she was in the Women's Auxiliary Air Force, but then went back to teaching. Barbara was quite tall and had a good figure. She wore skirts that flattered her narrow waist and her easy movement. One would have guessed, from watching her walk, that she taught games.

PART ONE

She found it a good subject and was energised by it. She was a good skier, played tennis and netball, taught remedial gymnastics at one stage, and was good enough at ballroom dancing to teach that too.

There was, uncharacteristically perhaps, an indolent quality about her as well; and I liked this. I remember her as passive and resigned. There were times when she looked so sad. I found it difficult on those occasions to imagine her in fields or playgrounds surrounded by young girls in gymslips. She said little about herself. She did occasionally mention her childhood and the rather sumptuous life the family had led in Penang. It had given her a high sense of expectation, reinforced by the settled family life focused on her widowed mother, Edith.

I think I absorbed all this greedily, possessively, knowing how much it meant to my father and wanting, because of that, to make importance out of it, perhaps beyond what it deserved or merited. When she was free, we spent afternoons together, and, being a curious youth, I sought to know everything about her.

We went to the Festival of Britain. This austere event was to celebrate the centenary of the Great Exhibition of 1851 and was a showcase of British industrial, commercial and inventive endeavour. It was less a festival than an exhibition, boring in places but crowded all summer with curious visitors. Until I suggested it, she told me, she had been reluctant; such events, she thought, were bland and predictable. I, on the other hand, had already been twice, once from school and then a second time because I was doing a holiday project about it, chosen by myself with encouragement from my form master. I did not tell her that I agreed; that in fact I had found it tedious and tiring, the crowds of visitors to the South Bank of the Thames looking vacant and bewildered as they tried to make sense of the broad thematic programming of it all. We were invited to visualise 'the sea', 'the land', 'the living world'. With Barbara, it was different. I held my breath and hoped she would agree.

I was so proud to go with her and visit the Festival, the two of us together. I do not know who brought whom. I only know that she transformed it for me. She ignored the thematic planning. She remembered, right at the beginning, what she must have read months before about the artists involved in the project and suggested tentatively that we seek out some work by Lynn Chadwick. It was in the courtyard of the Regatta Restaurant, one of the largest of a dozen or so places of refreshment. When we found it, she told me a bit about Lynn Chadwick's sculpture and I asked her about other artists.

She suggested we might find them. We bought the guidebook and it became a game of hunting in crowded places, mainly for works of sculpture and for murals. At the age of fourteen the names of Henry Moore, Victor Pasmore, Jacob Epstein, John Piper, Barbara Hepworth and – rather specially – Feliks Topolski became known to me. They did so with a relevance and a vitality that began to explain the nature and purpose of art to a young schoolboy. I loved the day out and I adored Barbara.

I was no Vladimir Petrovich, nor was she Zinochka, daughter of a princess, but love comes in many guises, and in part I saw her through my father's eyes as well as my own. If he was inviting her, in an unseen and unwritten script, to be part of his life and thereby qualify to receive his innermost fears and aspirations, then she would in part be taking over a role that I had performed, largely on my own, since my mother's death. Of course I had been privy only to the more benign aspects of his struggle. He remained a hero in my eyes, rather than a victim. I was unaware of the exceptional cry to her of passion and love, and came to know it only decades later. But instinct and dropped remarks help the child to know much more than the adult thinks. And children ask questions, a matter that will become more evident with later letters.

As the summer holiday drew to a close, I came to love that part of London where my father was then living – Pembridge Villas – and to enjoy the increasingly familiar journey we made to Chelsea and to Sydney Street. She had returned there in preparation for renewing her teaching duties. During the daytime, as my summer holiday ended, we went on other outings – most of them I recall connected with art. She did not collect. She was too poor. But she had attractive pictures and pieces of furniture in her flat, among them reproductions of works by Degas, Parmigianino, Rembrandt, Leonardo. Incessantly I asked her about them and other artists. She took me to an exhibition of Leonardo drawings. I remember being enthralled by the silken beauty of his drawing of Leda, the stern ugliness of the 'Grotesque Heads'.

Only some evenings were spent with her. There was a restraint that I did not fully understand then, but is now made clear in his letters. This was the fact that he had not yet secured her. He did not have her love. Naturally enough, and with growing pleasure, I became a spectator of both of them. I was trying to understand what was happening between them and wondering where it would lead them and how it would affect me.

After the August letter, pregnant with his uncertainty, and clearly indicating a prevarication on her part that was to become characteristic in so many of her reactions, there were five months without any letters. I can only think it was because they were together much of the time. I returned to school early in September, my heart full of longings about the future. There were my own apprehensions as well in all of this. I was now fifteen years old. I worked hard on the project, and, inspired by the way Barbara gave a new artistic focus to that strange, frail Festival of Britain, I was able to turn it into something that had greater meaning for me. Back at school I delivered a finished explanation based largely on her views. This was commended by my kindly form master, a man already well disposed towards me because he was also the music teacher. I was noted down as a new authority on modern British art.

In October Winston Churchill was returned to power. He had been in Opposition since 1945, and yet his political stature was such that he had remained a dominant figure in all our lives. We followed the general election at school, reacting to the result with unusually strident debate, much of it, of course, inspired by parental attitude. My father's views were mixed. Churchill was a warmonger; Churchill saved us. War was a necessity – it had to be, but when the blast of peace blew in our ears, in 1945, a different order emerged. By 1951 this had changed. Once again, with a new enemy in the East, Churchill took on ancient attributes and was again admired. We were forming our opinions and testing our judgements against a backdrop of world tension centred upon Europe and on the great divide between communism and democracy. Earlier in the summer Guy Burgess and Donald Maclean had defected to Moscow and a yawning gulf had been exposed in Britain's protection and security. Spying and treachery became hot subjects at school. Though many shades of opinion were expressed, the underlying sense of national safety being threatened was paramount. Protection of our island, whose shape and nature had been exemplified in part by the 1951 Festival of

PART ONE

Britain, was coming once more under the control of that ageing political fighter, Winston Churchill. This met with my fellow students' approval.

So there I was, the child of circumstance, governed by a strange principle – that of the perseverance of circumstantiality. It governs us all, or should do so. The trick is to know the logical surroundings of an action. Where lay the state of my own affairs, and I little more than a child struggling towards understanding? What, in the circumstance of small things, be they ever so humble, mattered at that time?

One needs to know the answer in order to persevere and to judge whether or not what one seeks to achieve is possible. Out of this grow not the principles, but their use for oneself. I did not *know* this. Circumstance is not always rational. It is judged by the subconscious mind, by instinct and by inference. And that electric principle guided me then.

What is it, to persevere? It is one's continued application to that voyage on which one has embarked. I had so embarked, and upon changed circumstance, just as much as my father. But whereas he was able to dictate his actions and pursue his ends, I was not free in the same way. Nor was I independent. I went along with what he did. And whether he was right or wrong, I could not dictate either the direction or the determination. We persevere towards success and hope that we shall find it. But what is success? I knew, by instinct then, by reference to the letters now, more than fifty years later, what it was to him and how elusive it was.

II

I CAME HOME from school on 18 December 1951. My father met me at Paddington Station, as he always had done, but this time with exceptionally good news. For whatever reason, he had been tried in some strange, domestic refining fire of family judgement and had come out of it with sufficient credit for Barbara Young's mother to have issued an invitation that we should spend the Christmas of that year with her family at St Leonards-on-Sea. I was over the moon with excitement. We were to become part of their family Christmas, and into this huge change in circumstance I read conclusions I thought irreversible. George and Barbara would marry. That was an immediate thought, though I did not express it to him. I would come to know all of them better. Georgiana, Charmian and Ulick would become 'family' in some strange way. And the family home, as yet unseen, would welcome us.

Both together and apart, during that year of 1951, my father and I had negotiated some of the difficulties of knowing and understanding the Young family and the Lorings. The summer visit to Steyning, the meetings with Barbara's sister Roberta Loring (the mother of the three children I had spent that short holiday with), days spent with Barbara during my summer

PART ONE

holiday, some of them accompanied by one or more of Roberta's children, had constituted new ground in family relationships. And quite separately from me, my father's own prospects must have been transformed in the autumn months while I had been away at school. Uncertain longings gave wing to my thoughts and I constructed from them a Christmas empire of expectation. It was a transforming exercise never before experienced. I contrasted it with the previous, rather gloomy Christmas in Sanderstead. My mind ranged back before that to the fairly dismal and lonely occasion, faintly relieved by the strenuous efforts of Irene, in the Christmas of 1948, for example, which we spent in the bed-sitting room at 27 Clanricarde Gardens.

I had become used to day-to-day uncertainty. In what I think of as the Notting Hill Gate days, which lasted from 1947 until he met Barbara, addresses and locations crowd into my mind, as do the initial encounters. Before that Christmas of 1951 I was the creature of uncertain expectation. And climbing down from the Kingham train at Paddington at the beginning of each holiday, the question high on my diffidently handled list of questions were those that for many people would have been superfluous: where are we to go? What is our new home? (for almost always it was new). And what then? Who will the people be? What friends will I have? I can name the indifferent residences and remember the numbers. It is all done from memory since the early records are few: 27 Clanricarde Gardens, 35 Ossington Street, 1 Hillsleigh Road, at different times 11 and 13 Holland Park Road. Then there was a time when my father worked at a tennis club at the top of Campden Hill Gardens and lived in a house there, Number 25. I see myself approaching it, up the hill, knowing what I would find; I am still able to recall the shock of discovering the landlady being comforted in his arms, sitting on his knee, her face streaked with tears. He spread the largesse of his loving nature and his comforting protection more widely than I ever knew. Did he offend my innocence? I cannot recall, at that stage, though later he did. I have mentioned already Sanderstead and Pembridge Villas. So was this now to end? I believe I began to think so as soon as I had absorbed the news.

Such preparations there were! Such planning! Such buying of presents! Nothing could have been more exciting. The news was doubly welcome since it gave, in addition to the excitement of the invitation, tangible reality to the longed-for continuity in my father's relationship with Barbara. What had been transient and uncertain had now been given the strange seasonal endorsement of the greatly enhanced Christmas holidays from school. In addition, it was coupled with a special place to go to on the south coast, a new 'home' as it at first seemed to me. Place matters so much more when you have no place, or when it shifts underfoot without due warning or logic.

George was still working at the London Bedding Centre. He had changed his lodgings from Pembridge Villas, where we had been in the summer, to a double bed-sitting room at 43 Carlton Hill, in St John's Wood. I have no memory of it. We had moved away, temporarily, from Notting Hill Gate. He worked in the Knightsbridge shop until Christmas Eve when we left together for Victoria Station and the crowded train to the house in St Leonards-on-Sea. Together we walked up the short steep climb from the station, and under the clear night sky approached the large, rambling three-storey house at 29 Chapel Park Road. The house was rather overwhelming. We were latecomers, the last to arrive. We had to catch up with the festive spirit, which quickly we did. I was in a strange position, either the youngest of the adults or the eldest of the children,

PART ONE

but undeniably placed in an uncertain territory in between. My sense of it was reinforced by wisdom beyond my years and clearly beyond the boyishness that still marked my appearance.

The upbringing of Barbara and her three sisters had been very protected, from their early days in Malaya and then after their return to England. The family were very matriarchal, and there had been no strong male figure. Their father was forty-five years old when their parents married, and would have been quite elderly as they grew up. Roberta was the only one of the sisters who had children, and she was devoted to them; after her marriage broke up, she showed no interest in men but lived only for her son and two daughters.

That Christmas holiday was memorable to me because of my three younger companions and the natural charge I elected to have over them when we went out together to walk down across the railway and onto the seafront. We did this on Christmas morning, before church. I think there was a maid in the house – certainly someone who cooked – and perhaps there was someone who came in to clean the rooms, of which there were many. I slept alone in one on the top floor, but near to the three children.

Georgiana was the eldest of Roberta's daughters. Such a pretty girl she was, long straight hair to her shoulders, parted on the left, held back with a hairclip on the right. Her gaze was clear and direct, her expression at times quizzical, often the case with the eldest of a family having to face the larger share of mixed responsibilities. Charmian was two years younger. She had softer features, a more ebullient, welcoming nature. Then there was Ulick, the youngest, with his wire-framed spectacles and thick lenses, clutching my hand and racing in excitement along the seaside promenade and down to the beach.

The eldest of Barbara's sisters was Margaret, known as Marg, who remained unmarried and lived at home with their mother. Ursula, the youngest, was married to Bernard and lived in Paris, but they had no children. According to her nephew, Ursula was precise and practical – she was the only one who saved money – and she lived very modestly in Paris without any expensive tastes. Ursula hated the sight of blood, though she had been a nurse during the war. Always very kind and generous to her nieces and nephew, Ursula was quite opposed to religion. She and Bernard later retired to the South of France where he died. After that, Ursula returned to England.

I knew Ursula and Bernard only through that Christmas visit to St Leonards-on-Sea. I may have met her on one or two other occasions in London during the 1950s. I also met the eldest sister, Marg, for the first time, later getting to know her better through Barbara.

Bernard was very French in appearance, a small, lean-looking man with sharp features and close-cut grey hair. He got on better with my father than James Loring did. Perhaps he was more detached, not a neighbour of Barbara's in Chelsea, not as much aware of the developing relationship between his sister-in-law and George. This was also the case with Ursula. In my memory, the family was always surrounded by the golden glow of happiness that I associate with that particular time. I romanticised them further, without grounds for doing so, perhaps because they lived in de Gaulle's France. They had a certain *je ne sais quoi* of French Left-Bank radicalism, as I may have thought at the time, and certainly did later. Bernard conformed, if conform is the word, with my early images of what France was like. These were culled enthusiastically in those days in the early 1950s from the films Barbara used to

PART ONE

take me to in the Chelsea Classic, a cinema then offering a wonderful programme of continental films.

My views on Bernard, on his politics and disposition, turned out to be completely wrong. Bernard, to begin with, was much older than James Loring. Bernard had been in the British Army in World War I, but then in the Royal Air Force in World War II. In the 1930s, when he would have been in his forties, he had been an active member of the British Union of Fascists. He belonged to a branch of it in Chelsea, as did James Loring, in the same organisation. It was where they met. They regularly attended meetings together, took part in demonstrations, went on marches and were at times involved in violent encounters. They did not materially change their politics for years to come. They both had some contact with Oswald Mosley, and James, according to his son, had correspondence briefly with Ezra Pound, an American fellow-traveller with the European right-wing political parties. Indeed Pound was a protagonist, through that controversial period, and had been interned.

Ulick was influenced later by his Uncle Bernard, whose background was something of a mystery, in particular by his views on philosophy and religion. He never really settled after the Great War and, though clever and profound in his thinking, was something of a dabbler. In fact Ursula was the breadwinner while he effectively gave up working altogether in the 1950s. Highly strung, no longer young, it is possible he had difficulty holding down a job.

The Christmas festival included church and outings, walks and drives, as well as visits to and from friends. The Young family were Protestants, but James was a Catholic. His wife Roberta was a convert who thought the Church of England 'ridiculous' and used this as part of her childhood rivalry with her sister Marg, whose faith had been important to her at a particular time of wartime crisis when she was interned by the Japanese in Changi Gaol in Singapore. Roberta's three children were brought up as Catholics.

I reconstructed that Christmas in my first novel, *A Singer at the Wedding*. Changes are made. Roberta, mother of the three children, is portrayed in the character of Madge Springer. She has already been established in the entirely fictional encounter between her and the narrator at the beginning of the book. There, her three children have been transformed into one, Babette, and she is the focus for the narrator's first indulgence in the adventure of love. There are other inventions and changes, but essentially this portion of the novel – indeed the whole of that first novel – is built around the idea of gain and loss, the magical promise of a new life for George, and necessarily for the narrator – who is still a child – with the Ursula of the story, based closely enough on Barbara.

That Christmas story – which I think of now in the light of so many other Christmas stories so faithfully and dramatically told in fiction – is a presentation inspired by remembered or imagined warmth and happiness. It is enriched with fictional event and created emotion. Conflict between characters and interests within the family are a product of the larger story I tell. Inevitably, since Madge's husband Robert is based on the man who in a sense had assumed the senior position within the Young family, there are frictions that develop with the narrator's father. Those frictions become the shadow overhanging the narrator's high expectations.

I think when I came to write the book, many years later, I had read *A Portrait of the Artist as a Young Man*, and may well have been influenced by James Joyce's handling of Christmas in the opening pages of that book. But then Christmas, as I say, is a festival that has a natural attraction for novelists and many have used it for diverse purposes. There is certainly not much in common with Joyce's purpose and my own.

At the end of that part of the story, the important central chapters, there is the inevitable farewell and departure of the narrator back to London. This, as is revealed in the letters, took place well after my father had left. In fact, as I remember it, one by one the adults left the family home. All those years later I did conceive of this as a suitable way of ending the novel. The precise detail of anticipation leads to rich enjoyment and then fades towards sadness as the boy's own time for departure approaches. He yearns for his stay to continue. But all such happy holidays must end; his own attenuated and enriched by the happy times he then spends with Babette. The narrator leaves some days after George. Babette sees him off, walking with him to the station on a cold January afternoon.

When he had arrived for Christmas and had walked into the house with his father, George had said to him, 'Say hello to Babette, and give her a kiss.' But a kiss is too much at that point in the story. The narrator records: 'I said hello. We smiled at each other. We did not kiss.' At the end of that Christmas holiday, emboldened by the shared days of happy and carefree enjoyment, they do kiss goodbye. He is conscious of her lips, cold on his cheek, and he tells her to hurry back home, on account of the cold perhaps, or her being on her own. It is an unconscious moment of solicitude, learned from his father, and it makes her laugh. She says to him, 'You're so like your father. Don't be too like him.'

Babette is a creature of the imagination, inspired by the three children, not an amalgamation of them. She is made wiser, more sophisticated than they could ever have been. She is made to add to his faint foreboding, and to intensify the feeling of sadness. I puzzle now, as I did when I wrote those words, about the different levels of awareness that are represented by the episode, whatever it was drawn from, and by the description of it with the emotionally charged feelings of the narrator, compared with the calm, even cool, demeanour of Babette.

The boy judged events within the narrow single dimension of immediacy and of his youth. I make him believe that all is resolved, and yet, at the same time, fill him with a sadness that is reinforced by an inexplicable foreboding. He could not know what, if anything, had been resolved. And his response is to the parting between himself and Babette. She represents all that he hoped for at the time. And of course the writer, in trying to recover that feeling, sets aside – or tries to set aside – the knowledge that he has when he writes. It was a watershed. This was clear from first news of the invitation until after everyone in the Young family, as well as my father and I, had departed back to London. The purpose in the writing is to hold the reader in suspense. Tears do that.

Journeys to London, at that stage in my life, were always exciting. They were usually my coming home to my father, and, if not, they were outings from school, like the visits to the Festival of Britain. But on this occasion it was different. Things had happened, in their way irreversible, and the prospect – moving out of the family environment and back into the wider world – was filled with perplexity and doubt. As it turned out this was justified. What I did not know, either then, or at the end of my father's life in 1975, or when I completed and published that first novel in 1978, was what the letters would eventually tell me: my father's struggle to win Barbara's heart was not over.

George at that time was not a free man. Perhaps he never

PART ONE

was. He laboured in chains. Like Marley's Ghost, the chains were forged out of his own past, and perhaps for that reason they always disturbed the wake of his progress through the world. If there were to be a life with Barbara, then he had to make himself free. And this formidable task faced him in the days that followed. Freeing himself, in the sense that mattered to all of us, could happen only with a divorce from Connie. And so Connie enters the story.

Connie. Such a sweet name. So much part of our lives. So much of a handicap upon his chances of happiness. It was only ever a name to me. I never met her. But in 1951, and in the following year, Connie's name, part of the paraphernalia attached to my father's chains, rather like the bolts and locks and boxes that hang on Marley's chains, came to mean so much. She stood in the way of him realising happiness with Barbara, if indeed Barbara could learn to love him. And now I understand, as I did not before, that the issue of Connie being still married to George came to some kind of a climax at that point in his life, the memorable Christmas of 1951.

That it emerged at all must have been provoked by events over the Christmas holiday. Yet my father's first letter of 1952 was written at the end of my school holidays, when I was out of the house. It was dated 9 January.

> I have seen Bruce, he is out with his friend, and apparently he has enjoyed himself thoroughly, so I don't quite see where the boredom comes in. I think he will be writing to Granny – it's been very pleasant and *always* grand to be with you –
>
> Lots I would like to say but I must be careful as I would very likely say it the wrong way –
>
> But there are definite things I want in 1952 –
>
> A greater love from you –
>
> Something substantial and definite to aim for –

And plenty of other things –

I worship you Barbara and would literally give my right arm to be married to you – That's that, and I've written to Peggy for Connie's address, as I must get cracking about that.

The flat should be finished by Sunday night easily – fire will be laid and I'll top the coal bin right up – It's not looking too bad – I'll put the curtains up after giving them a good shake – And now I must go back to work – Look after yourself. Love to Mother and Georgiana.

Love from George

So there it is; the main problem he faced was Connie. And then of course my Aunt Peg as well, the middle of the five children of George Barrett Arnold and Jessie Croft. This problem of Connie further complicates the story and has to be unravelled before we move on. So, too, does the involvement of my Aunt Peg. In due course she was to move to London from Folkestone and this meant that we saw more of her. Aunt Peg *was* a free spirit; free in every way that mattered. Her eyes sparkled with the welcome task of meeting each day's challenge, and the look she bestowed was always full of love. I always remember her wonderful laugh, suffusing conversations, filling the room with welcome. She had little enough to laugh about. She lived in genteel privation; a pensioner with a small income from investments and probably a tiny residual income from her late husband's writings.

It was my Aunt Peg's liberal and open nature that endeared her to my father. In part also it was because my other two aunts, Jess, who lived in Bexhill-on-Sea, and Joan, who lived in Bermuda, were less accessible. In the case of Aunt Joan, this was obvious enough: an ocean divided brother from sister. In the case of Jess, it was more complicated. Her husband had been reluctant for a time about too much closeness between

PART ONE

the families. It had to do with my father's dubious reputation and the threat his drinking represented, as an influence, as a bar to closer relations between cousins of roughly the same ages. While Jess did her best to ignore this, and visited us all as children, and loved us in her way, because she loved her brother, the difficulties were there residually. Perhaps Aunt Jess, the eldest of the five children, with Father next to her in age, had a sense of moral responsibility reinforced by her own religious nature which she shared with my grandmother, then dead only five years. We saw little of our cousins; even later I only came to know one of them, Jane, at all well. She had become a guardian of family memories. Uncle Reg, Aunt Peg's husband, had an even greater distaste for George, but by this stage he was dead and it did not matter.

Aunt Joan was the youngest. The one between Aunt Peg and her was my Uncle Matthew. He also was at King's School, Canterbury; younger than my father and an even greater sporting success there, outshining George's career as a rugby player and playing a significant part in competitive school athletics. But by 1951 he was dead, knocked down by a car.

Whatever it was that brought Father close to Aunt Peg, who was next in age, they shared a bond of affection, never more so than in his early years as a naval officer when he wrote her loving and informative letters. The first that I have dates from August 1918. He had first been promoted to acting sub-lieutenant and had been posted to *HMS Verdun*, on which he served for more than two years. Before that he had been on *HMS Tiger*, first as a Royal Naval Reserve trainee from the training ship *HMS Worcester*, and then, from September 1917, as a midshipman.

That first letter from George to Peggy has much in it about marriages; their friends in Folkestone were marrying and also the eldest in the family, my Aunt Jess, who became engaged and was married that year. At the end of the letter George comments on the Great War, then drawing to a close. It had been less than glorious for the Royal Navy. George says: 'Peace looks a bit more hopeful now, but we want another Naval action first or we shan't be very popular.'

My father was a keen rugby player. At that time he was, I think, up at Scapa Flow in the Orkneys. He went round the ship's company, successfully recruiting a team and then searching for one to play against. 'My great ambition is to play for the Navy at rugger and then for England.'

He wrote in November 1918 of having played rugby four times in a week, once against *HMS Queen Elizabeth* 'and the destroyers', twice for the 13th Flotilla against the 15th, as well as one 'lower deck game with the sailors'. He anticipated a 'Great Naval scrap coming off soon, everybody says so and the Huns are going to give us a surprise'. What worried him most about the possibility of dying was the fear that they did not play the game in Heaven. 'I'm rugger mad. They are organising rugger teams for peace time and things look very hopeful.' It was seven days before the German surrender and so the 'Great Naval scrap' never came off. Instead, with his ship he sailed to take part in the most remarkable event in twentieth-century naval history: the surrender of the German High Seas Fleet. This took place on 21 November 1918 and was a key condition of the Armistice signed ten days earlier. Though the war was over, there was still great tension about this handing over of vessels. The two greatest fleets in the history of civilisation went to meet each other; the German vessels flying the white flag of surrender, the Grand Fleet under Admiral Sir David Beatty sailing out of the Firth of Forth with guns ready to fire if necessary, and with an aircraft escort overhead.

PART ONE

The line of German battlecruisers heading into captivity, for all the world like Ptolemy's fleet submitting to Demetrius after Salamis, was led into Scottish waters by *HMS Cardiff* on a beautiful clear late November day, 'a school of leviathans led by a minnow'. They were stretched out in line ahead as far as the eye could see and beyond. So many warships were at sea at the one time that no one could see them all. In calm waters, hardly flecked by the breaking of waves, these great vessels were a pageant of capitulation. From their grey and awesome superstructures, the guns now silent, great dark clouds of smoke from the furnaces deep below the unthreatening decks softly spread eastwards in the light prevailing wind. More than any event witnessed on land, this was an expression, devastating in its grandeur, of the end of a huge carnage.

The High Seas Fleet moved to Scapa Flow. The vessels, not greatly used during the war, were in excellent condition. Their surrender had made the Grand Fleet, which was essentially British, the greatest naval fleet there had ever been, and effectively in possession of richly equipped additional vessels. But just over a year later the skeletal crews of German sailors, caretakers for the captured vessels and under a German commander, opened the seacocks on seventy great vessels and scuttled £50 million worth of shipping while the British Fleet was out on exercise.

George wrote to his sister Peggy in April 1920. He was on a new and dangerous posting in Irish waters. He was at Buncrana first, as he said, 'presumably to keep order during the Easter holidays'. Then he sailed to Queenstown (now Cobh). He was still on *HMS Verdun*, his promotion to sub-lieutenant having been confirmed, and he was wondering what to do with his life. He was at a crossroads in two respects. The Navy was scaling down its officers under a scheme known as the 'Geddes

Axe', but only offering a bounty of £500 for men to leave the service. He liked the life. It had many advantages, playing regular games of rugby being a high priority, and he had effectively decided to stay on. Earlier, he had been in love with Connie Innes but she had become engaged to another man. In his letter to Peggy, he told her that this engagement had been broken off: 'we write to each other again but don't tell anybody else, wrong impressions get about – I don't quite know if I am glad or sad. There won't be a ghost of a chance for me and she thinks she is going to be an old maid.' But he did marry her eighteen months later, on the last day of October 1921. They had a child within a year. He wrote to Peggy on 16 September 1922 to tell her 'there is another George in the world'. This was my half-brother 'Chips'. 'He is going to be a big fellow and good at rugger and tennis. He was christened last Sunday.'

My father's career as a naval officer meant a great deal to him during those years. He was posted to *HMS President* for six months after his service in Irish waters and then to *HMS Dryad* before joining the light cruiser *HMS Danae*, on which he served for two years. Together with four other cruisers and the battlecruisers *HMS Hood* and *HMS Repulse*, she formed the Special Service Squadron. This then went on a world cruise of goodwill.

Yet another George was on that cruise. Prince George later became Duke of Kent and died in a mysterious air crash in 1942 on his way to Iceland. He had a long naval career and was the close friend of Edward Prince of Wales, sharing his taste for affairs of the heart, but also having a liking for drink. My father wrote: 'Prince George is on the cruise with us and is quite a cheery bloke. Spoke to him the other night and asked him to have a drink. At Revel he got quite blotto.'

George was on the *Danae* with Mark Pizey, who served in

PART ONE

the war and commanded *HMS Campbell* in the attack during the celebrated 'Channel Dash' by the *Scharnhorst* and the *Gneisenauer*. Pizey was one of the Royal Navy's finest destroyer captains, had many commands and was knighted.

After serving on *Danae*, my father did what was known as 'the long "N" course' – four months of pure navigation – which he loved. He was qualified as a navigation officer and, after a period of leave, served on the *Abdiel*, a minelayer, for six weeks. This was in the summer of 1924. Towards the end of August he was posted to *HMS Crocus* where he served for a year before his last posting, to *Heather*. In each case he was the navigation officer. This concluded his last eighteen months in the Navy.

He gives some account of his life on board *Crocus* in letters to Connie in April 1925, thanking her for snaps of herself and of 'Chips', as well as of their second child, Elizabeth. These he stuck into an album. 'Chips looks very fat, doesn't he? And happy – he must enjoy that tricycle. And Elizabeth looks splendid – And you'd look perfect dear if your face had been clearer. Have had the powerful magnifying glass onto you, which makes your face a little clearer. I like the coat.' He also had a camera and got a signalman to photograph him – a photo I still have – but could think of nothing else to take. He was reading Shakespeare's *Measure for Measure* and found it funny but 'dirty'. When he finished it he moved on to *A Midsummer Night's Dream*.

It was Easter, and on Good Friday he went to church, 'not the 3 hours service, but a short military service at the Garrison church.' He gives news of other ships and visiting them, the *Nagoya*, the *Baroda*. He also helped 'No. 1' to entertain guests and ended a 'pleasant day' having consumed 'perhaps a little too much alcohol, but it was all free to us.' The mail came once a week and there were more snaps. 'I feel so bucked that I've got such a pretty wife.' He *passe partout*-ed them and had them hanging in his cabin.

George was concerned about Connie taking exercise. 'Yes, I *know* darling, you get plenty of exercise with the children, but it's not the kind of exercise that does as much good as outdoor exercise, when your mind is free from work & you are enjoying your sport whatever it is – your limbs don't get supple with work but they do with sport – a bricklayer gets plenty of exercise (or used to, when they worked), but I bet he couldn't bend over and touch his toes or do a splits over a horse.' Time hung heavy on station, and he was often very bored, longing to be with her. 'Your photos are looking down at me and you look so happy and lovely that I'd give my right arm to be with you always.'

Something terrible happened then, never fully explained, though perhaps related to events that were to follow. He wrote a brief, puzzling letter at the end of April 1925:

> My darling wife,
> I've gone off the deep end I'm afraid and I'll write and tell you all about it next week. I can't go in my cabin and face your photos –
> Your always loving husband, George

The end was sad. He had had a love affair with his admiral's wife. It is not certain that it started at this stage, or was directly related to that letter, but it certainly became the cataclysmic event of 1925, destructive in a way that simply could not have been foreseen.

At one stage George and the admiral's wife went together for a long weekend at the Dorchester Hotel in Park Lane,

PART ONE

staying there at the admiral's expense (the admiral ran an account at the hotel). The two of them ordered extra hampers of food and drink from Fortnum & Mason. Unfortunately, on this occasion, my father outstayed his lubricious welcome and very unmilitary engagement, and was late returning to his ship, a grave offence that merited a court martial. It did not happen. The Navy knew all too well the scandal that could have occurred, with the circumstances reported in the press, and instead George was 'invalided out' of the service. The process, whatever it was, took time. When in 1992, many years after his mother's death, Chips sent me copies of the letters summarised here, he confessed to feelings of embarrassment between himself and his mother over this and other questions about George. He wrote also of his own painful shyness, during his childhood, concerning his father's absence. 'I'm sure there was a time when I ought to have shown an interest in knowing the whole story, whereas something of a cloud obscured that part of our horizon and was never dispersed.'

Chips never saw the letters until after Connie's death, but his Aunt Nell, the closest family member to Connie, who for many years lived with them, told Chips when he was still a boy that 'it was largely due to my mother's testimony that Father's discharge came under the form of being "invalided out"'. And he went on: 'Since the letters were fastened with a split-pin I *guess* they were adduced in evidence.'

The Royal Navy later promoted George to lieutenant commander and put him on a life pension. His marriage, damaged by these events and by long absences at sea, ended with this catastrophic dismissal. In January 1926 he left the Navy. I think he felt he was stripped of everything. He certainly never got over it. He and Connie parted, she taking the two children. Connie would not grant him a divorce. She had two young children to bring up and feared the loss of her share of his pension.

How much suffering and confusion had pivoted upon that love affair and on the weekend at the Dorchester Hotel? I cannot pass down Park Lane and see the plump, brown-coated figures of the senior porters outside without a shiver of terrible regret at what the world they protected stood for in my father's life. As a child, in his company, I must have walked by it on many occasions, hearing from his saddened lips some oblique and puzzling reference to it that seemed to show me that in an earlier life he had known its luxury and temptation at first-hand. But apart from faint and, to me, impenetrable allusion, he never did tell me about it. He did tell my eldest brother, Hugh.

Years later Hugh, in an almost casual way, told me. We were walking by the Dorchester Hotel, on our way from looking at paintings by Rubens in the National Gallery and it suddenly occurred to Hugh that I did not know. I had made a remark about the puzzlement I felt over the ending of what promised to be a distinguished career. Hugh just said what had happened, and what he remembered being told. I had more to add to that. I had never told him about Chips's letter and the three letters written from *Crocus* at Easter time in that cruel month in 1925.

What can I say of Connie? Her impact on my life was large enough, but on my father's it was enormous. But then so was his on hers. What they decided to do and how the decisions were made remains a mystery. I never met her, and my only contacts were indirect ones through Chips and his younger sister Elizabeth. Their mother was the fourth child of Henry Lewis and was descended from Robert Hugh Innes, whose name was taken as a second Christian name by his great-great-

PART ONE

grandson, my half-brother. 'Chips' probably met Barbara, though Elizabeth never did.

I can form no clear view or opinion of Connie. I am still confused at the shadow she cast over our lives, as she also did over George's life at this time and over Barbara's future. She seems to be there now, as she was then, a blockade on his advance towards the dual objectives outlined in the early letters to Barbara, the 'greater love' he wanted with her, and 'something substantial and definite to aim for' in his own life.

If I am confused now, how much more was this the case then? It is almost as though Connie and the obstacle she represented obscured the life and existence of the family to which I belonged. It also is part of the story since he told it in full to Barbara and the details are referred to in letters at the time. After the break-up with Connie, he moved to the north of England for a time and worked, among other places, in Birkenhead. He occasionally referred to jobs he had in the early 1930s as a salesman. He met Margaret Shaw, always called Rita by him, in 1929 and they became lovers. A son was born in April 1930, my eldest brother Hugh, and a second son, Guy, in May 1932. Connie promised George that if, after two years, he and Rita were still together, she would then give him a divorce. She went back on that when the two years had elapsed, but I know nothing of the circumstances. It may be that George did not pursue it.

The family had moved to Croydon by the time I was born in 1936, and we lived in the house at 21 The Waldrons from then until my mother's death. George was a salesman in the town, in a store in the main street called Allders, but he had other jobs. My two sisters, Marion and Lena, followed. Marion was born on 14 January 1938 and Lena on 4 June 1940. In August 1943 my mother died. My brothers were sent to

Kingham Hill Homes for Boys, in the Cotswolds, originally an orphanage but at that stage becoming a boarding school. I went there six months later, but to the junior school some way from the main establishment. Hugh and Guy often came down the hill to visit me on Sundays, a high point in my week. My two sisters went first to my Aunt Dorothy, my mother's elder sister, and were later adopted. I remained with my father. It is for this reason, and the many further complications and changes that followed, that I describe these experiences involving Barbara from a solitary point of view. It was not entirely so, but my siblings enter the story infrequently, and by then had, for different reasons, dispersed. In these early years after my mother's death, this process had begun with my two sisters. I and my two brothers were still together, for only a short time as far as Hugh was concerned, since he left school in 1946 to train for the Navy, but for Guy the period was longer.

George was not able to cope with even one child. He was drinking quite heavily and, through my paternal grandmother, arranged for me to live for a time with the Rector of Beckenham, Bernard Mohan, and his wife Christine. They had two children of their own, John and Patricia, and had in addition taken in a Jewish refugee child, a girl called Ursula. Christine's mother, Mrs Dickinson, then very elderly, also lived in the rectory. It was she who had known my grandmother; the two had been friends from the time of their young married life in Calcutta, first meeting as maternity patients in a hospital there.

Christine Mohan took a great fancy to me. She offered to adopt me. My father considered this and also my Aunt Dorothy, one of the trustees for our family. My grandfather on my mother's side had left us a small legacy, but there were conditions surrounding any arrangements that might be made for my adoption. Whatever the legal advice may have been,

PART ONE

my Aunt Dorothy opposed any transfer of my share of the legacy to my adoptive mother and the adoption was abandoned. In February of 1944 I went off to Kingham Hill, following my brothers there.

I did not know it then – I learned it only after his death – but George kept, in a small blue 'Century' notebook bought for ninepence, a record of all the early visits to the school when my brothers and I were there together. The first record is of Easter 1944, a full account of the visit, from a Saturday to a Monday. Then in June of that year he came again, for Prize Day, my brother Guy being a recipient. In October of that year he set out to cycle from Brickett Wood near Hemel Hempstead, but then it rained and so he took the train. Those journeys were not recorded, as the later facts were recorded in his diaries in the form of a chronology of events; they were little essays, the first of them headed 'The Perfect Weekend'. He said it was 'one of the happiest times of my life – the boys are so wonderful and loyal to me that they deserve a better father and I pray that they will get on in life and have many happy days and years.' Hugh, my elder brother, was on his mind. 'He worries a good deal and now feels the loss of Mummy very much. He has a good voice.'

We all had good voices and we all sang. We walked everywhere during the second summer visit, and after the prize-giving and the main speech, we went down past the school farm and sat on huge logs where some elm trees had been felled. 'The boys sang some of the old Waldron songs', my father recalled. The Waldrons, which had been our home in Croydon, was the place where my mother had died the previous summer. We walked in perfect weather and I had to be left back to the junior house well before Hugh and Guy, who walked with him some way towards the station at Kingham.

They turned back at a signpost and he waved them out of sight.

The entry concludes: 'Life is a series of heartbreaks.' Leaving us was always a terrible wrench for him. In a later entry he says, 'Parting from my boys is always sad', and recalls walking in the still, silent October landscape by moonlight, remembering the swiftly passing days, the imminent return to his un-recorded work somewhere near London. What it was, I think none of us knew. He does not mention it in his diary of those very first visits. They are distilled as a precious spirit out of grapes of wrath. My father came from the same area of Brickett Wood, on the road between St Albans and Watford, and in those days – at least as I remember it, from one holiday only – it was all farming country and woodland.

When I read now the carefully composed and at times heart-rending pages of that sad little blue book, 'The Perfect Weekend', I realise that desperation, even then, was nagging at his heart. Whether he could deal with it or not, he was facing the disintegration of his family. The two girls had been taken from his care. The youngest of the five, my sister Lena, was adopted by the Knapp family, who lived in north London. My other sister, Marion, much more of a handful, even at that stage, was for a time with him, then with others in the family, and finally she too was 'adopted', though neither in as regular nor as successful a way as Lena had been. As to the three of us, at school in the Cotswolds, we in a sense had also been 'adopted', embraced by the strong arm of care and charity extended by that remarkable school, founded to take care of children from broken homes.

To begin with, during the first years at Kingham Hill, we did not go to him at holiday-time. Both the Easter and summer holidays of 1944 were spent in school houses especially kept open for the purpose where I and my two brothers remained in what was then remote countryside. It was not very different from the fate of many children in England at the time. With the war still on, various forms of evacuation had been introduced. There was an exception to this pattern: the Christmas of 1944. On 22 December we went to my father for ten days and lived in Brickett Wood in a green derelict van that had been converted into a mobile home that was no longer mobile; in fact it was hardly a home in the practical sense. It was cramped and cold, heated by a paraffin stove, and I slept in a hammock slung above the two beds in which my father and brothers slept. Mercifully, I remember no more and the holiday effort was not repeated.

On one occasion, before Easter of 1945, in February, Guy and I were sick in the school sanatorium and my father's visit was spent mainly walking with Hugh. On one day alone Father reckoned he walked twelve miles, from Bledington to Kingham Hill, from Chipping Norton to Great Rollright and back, from Churchill to Kingham Hill again and then back to Bledington. Hugh was his walking companion for part of this only. I was an unspecified worry to him, though he thought I looked run down.

It was around this time, possibly in the light of that Christmas experience, that George attempted a reconciliation with Connie, but nothing came of it. He did, however, write to my half-brother Chips from that same Brickett Wood address:

Dear Chips,
Would you like to meet me sometime? I very much want to get to know you and Mother tells me that you are coming on leave this weekend, so if you have any spare time I will meet you any time from Friday (Good) to Monday (Easter) in St Albans.
Yours sincerely, G.C. Arnold

Funny the formality of it, and what a strange letter to receive from one's father! So, many years later, far too many years to be of any lasting benefit, he was trying to make good my half-brother's childhood shyness about not having a father. In a way, I suppose, it did work. I was the only other beneficiary since I had Chips as a companion in the second half of the 1940s when Hugh was much at sea as a naval officer and then in the Merchant Navy, and Guy was more formally detached from Father at his own wish. But the wider scheme George had – of getting together with Connie for the benefit of all his children – never materialised.

We stayed at school for subsequent holidays until the Christmas of 1946 when George was in charge of a German prisoner of war camp in Chipping Norton, not far from the school, and Guy and I went to him there, though Guy did not stay for Christmas; he had made other, independent arrangements, through a friend of my mother's called Kathleen Sperring, and it signalled a detachment from his father that became complete for a number of those early years. After that, I was more or less the only child left with him. In the summer of 1947 my father was in charge of a Polish Camp in Duns Tew, a small village on the east side of the road from Oxford to Stratford-on-Avon. Such camps temporarily housed the soldiers from Poland who had fought for the Allies in Europe and, at the end of the war, had been repatriated to Britain. After that, my father moved to London.

Going on holiday from school, I never once, then or later, went to join him in the same place. He was apologetic and a bit evasive about this. Things had 'not worked out', the job had not been right, the employer, often a woman, had been either a 'battleaxe' – one of his favourite epithets – or for some other reason he had fallen out with his employer.

PART ONE

So, at this uncertain point in his life, with his children being dispersed, with him wandering from job to job and from place to place, with his attempt to effect a reconciliation with Connie failed, both their long-defunct marriage and the sprawling residue of his later union with my mother were in bits. He had been at a loss as to how he might manage five children. Five children became four with the adoption of the younger of my two sisters, Lena. In 1946 my elder sister, Marion, was still with him, but he could not manage this responsibility. She lived for a while with his Aunt Bertha, his mother's sister, in the village of Great Milton, south of Oxford, off the main road to London. Then Marion too was adopted. After the Christmas of 1946, Guy moved away. Hugh was already a creature of passage, being in the Navy. Possibly my father's deepest concern was how he might manage himself.

It is evident from 'The Perfect Weekend' that he attempted to monitor us all. At different times we worried him. Our health was a matter of concern. He fretted over Hugh's future and then was pleased when his life became more settled. He had followed his father into the Royal Navy, beginning his time in the same way, on the Thames training ship, *HMS Worcester*, in January 1946.

Those visits, in the years immediately after my mother's death, created their own small rituals. There was our place for resting among the fallen elms on the way to Chipping Norton. There was also the special love we had for the artificially perfect village of Cornwell, tiny and tucked away near to the school. In the summer of 1946 we watched him as he lay beside the stream there and successfully tickled a trout, spinning the silver creature out of the water and onto the bank. We later shared the freshly cooked white meat at tea.

III

*I*s it any wonder that George wanted a 'greater love' from Barbara Young? For how long, and with what heartache and regret had he wanted 'Something substantial and definite to aim for' in his life, as well as 'plenty of other things'? I shared with him in those wants as he expressed them in the letter of 9 January 1952, though I knew nothing of his uncertain state of mind.

Did Barbara come to love him at that time? Did things change, bringing them together? I only know that the day after he wrote that January letter, giving nothing of his thoughts away to me, I left him and went back to school.

As I have said, I was beside him when at home during my holidays, a close observer. And when I was not there, I was the unseen monitor of what he did. He wrote regularly and came down from London for half-term visits, though this did not happen that spring of 1952. My involvement in what he did and felt, some of it directly imported, some learnt by instinct and guesswork, had a pattern based on the unchanging routine of school and holiday; the one joyful and indulgent, the other a separation keenly felt.

He sent me gifts of things hard to get in those days, using up his ration allowance for sweets to buy bars of chocolate and tins of Sharps toffees. These he sent in tightly wrapped packages, tied, as a sailor might tie them, overdoing the firmly knotted white string and addressing them in such clear and authoritative handwriting that they seemed to carry treasure well beyond the importance of sweets. I believed then and still believe that my happiness was among the 'plenty of things' he wanted as he set out on this new stage of his life with Barbara.

I shall always be uncertain about that transition from the desperate need he expressed for her in the early letters to the infinite comfort in small things that suffused the letter, dated 27 February 1952, from Carlton Hill, in a new bed-sitting room to which he had moved shortly after my return to school. I give the letter in full:

Dear Barbara
I'll start my letter tonight and finish it at lunchtime tomorrow after seeing the solicitors –

I miss you like —— and am counting the seconds as they go by to seeing you again – But I somehow feel very happy while thinking of you (sounds as if I do it in spasms, but not so, it's all the time) –

This morning I went to Kingston (John Perrings H.Q.) to a meeting of the Ideal Homes Committee – all the directors and me! Apparently I am going there for some of the time (or so Mr Hyde told me), but I've told Mr Hughes that I want to go for all the time and I think he may be able to push it through. I had plenty to say at the meeting, showing interest, so it may help? The Hall of Sleep is being especially featured by the *Daily Mail* and its John Perrings – it has cost them about £15,000, and so should be good.

Try and keep Sunday as free as possible because I am not going to Bruce and if it's fine we will go out and I must have some more snaps of you – *Remember please* darling and don't go and make any arrangements.

Mrs Duncan Sandys came into the showroom today,

Churchill's daughter as I expect you know. I spoke to her, but did not ask her how her old man was. She seems quite pleasant –

And now I must do ironing, write out my report for the lawyer, have a bath and go to bed early.

I worship you darling – Good night –

Thursday noon.
I have just come back from seeing Mr Newman and he says that I have more than a 50/50 chance, but he can't say it's a walkover – He gave me a good deal of advice re my report and I must amplify the points where I can stress my own grievances – such as – short marriage trial in 1926 – the suddenness of leaving me – quarrelling due to unsatisfactory sex relations etc. – also 1945–46 the reason for cooling off, the fact that Connie would not help me re the looking after of Marion –

The points for a divorce:

Short trial in 1926.

Sex relations constitute cohabitation – this apparently definitely annuls separation agreement.

Her refusal to have me back.

The drinking business he did not seem to be much worried about.

Points against:

My adulteries apart from Rita.

If she defends – what she may bring up. Living in a nudist colony would not go down well with some judges.

The adultery with Rita was quite understandable and he said that most judges were reasonable, practical men, and with most judges discretion would be exercised regarding my other adulteries.

I shall not go round to 81 [the house in Sydney Street] tonight (or I may do later if it's not too late) but write out my report at home and send it off to the Law Society –

And now I must go to lunch –

The interview (my present reaction) was satisfactory

PART ONE

without being over hopeful, and I have the feeling that with luck I shall get through – Mr Newman was very pleasant (fairly young, I think Ex NO) and at the end indicated that he thought I was justified.

No more now – Longing to see you again more than ever – Goodbye, George

In particular I consider the opening sentence where he writes 'I miss you like ——— ' and concludes with a dash, finding no possible simile for the aching void she had created within his heart. She was obviously returning to town, perhaps after her half-term which no doubt coincided with my own. And the absence of letters at this time – it will be so different later – can be explained only by the fact that they were together. They were lovers, in each other's arms, their lips joined in tender, soft, exploring kisses that represented their passionate union and about which he expressed himself with such forceful and positive pleasure. And when she went away, just briefly, to her mother's house in St Leonards-on-Sea at the end of February – she was away from Wednesday to Sunday – he wrote of the sense of loss, the gulf of emptiness.

At the time of his letter, saying he would not be coming down to see me, that February of 1952, I was preparing for a new musical role. By then I had been a treble in the school choir for four years. I had the best treble voice in the school at that time, and it was important for the school music. This subject had not really been developed until Stewart Brindley returned from military service in 1948 and began to treat it seriously.

From the start I was an asset to the choir he built up. He had said so in my summer term report of 1948. I sang most of the solo pieces that good trebles had sung since Ernest Lough set a certain standard for such music in the 1920s, and recorded boy soprano pieces on HMV 78s. Stewart Brindley sometimes played them to us. In the summer concert of 1948 I sang Handel's 'Silent Worship' as a treble solo, and the following year, in its English version, 'Ye Who Can Measure Love's Loss and Gain' from Mozart's *The Marriage of Figaro*. Music competitions between Houses were introduced in 1950 and I sang 'Hush Thee, My Baby' by Arthur Sullivan. In the summer concert that year I sang, with a friend, John Hunt, the duet 'Let us Make the Best Use of Our Leisure', again by Mozart. I loved the simplicity of Mendelssohn's 'I waited for the Lord'. I remember well the sense of fear and tension as the introductory bars to Handel's 'I Know that my Redeemer Liveth' were played with their sequence of trills and their build-up of expectation. And then there was the relief at dropping down upon the E natural with 'I *know*'. How infinitely well one knew, and how transient that first-hand knowledge was. How wonderful were the guiding instincts, and the training, and how wonderful once one had embarked.

It was a gift outright, having a good treble voice. Yet it was like a loan, to be recalled with little warning as a price for adolescent development, the process of maturing. It was as good as having an eye for a ball or the ability to draw a likeness, though these have longer life as gifts. For me, the shutters of time were coming down by the end of 1951. Fate was set against that wonderful gift. In the Easter term of 1952 my voice broke. I had been cast in the part of the plaintiff, Angelina, in Gilbert and Sullivan's *Trial by Jury*. Stewart Brindley was already rehearsing me in some of the songs before Christmas, although we were not putting it on until towards the end of the Easter term. Then I was struck by what I thought was a sore throat. In fact it turned into the loss for ever of my soaring treble voice. I was relegated to the role of

PART ONE

one of the barristers and attorneys, with little to sing and no substantial part to act. I thought that Carl Browning, a younger treble in the choir, took over the part, but in fact it was a boy called Richard Huckle, of whom I have no memory. Browning sang and played the part of a bridesmaid.

I think that, with these and other pursuits, the absence of my father was not of overwhelming significance to me. Later, when we put on the public performance of *Trial by Jury*, the school was cut off by snowstorms and the audience much reduced as a result.

So in one sense he and I were separating a bit. I was growing up, leaving childhood behind, in my mind always associated with the glorious magic of a pure treble voice, but of course associated as well with the changing relationship with my father. I dropped through the musical register, pausing briefly as an alto but then descending to being a bass. And inevitably it coincided with an enlargement in the complications of my still youthful life.

Inspired by Barbara's love, the warm response from her that his persistent desire had achieved, he embarked upon a programme for himself aimed at greater respectability. He wanted, at fifty-four, to make something of his life. He wanted to realise, all over again, the lost potential of his naval career, so long ago rendered a ruin. He wanted to make money, craft out a job for himself. No doubt at Barbara's demand he wanted to resolve the contradictions in his personal affairs that existed as a result of Connie's refusal to grant him a divorce after their separation in 1926.

It was part of the good side of my father's strange and complicated nature that he had always seen himself as being at fault in the collapse of his marriage to Connie. Rightly so, no doubt, since a primary cause had been the crisis brought on by the wild weekend in the Dorchester Hotel. That event certainly cost him his career and must have left his sense of personal pride, his great early achievements as a naval officer, in tatters. But there was more to it than that.

In his mind and heart he was always deferential towards that first family. He had a keen sense of guilt at what he had done in breaking it up because of his own brief episode of infidelity. He suffered from the shame of this. He was haunted by the loss. The sudden and appalling break in 1926 – discharge from the Navy, loss of his children, rejection by Connie – turned him to drink. The happiness he gained with my mother, Margaret Shaw (Rita), and the life this gave to the children he then had, including myself, were made precarious by the intense and volatile pattern of his drinking. He was wild and flamboyant in drink. It ignited within him rage and sentimentality, nostalgia and confession. He could stare into the star-studded firmament and see himself pinned there among the stars that had guided his sure hand and eye when he had learned to be so good a navigator in his young manhood. The pain of this and the shame of it fell like a torrent upon his bewildered head.

His life and nature took on a schizophrenic character. In drink, he was full of wild fluctuations, most of which were expressions, in the end, of guilt. When not drinking, he became quite a puritan, turning his energies – which were prodigious – to excessively good behaviour, hard work and to an almost sanctimonious determination on recovery.

By the time he met Barbara, I had experienced many of the variations in his nature, seeing him lose jobs, pick himself up, find new employment and recover his confidence and self-respect. I was a sceptic about the lasting power of his transmutation into a hard-working man and a good father, and wondered if he was deluding himself. My scepticism, even as a child, was rational. I saw things as they were, and not in some imagined perfection such as he envisaged, though with woeful lack of realisation. And I should have sustained this cool view of him during the events that were now to develop. But I did not. The reality of what I experienced from the age of seven to the age of sixteen was punctuated by his drinking bouts every four months or so. Sometimes he lasted longer, sometimes he turned aside soon enough from the abyss, and the bout did not necessarily lead to the loss of his job and then a move from one lodging to another. But in general the outcome was dismal and unhappy.

Barbara knew all this and still clung to him. George was told by the lawyer Douglas Newman to amplify the points where he could stress his own grievances. It seems so remote, the prospect of an unflinching court and a surly judge, and of their having to be persuaded that a marriage that had foundered almost thirty years before should be dissolved. Divorce was a combat zone in those days. One didn't always win freedom, as it might be seen today. It was all judged differently. My poor, vexed father wanted the marriage dissolved finally. And then his aching spirit would be set free in order to let him start again.

He wrote his report on the night of the letter, 27 February 1952, and sent it off to Douglas Newman at the Law Society. He set out in it the brief trial at marriage ending in 1926, the unsatisfactory nature of their sexual relations, and Connie's refusal to have him back. The attempt he made at reconciliation, at the end of the war, came as a surprise, as did, to a lesser extent, the fact that he had lived and probably worked at that time in a nudist colony. The lawyer saw this as something that would not go down well with the judges.

I am amused now at the thought of it. I was amused at the

time, some six years before this letter when I, a boy of eight, had gone with him to visit the nudist colony – 'naturist camp' I suppose we would call it now. We were met at the door by a balding middle-aged man smoking a pipe. He was wearing socks and shoes and a waistcoat and jacket, his genitals and pubic hair exposed with casual indifference to the surprised and conservative gaze of a child who had already met with many surprises but none as eccentric as this one. It was strange in that the encounter was in the depths of winter in a woodland of bare trees. It was indeed Brickett Wood where it happened, that Christmas of 1944. Not only does the encounter remain with me; so do quite strong recollections of the wood itself, the stillness and the cold. The ground was flat, the trees comparatively small and unimpressive, so that the grey sky was visible through the leafless branches and the thin, silvery stems of the birches. Underfoot, the leaves, crisped by frost, made a rustling sound as we walked through them. I went alone with my father to the nudist colony; my brothers were playing elsewhere.

My knowledge of these events at the time was greater than either my father or Barbara knew. The 'silent witness' in me, quite apart from the tense expectation that governed my view of them both during these early years of their growing love, also persuaded me towards a very careful surveillance of his correspondence. I was frightened at doing it, but felt it was justified in the circumstances. I don't remember seeing the report he wrote. It was no doubt a single copy, written in longhand and, once sent, not part of the record kept at this time. But in a soft green leather folder he did keep letters, and on one carefully managed occasion I did read, without his knowledge or later detection, some of the correspondence that revealed to me what was happening.

PART ONE

At the time, early in 1952, when the golden glow of George and Barbara's realised love for each other was taking on the practical issue of divorce and marriage, the revelation from the letters that I did actually look at, long since forgotten, had a profound but beneficial effect on me. I have to assume that they are related to the letters I now possess, written to Barbara, but I cannot be sure of the detail. The letters gave logic and specific purpose to the anticipated changes for which I so desperately hoped. I already knew of Connie's existence. I had met Chips more than once. He had grown tall and was well built, fulfilling my father's expectation of him when he was born, that he might play rugby and tennis. He did both, with some success, at King's School, Canterbury. And hearing his deep and musical voice addressing George as 'Father' opened up for me a wider complication of the meaning of 'family'. But it did not have much to do with letters from the lawyer, and the drafts of George's own letters showed me a new and infinitely appealing future, and for a time I had reason to hope that it would come about.

King George VI had died early in February 1952. It was a grey time in all our lives, certainly as I remember it, perhaps in every way. Grey clouds covered the winter sun. Our spirits were grey under post-war privation and hardship. A brief moment of colour and excitement was covered by the newsreels which always accompanied the films we saw. This was when Princess Elizabeth left for a Commonwealth tour with Prince Philip, seen off by her father. The King stood on the runway, severe-faced and stoical in a grey overcoat. Beside him stood the Queen who, as Queen Mother, would live for another half-century after his death. The tour was cut short by the death, and the princess returned, to the solid grey of grief, a queen.

Three queens gathered to mourn King George VI's passing and were photographed standing together on the platform at Paddington Station, waiting for the coffin to arrive on its way to Windsor. I loved that occasion of grief. It was so real, so palpable; the black veils like curtains, symbols of privacy in public. At school I kept the newspapers and magazines and remember the mauve and black used in the printing of some of them. I must have designated myself as unofficial archivist for those days, a status accepted by other boys in my house who recognised some strange intensity in the grief I had elected to observe, and condoned my collecting and keeping of newspapers. In the library of the main school, where I was already a keen reader, I was assistant to the master who acted as librarian. Later, as magazines were replaced, I gathered them for myself. There were those like the *Illustrated London News* that gave page after page to the stately rituals surrounding the King's death and burial. His reign had covered almost the whole of my life; from peace, through war to peace again. He and Winston Churchill, opposite in almost every way, the King gentle where Churchill was truculent, the King calm when Churchill was being dramatic, yet mutually respectful, even affectionate, were emblems or icons, and I was shaped in consciousness of them as presiding figures.

Earlier, as a child, perhaps in 1947, sitting on my father's shoulders in Parliament Square, I had watched King George and Queen Elizabeth going to the opening of Parliament and had cheered him for leading us through the war years and helping us to survive the austerity that surrounded my childhood. He had the same frail truthfulness towards his chosen purposes as were reflected in that other memorable event of the time, the Festival of Britain, which I always associate with the end of his reign. Whatever lay ahead, the King, in his

PART ONE

quiet, undramatic way, had been a stabilising force. Now for a time he lay in state in Westminster Hall. More than 300,000 people filed past the coffin. Then his body was carried away on a gun carriage. At one stage the solemn procession passed Marlborough House where his mother, Queen Mary, stood at a window over which a blind had been half-drawn. She bowed her head. King George VI was the fourth of her sons to die before her. It is an image that expresses the time; the long, sad moment of his going. Another striking image of Queen Mary: her tall form, taller than her daughter-in-law and her granddaughter, but clad, like them, in heavy black veils over black coats, hers full-length, and on her head a black toque hat. They stood and waited in silence at Paddington and no other State grief that I can remember, save that for Winston Churchill when he died, came near in compassion, then or for the next fifty years.

For my father it was different. He was clearly made happy by the turn of events at this time. Grey, for him, was the colour of doves and of sunrise, of love and of understanding. It was like that magical, unstable grey made by the watercolourist from mixing alizarin crimson with viridian green, a grey that is warmed with the flush of red, softened by the doubtful, difficult viridescence. Out of the grey, for him, came new life. Though the events at this time have never entirely fallen into place, making them hard to piece together with complete satisfaction, nevertheless there is a strong perception of relief and happiness.

There are gaps in my father's correspondence with Barbara. Later on in their lives, these gaps came to represent separation and even more woeful circumstances that struck at the roots of their love. But at this time the gaps meant they were together. This is indicated in the letters when they follow such periods. I was in part responsible. Home from school, I shared whatever accommodation he had. And he wrote letters then as he did when she was away or when he was away. Whatever they faced, he wrote of his love. When I was at school and they were together, he told of it.

This was how it was, a mixed kind of engagement, in the early part of 1952. He saw her often and the encounters were loving ones. These were happy days. She represented all his hope, and the letters expressed this hope, linking it with the future. There had been a burial of past uncertainty. And I am able to read, out of nine letters spread from January to September 1952, with large gaps when I surmise they were together, a sustained flood of loving interchanges, and evidence also of them being much of the time together.

In the break of silence, from the end of February until the high summer of late July, another love affair, which also lasted all his life, grew out of visiting Barbara and then living with her. This was his love for the house in which she lived, in a flat on the top floor. It was one of a terrace across the road from St Luke's Church in Sydney Street, Chelsea. The buildings dated from the 1760s. Even then they were condemned, yet for many years after that they were not demolished, and for love of them I returned, many times over the years, quite often to relive the experiences I had with him there at that time. Then, one day, they were gone.

The next group of letters ran from July to September 1952. In them he dwells on what the house meant to him and how inextricably it was linked to their love. 'I have just come back from Sydney Street. My sacred Sydney Street! And I saw you walking along and smiling up at me when you saw me. I shall go back to that street in a hundred years' time, when I am dead. And I will get my happiness again, and perhaps a little sadness as well – my darling I love you so much and every place connected with you is sacred to me.'

The house in Sydney Street in Chelsea had been connected with the Young family for a number of years. During the war Edith Young, Barbara's mother, had lived in the house. At the end of the war Sheila Stewart, a South African who had been in the WAAF with Barbara, lived in the top-floor flat that later became Barbara's. This would have been in about 1946, since my brother, Guy, stayed there with Sheila at that time without knowing anything of Barbara Young. After the war, Sheila Stewart had been invited by my headmaster, John Woollan, on his appointment in the summer of 1946, to help teach in the junior school at Kingham Hill. She told me many years later that she was John Woollan's cousin. She taught history. I cannot imagine what history it was, Alfred burning the cakes perhaps. My father had first met her on a visit to Kingham Hill; much later she may have been the person to introduce him to Barbara.

George was practical in his love for her flat and her things, looking after her window-boxes and her sempervivum, making sure her plants were well watered. 'They are looking splendid and I think should be moved to a larger place as they are spreading and would then be able to spread more. Let me have your orders please. They don't require much water as they are alpine plants and there isn't much rain in the Alps.' He knew something about them, whatever his knowledge may have been about the rainfall over high ground. He had worked at one stage in a nursery in the Cotswolds specialising in alpine plants and I had worked beside him, a gardener's boy, during a holiday from school. We potted up all manner of rock plants and dispatched them by mail. All I remember is the epithet 'slave-driver' my father applied to the man in charge.

His gardening always underpinned his life. In London it meant jobbing gardening and, since this was summertime, with his abundant energy he took on clients in the evenings. He told her everything, even recording, in that particular letter of 5 August about the sempervivum, that he was 'going to bed in pyjamas – many thanks again, my sweet. You have been in my thoughts all day.' She must have given them to him, a pair of pyjamas. I, who shared a room with him in those years of growing up, and never thought that anyone else did, can well remember his perfunctory style of dress at night – a vest and pants – and his necessarily cavalier view of more elegant conventions. He was always poor. Carefree of spirit, simple in his tastes, eating well but inexpensively, he forged on, at very best making ends meet.

It is interesting how much he told her about everything, and related to her in his letters when they were apart. These were the days of the three-minute phone call, the archaic telephone rituals, the small change balanced on small ledges or on directories in booths while diaries or address books were consulted. How wonderful that it has given us letters spelling out intended actions day by day. He was no Diderot offering his *Pensées Philosophiques*. And yet it could be said that his own letters were akin to *Les Bijoux Indiscrets*, the soft jewels of thought savoured and exchanged.

He fashioned out of words his many acts and dropped them in total trust before the attentive gaze of Barbara's brown eyes. The proof that she attended, that she cared, is to be found in his words to her. Hers to him have long vanished. But there is the additional knowledge of my own watchfulness as their love grew.

I came home to him that summer of 1952 full of my own adventures. It had been a good term for me. I was fifteen years old and doing well at school. I had won the senior reading prize for the second year running, no small achievement in itself but made special for me because I coveted most of all the element of proud performance by which it was gained; a dramatic recitation, usually of Shakespeare. It may have been Jaques in *As You Like It* deliberating on the Seven Ages of Man, or Hamlet's 'bare bodkin' speech. I do not remember which, but I have the prize itself for that year, *The Oxford Book of Modern Verse*, chosen and edited by W.B. Yeats. I have ambivalent feelings about it today, recognising the bizarre nature of Yeats's selection, but then it was a new form of magical inspiration, a leapfrog game of thought and feeling from Walter Pater to the poet I would come to love and read above all others, Louis MacNeice. He was not well served by Yeats, nor was Auden, nor Eliot. In fact the further Yeats got in the book, the worse his choices became. Many years were to pass before I came to a critical understanding or a better-ordered love, generated in part by my own efforts to write, then just visible above the entwined web of a thousand different enthusiasms.

I came home also that summer with an altogether different experience: that of exploration and adventure. Instead of leaving in the normal way to travel in mid-July to London from Kingham Station, four of us went north to the Lake District. We travelled in the Bursar's Wolseley motor car and met at Brathay Hall, in Westmoreland, with a further fifteen boys from other schools. We had volunteered to do work for a geographical society in Cambridge, mapping the land beneath the surface of a number of small lakes or tarns. It had not been done before. This was mainly because of the difficulty of bringing a stable enough boat up the thousand or so feet of difficult climbing. We were exploring these small scooped-out glacial tarns that lay on the lip of land looking down the valley and backed, usually on the other three sides, by much higher crag and scree. A master had solved the boat problem, designing a collapsible dinghy made of canvas and wood.

A record kept and published in the school magazine tells me that we explored Codale Tarn and then Hayeswater Tarn. From memory I recall another beautiful teardrop of dark water, Blea Tarn. It lay still and undiscovered. It was cradled in a valley that seemed fashioned by a pair of giant hands. They were held together in perfect symmetry, the curved fingers representing the steep wall rising above the water, the fingers representing the striation of tumbling becks and rills, forever there above us in the uncertain weather that made our work more difficult. The large-scale Ordnance Survey map showed clearly enough the presence of whichever tarn we explored, but there was a small and intense feeling of wonder and excitement at the unexplained depth before us. Knowledge turned into speculation at the water's edge. Would our plumb lines sink to unimagined depths? Would we discover undreamed-of phenomena? Beyond the mix of turf cropped by sheep, of boulders and small rocks and the mirror-like surface of the small lake, was the inscrutable challenge facing us.

So there we were, on that day in late July, straight from the much softer climate of the Cotswolds. We came like explorers, climbing up the steep and rocky fell side and carrying with us equipment of which Patrick White's eponymous Voss would have been proud. We shared among us the awkward burden of the collapsible dinghy, with its crude wood and canvas construction; we had paddles, plumb lines, tripods, alidades, measuring and righting instruments, our two-man bivouacs and our own personal kit.

The more adventurous swam naked in the cold water of

PART ONE

the lake each morning and then we set to work. A team of three manned the dinghy: one to row, one to keep to the sight line and respond to signals from the lakeside, directing the boat with gestures when he strayed off its path, and a third to drop the plumb line and measure the depth. Two more pairs of boys on either bank guided the small boat along its invisible course line. Then, from a third triangulation point, the course of soundings was followed with the alidade and recorded on a flat table on top of a tripod which had the map pinned to it.

What did we expect? We teetered between the fabulous and the prosaic. Fathomless depth, or a natural incline down, across and up again? The reality of discovery is to render the known out of the mysterious. All day long we did it, and then in the late afternoon we bathed and walked and read and chatted. For meals we fed largely on concentrates and dried vegetables, biscuits and chocolate. We had brought our own supplies of a regional mint cake sold as a source of energy. I seem to remember that the school was trying some of the foodstuffs on an experimental basis for a company supplying comestibles to the army. The army was on all the older boys' minds. National Service was not only not far off but was the most common experience coming back to us from boys who had been at the school, as well as from elder brothers now serving their time. The messages were rather ominous; hard times lay ahead. We needed to prepare for them. Modest though it may seem, this mountain exploration was highblown adventure: a carefully planned examination into the nature of things. It was that in different ways, however. The setting was sombre, the atmosphere melancholic. Cold nights, cold water, rain showers, and a wind blowing off the much higher fells that surrounded us at times induced what was an atmosphere of foreboding, even of Wordsworth's 'blank despair'.

The poet was a presence as well, I remember. It so happened that the more senior among us who were doing A-levels and studying English had already embarked on Wordsworth's *Prelude*, part of the giant task of absorbing the Romantic poets for the A-level examinations. When we looked up at dusk into the stars, and saw the harder edge of the darker horizon encircling us on every side but one, we were perhaps oppressed. And when we descried, through the v-shaped gap, the lighter sky to the west, we were at one with what we had begun to read and conscious of other levels of exploration that went deep inside us.

I had to consider what I faced in my final two years at school which would begin in September. I had to confront the question of whether or not I would get into university. I had finished the term on an indifferent note. At that stage, not having seen the term report on what I already wanted to forget, I was not too painfully aware of the criticisms, principally that I was skating over the surface of work. But those who taught me had conveyed enough of what they thought to create a mood of uncertainty about the future. The lake and the work we were doing took my mind away from such gloomy concerns. But in the evenings, and often in the cold mornings, sitting alone outside the bivouac I shared with Tim Rogerson, I did worry about myself.

I had brought the slim volume of Wordsworth's *Prelude* books I and II which we had been asked to read that holiday. How well it suited the occasion. It offered answers to the perseverance of circumstantiality. It invited a harder look into the meaning of things and the light that meaning might shed upon future time.

PART ONE

We carried down from the mountain complete manuscript maps of what had never been mapped before. Blea Tarn, like the other tarns, surrendered its secrets. They were as one might have imagined: normal in depth and with an evenly curved cup shape. But, oh the difference between prediction and speculation on the one hand and the firm reality of what we had discovered and recorded on the other! The ice had done this. The wonder of its power, now that the evidence of its existence had faded and changed with the green landscape, was brought more vividly back by the inverted contours we recorded.

We had been changed. Filled with pride, we struck camp and descended the mountain, struggling with the heavy dinghy and our kit.

I felt less of a child coming back to my father that summer. Stress had generated energy. Companionship on such a scheme had made for greater confidence. He listened patiently to my detailed account. He, of course, knew all of it and much more from his days as a Royal Navy navigation officer. But this made him more keenly interested and quickened the early conversations between us.

Barbara had gone home to St Leonards-on-Sea to her mother in late July; the two of them, I surmise, having lived together. At least it seems so, since after the loving letter of February there are no letters for a time. Compellingly, after she departed, George sent her a short and loving note to tell her, 'Your letter has just been read and it makes me feel of course happy as possible – you are a dear.' He sent love to everyone and cautioned her 'Don't swim out too far'. He was off to see the youngest of his siblings, my Uncle Matthew, who lived in Kent. How I wish the letter she sent him had survived so that I might read the exact expression of her love for him that stirred his heart. He wrote to tell her of my impending return. He had got for me 'a large ground-floor room, here in Castlenau, Barnes, at 30/- a week'. Finding again the precise, over-informative nature of my father is a pleasurable memory of his care and forethought. He told Barbara that he had been unable to get me a temporary job. 'They are overstaffed with schoolboys so I expect he will manage to earn a pound or two somewhere else.' But he did take interest in what I had been doing. It reminded him of navigation, of his own prowess in that field, of the dark reality of still water under grey skies, and of the importance of knowing the depth of it.

He was pleased with me. My report that summer term had been 'quite good' he told Barbara. I did not wonder then, because I was confident of her, what she could possibly have thought of me. Now, years later, when all has been reduced to a bundle of forgotten letters in a cardboard box, I am not so sure. What did she think?

I was to arrive on the Saturday of that first week in August. The day he wrote the letter, a Tuesday, he told her she had been in his thoughts all day. And then, on Wednesday, going home at lunchtime, there was a letter from her. 'Your letter was waiting for me. It makes such a difference seeing your writing and, even if there is not much news, just send the envelope.'

Work was not going well. My father was not a man who trusted other men. He had good reason, given his chequered career as a salesman during the 1930s. In the war years, which were difficult for everyone, but an especially raw period for him, he had several jobs. And in the grim period of the late 1940s – up to the time of his frantic decision to make something of his life and to try and carry Barbara with him on that journey of new adventure – his job prospects remained

PART ONE

limited. In August 1952, in the wake of a successful time during the Ideal Homes Exhibition, he told her of a meeting he'd had at Cadby Hall, where I think the exhibition was to be held. It was with a senior person called Hughes, to whom he asked whether or not he would be made permanent. 'Nothing definite,' he wrote to Barbara, 'and I am not too optimistic – the job that I am doing now will last until the middle of September and then he and Dyer will see managers of other departments. In the meantime I think I will probe around myself, starting with the emergency department. In any case I would have plenty of warning that the job is coming to an end – as I told him, I did not want to be out of work. James still stands by his word, re writing...' The letter then ceases on that subject, moving on to gardening, the house and other things. James was Barbara's brother-in-law.

James Loring was always guarded towards my father. They approached each other warily. There was at this time a certain irony in their mutual positions, since James, who held a quite senior appointment in a London department store, was the kind of person who at that time would have employed – and indeed in certain circumstances dismissed – George. The reference to him in the letter was not for a favour that would be easy to take up. From James's point of view, writing on George's behalf would have been a last resort, and it would have been undertaken reluctantly. Would a word from James in any case have cut any ice? I doubt it. Life does not work like that.

During that time, on account of James's family, I too came to know him a little. I visited the large family flat in Cadogan Gardens once or twice. I liked his wife, Roberta, and she, I think, was sympathetic towards me on account of her sister's love for George and her children's fondness for him and for me. But then she also must have held something in reserve because I never think of it as a developing relationship, rather as one that held the future in abeyance. Did she have those same doubts that assailed us all, as to what lay in the future and how this urgent and passionate man would resolve these huge questions about himself and the woman he loved?

IV

BARBARA BECAME very much my father's life in that summer of 1952, and their happiness together lasted into the autumn and winter. It seemed to do so against the odds, and against the prevailing bad luck that dogged him in his unfortunate passage from crisis to crisis, from job to job. He was struggling with intractable problems. With the ending of the Ideal Homes Exhibition that year, his job on behalf of the London Bedding Centre did indeed end. By late August he was seeking employment through the pages of the *Gardeners' Chronicle*. The wording was very simple. 'Gentleman wishes to run large garden in the country. Is knowledgeable, and a specialist in many plants. Can take on all general duties, will drive car. Will work in family or guest house situation.' The same kind of advertisement was also inserted in his most favoured marketplace of all: the pages of *The Lady*. I hardly remember reading the magazine, though I did so once or twice. But it exercised a powerful influence on me and seems now, looking back, to contain in its forgotten narrow columns of 'Situations Sought' a sad chronology of George's movements in those years, criss-crossing England in what proved a vain attempt, either to make something of his life or to find permanent employment.

The mountain, as I say, was huge. Despite his energy, which was enormous, and his mind, which was quick, clever and resourceful, the material out of which the future would be fashioned was so frail. His naval career, which still meant so much to him, was a handicap. He carried it around as a measure of his shame. He had to explain its loss. He prevaricated no doubt over the detail, but accepted the fact of it, doomed either way, never able to explain how an able-bodied, intelligent 'Lieutenant Commander RN Retd' was advertising in the *Gardeners' Chronicle* or *The Lady* as a gardener or driver.

Years later, Irene endeavoured to explain the trap in which he seemed to be caught and her own remedy for escape, by no means a perfect one. At a time of crisis, after she had been helping him in one way or another, mainly lending him money, she wrote me a letter pointing out the futile prospect of any job in London where he took lodgings. 'Except for his brief periods on the water waggon, it simply means that when he is paid he takes his money to the pub, doesn't pay the rent, and by Monday he hasn't a penny left. He then comes down on me for the rent, and money to last him until the end of the week. Then the pattern starts all over again. The only solution is for him to have a residential job, so that when he gets his money at the end of the week, there is nothing to be paid out, and it is all his to be spent as he likes. When it has all gone, at least he has board and lodging till the next pay day.'

I knew part of this, though not all of it. While it increasingly became the dominant pattern for his existence, in the early days of his love affair with Barbara he was maintaining work in London and keeping to his bed-sitting rooms, mainly in the Notting Hill Gate region. Echoes of his disappointment over employment, which moved away from his being a well-

PART ONE

dressed salesman, are there, and there is growing uncertainty about gardening becoming predominant. But I was not terribly concerned; my summer was crowded with other things. I saw Barbara. We both did, and I went with her to exhibitions on my own. We had outings to the Classic Cinema in Chelsea to see grainy French black and white movies set in a rugged world of peasant love and rural animosity in Brittany, Gascony or Macon.

She was no lover of teaching as a profession. It did work for her. She did well and had a good relationship with her pupils, but she also found it boring and difficult. Yet she taught me so much. She had the knack of turning me into the discoverer. Discovery was the fountainhead of my youthful happiness. Discovery tells us where we are going. It draws the maps and sets the distances. Unlike my father, I was not burdened at the time with huge points towards which I was travelling and on which my future life depended. It was much simpler. I was learning how to use my eyes and my ears, developing my ability to understand and to move from one attractive vista to the next. I was associating the paint tones and colours of Vermeer with the grainy moodiness of Vittorio de Sica, the humour of Jacques Tati and the realism of Jean-Devaivre. I suppose I was conscious of what was going on around me, knew that a mood of near crisis was never far away.

It *was* a crisis. What hung in the balance during that month of August was my father's divorce. After the earlier meeting, when he was told he had a fifty-fifty chance of getting it, he wrote to the Law Society. Then he had to wait. He refers, in a letter of 7 August, to the divorce papers and a forthcoming meeting with the lawyer, Newman, after hearing back from the Society. This was to take place a week later in Chelsea. Barbara was passing through London that day. She had been in Oxford and was on her way back to Hastings. He wrote, 'Let me know what time you will be in Chelsea and we can meet. I must see you.'

There was much talk about 'snaps'. The term has almost vanished from use. The only snaps we have now are old snaps, woven into our past memories. It so happens that, among the letters there was a small collection of the photographs taken at that time. They included Barbara's friend from WAAF days, Sheila, and my older brother Hugh rowing with George, and Barbara sitting with him and her sister Marg on the beach at St Leonards. He printed them and sent them to her, got extra ones and lamented the fact that he had none of her mother. I have nothing, therefore, to remember her mother by. But those photographs that have survived do recall for me the summer events on the south coast of England. 'I have just been talking to you on the phone,' he wrote in the letter of August 7, 'and it was nice to hear your voice – I will keep this open until I get the snaps tomorrow – I shall get your letter on Friday – you must stick to your word, Barbara – I am always being told about my word but you are worse than me I think – Anyhow write as often as you can & don't tire as it is all I have of you at the moment.' She was herself a good subject for photography, much as he tried to make her do better. 'My lovely Barbara does not concentrate enough – I am determined to get a good one of you one day and then all the *Vogues* in the world will want it.'

I have always believed, of my youth, that unseen, even secret hands took care of me. I had a favourite story – is it any wonder? – as a small child, called 'Hidden Hands'. It told of a boy's adventures and misfortunes. The farmer for whom he worked ordered him to plough a huge field. It was a formidable task to be completed in one day. In the middle of doing it,

PART ONE

great hands came out of the sky and helped him by pulling the plough. He faced a fire in a house where a young girl was trapped in an upstairs room. The hands descended and helped to rescue her and scooped up water to put out the flames. The fanciful magic of the tale was reinforced in the old Victorian collection of stories, battered with re-reading, by charming drawings.

Of all the 'Hidden Hands' that reached down from the benevolent skies above my head, none were of greater help to me than those of Geoff Rocke, a trustee of Kingham Hill School. He was appointed in 1948 and came down for the School Speech Day that summer. Field Marshal Lord Wavell presented the prizes. The author of *Other Men's Flowers* and the former viceroy of India, Lord Wavell had also been one of Churchill's World War II generals.

Lord Wavell spoke about the school's founder, a man of deep Christian conviction called Charles Edward Baring Young. He described him as a man of great vision and generosity who wanted to make education available to those not favoured by the society they lived in. He had done so when this role was performed through philanthropy and not by the State. Baring Young, he said, placed an emphasis on craftsmanship and chose a beautiful and remote part of the Cotswolds to locate the school, one house succeeding another as the school grew in size. He told us never to cease learning and to keep our individuality and independence. He related these to the modern world, in which he had played a distinguished role, and to the threats which in his time and in the future represented a spiritual war 'between Christ and the Kremlin'.

I remember afterwards getting him to sign on the flyleaf of my prize and then carrying the book proudly under my arm.

He That Is Down Need Fear No Fall

My father did not come down on that occasion. He was living and working in London, but was unable to get away. We had all been instructed by the warden to ask visitors if they would like to be shown around the school. I approached the new trustee, Geoff Rocke, and introduced myself. He happily placed himself in my hands, and I showed him round. We set off on a tour of exhibitions, workshops, the art room, even my own classroom, where we had spent time preparing an exhibition of the geography of Britain.

Geoff Rocke was just forty years old. He was a big man, heavily built. He had been a major in the Grenadier Guards and had won the Military Cross in an engagement in Normandy after the invasion; in this he was wounded. The operations, involving the removal of bone from both legs, had left him without an obvious limp but with a slightly restricted walk; his big trunk and handsome head pitched slightly forward in order to give him better balance. This gave him a questing appearance, as though in search of truth, which indeed was part of his nature.

It was my nature, perhaps still is, to be exhaustively thorough. I showed him *everything*. He was grateful. Never again, after that first visit when his curiosity as a new trustee was entirely justified, would he have the same desire to acquaint himself about the physical extent of the trust he had undertaken on our behalf. Apart from showing him all I could, it was my youthful concern to make him understand what Kingham Hill meant to the boys who were lucky enough to have arrived there. I told him – and years later he reminded me of it – how much it had rescued our lives, how indebted we felt towards it and towards the trust he represented.

It was a school like other schools, and yet it was a school unlike any other school that I have ever heard about. Its

PART ONE

location was on a hill and among valleys where the fields were planted with wheat, barley and oats, and where the cattle gave us milk and cream. In winter it was cold. Snow fell and drifted; at times in winter we were cut off. In summer its seclusion and the unspoilt countryside brought it close to paradise. I was a beneficiary. 'Hidden Hands' had brought me there and had paid for me to be there. Geoff Rocke was a representative, to begin with, of the general concept of such help

Explaining the school to him inevitably led me on to giving details of life with my father, no easy matter at all. I must have summarised for him a strange enough story indeed, telling him about my mother, the rest of the family, life in London and the present set of circumstances. He took a close interest in everything I said. He was a shy man, probably at first uncertain of how much he should ask. But I was innocently forthcoming and by the end of the afternoon, when he drove away in a rather dashing Armstrong-Siddeley car with a canvas roof, he had expressed the wish to make contact again in London when I went on holiday.

Years later I asked him about that meeting and also about the trouble he later took to exercise the modest guardianship which then made such a difference.

He remembered my straightforward account of life in London with my father, and of the abundant, even exhaustive, detail I gave him. It was strange enough; I knew that. My truthful directness in dealing with it derived in part, I imagine, from the fact of my loving my father for his foibles and failures as much as for his strength of purpose. I may have thought, on my first encounter with this man who, after his war experience in France, had gone on to run a business in Philpotts Lane off Fenchurch Street, that my story was a strange one and outside his experience. Whether or not this was so, he was experienced in the trusteeship of young people, working in and for different boys' clubs in London. So perhaps the story I had told him was not so strange after all.

I may have mentioned my father's dependence on women, particularly on Irene Spindlo. This was some time before he met Barbara. In any case I am sure the question of my father's status would have been automatic. Anyway, however I explained it, it cannot have sounded as though my circumstances were particularly satisfactory.

Geoff Rocke saw, in a clear and logical way, Kingham Hill School and its pupils, how they were chosen, how they were cared for. In part, on that first encounter, I was showing him how the various ingredients worked in creating around us a safe zone of comfort, security and education. He valued this. And he valued, it later became clear, our moral education and our Christian faith. Having a dutiful and talkative guide made a memorable impact, or so he later said.

I saw him from time to time. My father, at first a bit uncertain, gave a guarded blessing but avoided any meeting himself. Geoff Rocke gave me holiday jobs to do. I met people, including both Dieter and Hartmut Schultz, who later became friends. I took elderly people, like his aunt, to railway stations. I carried their cases and put them on trains. We became, in due course, lifelong friends. There were almost thirty years' difference in age. He made himself aware of the precarious circumstances surrounding and affecting me and he offered choices. He held out to me 'Hidden Hands' of great help and long persistence and I salute his memory for what he did.

I saw much of him in that summer holiday of 1952 for all the reasons already given and because, by then, the friendship had become a relaxed and vibrant expectation on my part of his growing interest in my welfare, particularly the spiritual

PART ONE

side of my life. He was an evangelical Christian. Kingham Hill School had been founded by Charles Edward Baring Young, a member of the Baring banking family, and a man of strong, low church Christian principles. Geoff Rocke was slightly dismayed that this tradition had, as he saw it, become watered down. Among other events in 1952, he arranged for me to go on a 'Crusader Camp' on the Norfolk Broads. 'Crusaders' were pledged to Christian fellowship. I looked forward to the camp immensely, little realising how life changing that sailing holiday would be. It is briefly touched on in a letter from George to Barbara. He mentions receiving a postcard from me saying how warm the water was for bathing. 'I think he is going to enjoy himself,' he wrote on the Monday of that last week in August. I was away for a week or more, certainly including the following weekend. And while I was away, he was going to St Leonards-on-Sea on the usual weekend train, the 6.45 p.m., to be with Barbara.

Confirming this brief mention in the letter are the three inscriptions on the inside of the cover and the flyleaf of my copy of Bunyan's *The Pilgrim's Progress*. The edition has rather striking illustrations by Victor Bertoglio. The friendly messages were solicited as mementoes of that event. The first was from my friend Hartmut Schultz, met as a result of Geoff Rocke and invited to the camp also. 'Always your brother in Christ,' he wrote, then quoted in German the verses from St Paul's Epistle to the Ephesians about 'the helmet of Salvation, and the sword of the Spirit, which is the word of God'. It was offered me, through him, against those 'fiery darts of the wicked'.

The second inscription was that of Norman Gray, also a friend of Geoff Rocke's, and he quoted from the Book of Joshua: 'Only be thou strong and very courageous'. The book of the law was offered in order to make a man's way prosperous. 'Then thou shalt have good success.' Looked at now, more than half a century later, the words are timely for my father rather than for me. I was not looking for prosperity or good success just then. I was looking for understanding and revelations, for a permanency different in kind from my father's. He wanted to stabilise his life and focus it on Barbara; I think I simply wanted a home that would be the same each time I came back from school on holiday. Norman Gray, as far as I remember, was a doctor. This was his fifteenth Broads Cruise leading the Eastbourne Crusades.

The third of the inscriptions was from Ian Thomas, known by his initials 'W.I.T.' and revered by multitudes of young people who had been drawn into the evangelical fellowship of which he was a leader and an inspiring preacher. The organisation inspired events like that camp.

Ian Thomas did not quote other authorities. He wrote with his own authority: 'Faith says "Thank You" for all God's wonderful promises – and takes them, believing that God is as good as his Word! Those who have this faith are the friends of God – and he delights in them, as they in Him!' And, though he did not quote it, he offered a brief reference under his signature to another of St Paul's epistles, to the Philippians, Chapter I Verse 21: 'For to me to live is Christ, and to die is gain.'

Neither then nor later did my father ever understand what that part of my summer meant to me. He had once had his own faith, not much different, I think, from how it had been at King's School, Canterbury. It had been bred out of education at a public school and was spartan and moralistic, and also a bit emotional. I think he did not wish it revived. As first my halfbrother Chips turned to the Church, then my eldest brother Hugh converted to Roman Catholicism. My father developed

PART ONE

an antagonistic approach to their faith, a mixture of dismissive mockery or, alternatively, embarrassment. I expect that mainly unhappy memories were being revived, memories of a faith that had foundered long before and had never been any use anyway in the life he had led. Certainly those memories had vanished before he met my mother. This meant that none of us were baptised. In my case my baptism took place the night before my confirmation. Am I right in thinking that what he had once believed had now become a superficial memory, and that our spiritual welfare was more an embarrassment to him than anything else? I hardly think this is just to his school or his youth. Perhaps it is just a judgement on him? Whatever the truth, his faith had been battered by the vicissitudes of his life, losing all but frail remnants in the process.

Faith, for my father, was not the manifestation of need, at least not of his need. If his ambiguous but deferential respect for Christian belief came from anywhere, then it came from my paternal grandmother. She, I think, must have seen her own faith, and faith generally, as a defence for the female race against man's inescapable waywardness. If the need were greater, and the problem worse, then faith was a protection for women against the innate violence of men, particularly in drink. For me, that summer, my own intensely renewed faith was a discovery; what I experienced added a new dimension to what school had given me. And, sadly, all this was without any grounding from my childhood home. Perhaps that same religious force in the family, my grandmother, had turned my father away from his early belief at King's School, Canterbury, but I think the change within him was more complicated than this. What he had experienced had done him no good in the tribulations he faced later in his life. His first family with Connie – of Chips and Elizabeth – had been brought up in conventional Christian ways. They were sustained, even reinforced, after his departure into the wilderness. But his second family, myself a part of it, had no religion at all. School, therefore, had brought the first epiphany, strong if quite conventional, leading to confirmation and the practice of faith. It had led also to much youthful debate and was reinforced by my talents as a singer.

The summer holiday that year on the Norfolk Broads brought a second epiphany, infinitely more powerful than the first. I felt myself in the company of angelic forces, swayed by the power of the spirit, guided by an essential, unwavering love. The tented meadow beside the smooth calm waters of that inland sea, a veritable Galilee in its echoes and memories, became vital and alive. Those in whose company I spent that time were full of the energy of raw youth. The boys were from well-to-do families in or around Eastbourne. Hartmut Schultz and I were interlopers who had been introduced as a result of Geoff Rocke's friendship with Ian Thomas and Dr Gray. This was as much a mission as if we had been Hottentots. And in the evening, after a day's sailing under the hot August sun that browned us all like ripe pippins, we sat together enthralled by the word of God.

The spiritual strengthening encouraged in me a greater separation from my father. This was neither covert nor grounded in any disparagement, but it taught me to love him differently and to see him from a position of growing self-determination. My belief was an alternative and different form of comfort, reassurance and the acquisition of an inner life. It also gave me new friends, including the Schultz brothers. Perhaps it was also a natural part of the second climacteric in one's life.

Ian Thomas was a great preacher and he spoke truth. And while my father was battling with the loss of his job and the

PART ONE

need to branch out through the good offices of *The Lady* and the *Gardener's Chronicle*, I was imbibing beliefs that were magical and new. Many years later, when Barbara's nephew gave me the letters that tell this story, he spoke to me about his own attempts to write, and we discussed Catholic fiction. He was by then a Roman Catholic priest. I told him of my admiration for Greene, Waugh and Mauriac, but I asserted that the Reformation had created a guild of Christian writers of the reformed faith beginning with the man whose most famous work was in my hands on that summer holiday more than half a century earlier. Had Bunyan not written *The Life and Death of Mr Badman*, possibly the first English novel? Rudyard Kipling called him 'Salvation's first Defoe'.

I love especially, of all Bunyan's writing, that short lyrical poem 'The Shepherd Boy Sings in the Valley of Humiliation'. Words from it apply to my beloved father, particularly the beginning: 'He that is down needs fear no fall, He that is low no pride.' I often wanted a time in his life when he could also have said, 'I am content with what I have, Little be it or much.' But that did not come easily to him and was not part of his life that summer. The other words, however, dictated his fortune. The humiliation of Bunyan's shepherd boy was hunger and poverty. His spiritual pilgrimage was uncluttered by fullness. And it is in this state of austere grace that he makes his way.

The pilgrimage for me was just beginning. For my father, the pilgrimage was an endeavour to make a new start and in the company of a woman for whom he expressed at that time a love that verged on the frantic. Had I known all the details, I would have felt a greater pity for him than I did. But perhaps this was good. Why should I have wanted to pity him? He protected me. I diverged from him. I had my own life to lead, and in so many different ways, some of them barely perceptible. I was shifting into new spiritual and intellectual territory, while at the same time being in close physical, emotional and moral contact with him. Pitying my father would have damaged the high regard in which I held him on so many counts. Hope and expectation – that something, somewhere and somehow would turn up – would have been undermined and this would have damaged the unswerving love I felt for him. This love was instinctive, deep and visceral. Even now, sitting in the confusion and tumult of the letters, I am steadied by the regular heartbeat of that love and it brings tears to my eyes. They are such strange tears, representing a warm flood of feeling for him and for her. I am released within my heart by those tears. They are no longer painful as at first they were, when he was wrestling with the inevitable failures that nagged at him at this time. A perpetual fighter, who in one letter referred to his eldest son, Chips, as having told him 'Providence always protects you', he inspired those around him with belief in his invincibility when all the evidence told one that he was the most vulnerable of men.

I came back from the camp ready in every way to return to school. My father told me little of what faced him at the summer's end, but in his letters to Barbara in late August and early September he wrote: 'At the moment I am not absolutely sure what I am going to do. Certainly the outside life suits me and I think it would perhaps be worth sticking to gardening which with luck could be expanded and give me more money eventually.' But in another, later, letter there is a sad note, almost one of foreboding, when he observes, 'the light fades earlier now and soon evening work will end.'

The last summer letter, indeed the last letter of 1952, was written on 5 September, the day before my birthday. I was sixteen. My birthday present from him, though chosen by me, was a traveller's Bible, one of those that zip up so that the thin pages hold together and no notes fall out. I had notes from Norfolk to insert. I would always have notes after that. I think of it now as a pilgrim's Bible. The journey of a pilgrim is the journey of a stranger in this world. Have I always been that?

I always loved autumn in that part of the Cotswolds, the summer clinging on until the first frosts dispelled the dying hopes of late summer warmth, dispelling also all final illusions. The frosts came early to Kingham Hill. Though soft and curved in shape, the hill was often swept by strong winds and in cold weather it could be bitter. In the snows of 1947 access had to be dug through five-foot drifts. The eastern edge of what we always knew as 'The Hill' was not exactly an escarpment, but the long fall of the ground from the top of the hill down to the school farm, and beyond it to Sarsden Brook, exposed us all to the east winds that came across the higher flat countryside beyond Chipping Norton. From the southwest the prevailing winds came over the high ground around Stow, and from the Slaughters and the Swells. In that direction and on the horizon was Rissington, an air base from which, in wartime days, we had watched gliders depart for Normandy and the D-Day landings.

I knew it all so well and revelled in the knowledge. The importance of it grew with time. Coming back to school, from I know not what point of danger and uncertainty that governed my father's life, was a bit like coming home in that the place was familiar and constant in its certainties and comforts. I trusted it more, deep down, than I trusted him. I did trust in his love. That, in its essence, never failed me, but his wayward nature, his own struggles, his chronicle of problems, made him less reliable as the years passed, or perhaps made my own demands more taxing for him.

That term was the beginning of my final two years at school. It meant extra work, a more careful focus of energy, added authority over younger boys, as well as more respect and intellectual exchanges with staff.

There was extra music. Stewart Brindley's success with the choir had become a talking point locally. In November 1952 the choir was invited to sing at a wedding in St Mary's in the village of Steeple Barton The bride was Sylvie Catriona Fleming and the groom George Christopher Rittson-Thomas, a well-known rugby player. We sang the anthem, 'God be in My Head' and Carl Browning sang 'O For the Wings of a Dove'. He had replaced me as the lead treble in the choir.

We drove over in rainy weather through Chipping Norton and Enstone and we counted it quite a privilege to be invited to the reception in Barton Abbey afterwards. Many years later the bride's uncle told me 'it rained like hell'. I used my own experience at that wedding, together with creative imagination, to write the opening scene of my first novel, *A Singer at the Wedding*.

I cannot say with certainty that what I experienced made me a writer; far from it. But the seeds for a literary life were sown at this time by the yearning sense of isolation. And a number of the ingredients for later fiction – scenes, characters, episodes – had been absorbed and set in place for future use. Much more was needed, not least the capacity of skill and the quickening force of inspiration. But these I think were present in my response to teaching, to reading, and to my early fumbling efforts at self-expression, which were to take shape in just a couple of years' time. And there was something else, not yet realised. This was a more comprehensive understanding of the man who inevitably would take the central position in any work that was based on my life experiences up to this point.

PART ONE

Like the gentle touches of a brush on a painting that has been conceived, composed and partly executed, but needs to be brought to completion, this strangely isolated period of late adolescence was seminal. My heart was stirred by the occasion of that wedding. The nuptials reminded me of what had already begun to fall into place in respect of my father. This was the absence of such an event in his life. Photographs he did have. One of them was of my mother, her clear-cut and beautiful features set off and enhanced by an Eton-crop hairstyle. But of my two parents together, she in white, he in morning suit with a white carnation in his lapel, where was such an image? Nothing like that existed, nor had the event itself existed. And in the letters that I had looked at, secretly, fearfully, the full reason for this was now known to me. Known to me also was the pressing need for some resolution of the difficulties he faced.

I wanted it for him and I wanted it for myself. If it were to mean anything in his life, it had to be soon. I had seen too much ill fortune fall on his head. Unlike Chips, I did not see Providence smiling on him. He was reaching out for Barbara and it was already touch and go; the touch of love, the go of his or her possible departure.

For myself time too was running out. The demands of a life for myself were looming larger: the final two years of education, aiming at university and confronted by military service. Inevitably, my father's happiness and mine were diverging. This winter wedding gave to the select band of singers a glimpse of an entirely different social class. We were not privileged like the other guests, especially the families of bride and groom, but we enjoyed a privilege of talent that none could gainsay, and there were words of praise that made the occasion immortal.

The events of those years, beginning with my membership of the choir as a treble in 1948 when I was eleven years old, are memorable.

I returned home at Christmas to the very welcome, if now expected, news that we would be going again to St Leonards-on-Sea. The idea of a second Christmas there was a far sweeter prospect than the first had been. It gave tangible reality to the longed-for continuity in my father's relationship with Barbara. We were in lodgings in Castlenau in Barnes, which he had moved to from St John's Wood some time in the second half of the year. 'It must seem strange, this emphasis on the detail gathered from his letters and other sources.'

So the Christmas of 1952 was first of all memorable because we returned to that large, rambling three-storey house at 29 Chapel Park Road. The occasion was also memorable because my brother Hugh was included. This too had important implications. Instead of the comfort and happiness being confined within the symbiotic relationship that had developed among George, Barbara and myself, the more independent position of my elder brother gave an endorsement to what I hoped might happen in the future. In another sense, Hugh, who on the whole was indulgent towards me and relaxed in his feelings about my father by then, added to the normal enjoyment of the festival and diluted the intensity with which I was observing everyone. I already had quite a reputation for that. My father often commented, and with good reason, on my inclination to miss nothing. Hugh's approach – more mature, less affected – changed the atmosphere of that Christmas holiday.

PART TWO

Learning to Love

V

GEORGE'S LOVE for Barbara provoked a warm response from her. It grew and blossomed through 1952 and into 1953. The letters do not give the continuity to it for which one might hope. It seems they lived together when I returned to school at the end of that year, after the Christmas which we spent so happily on the south coast of England with Barbara's family. During that time they were together and there were no letters. Whether they lived together all the time or not is a matter for speculation. She certainly had her flat in Sydney Street, and for a time he kept his bed-sitting room in Barnes.

When he did write again to Barbara, on 6 January 1953, after his return to London and to work, there is almost a hint of desperation in his expression of his love for her. They can have been apart for only a few days. He writes: 'I was so pleased to get your letter and hear your voice again – I simply can't be without you and you've no idea what I feel like when you are not around.'

After Christmas and his return to London, I stayed on with the family at St Leonards-on-Sea. I then returned to him on 8 January. He wrote again on that day, 'Your letter has arrived, my darling, and so has Bruce, looking as fit as he has ever looked and full of his holiday which he has enjoyed. He thinks it's "the best he has had". Thank Mother for the eggs, sugar and butter – Bruce gave me all the details of what he has been doing these past weeks. Give Char my love and thank her for sending hers to me.'

Charmian was then twelve years old, the middle child of Roberta's family. In his letter, George write that we would meet Barbara's train when she returned to town in a few days, and that, if needs be, we would clean her flat before she came back. He was so energised by his love for her and I had been made so happy myself by the growing intimacy with all the family. We all belonged together.

I wanted what he wanted as desperately as he did. I wanted an end to our peripatetic existence, the uncertainty of it, the emotional impoverishment, the lack of friends, the break-up of our family, the sense of shame I felt at not having a permanent home and never quite knowing where I would be. A cloud was always there, an anticipation of some form of humiliation that would derive from having to explain myself, to answer the question that eternally posed itself even if not directly asked. I phrase it now because never before and never again afterwards would it have so poignant a context. How was it that this had happened? How could this man, with his stern and handsome demeanour, his soft and beautifully musical voice, be living so precariously? What good was his cultured accent and educated grasp of life? What did his background of King's School, Canterbury and a distinguished career in the Navy do for him? Why on earth was he now living so aimlessly, moving from one lodging to another, trailing with him his loving but bewildered and increasingly dissatisfied son?

I never pushed him or complained. I ameliorated what

humiliations there were, real or imagined, by the exercise of my own nature. This, as I remember it from the particular time, was loving towards him, patient with him, ready always to look on the bright side of his uncertain affairs. At the same time I was creating for myself a protective layer of calm dissimulation, hiding from him and others the inner feelings that derived from constant observation of the way things were. I was disillusioned so many times, yet went on hoping. It seemed then that what I was hoping for was some kind of settlement. This, after all, was the beginning of the tenth year since my mother's death. Hers and my father's five children were dispersed save for me. And what kind of family did we two constitute as we explored the ever-changing territory of new lodgings, new jobs, new and different acquaintances, and women who had never measured up until Barbara came on the scene? Would one not expect me to be half-frantic at the age of sixteen as my childhood disappeared from me, consumed in school expectations of the advent of manhood and a domestic environment that was as dramatic as any of the plays then on in London town? Yet it was not so; I looked on in a quiet and dignified way, a self-protective adolescent hiding my bewilderment, learning to live on the edge of expectation, longing for resolution but doubtful about it.

On more than one occasion, my father commented on my calm, even calculated, observation of him. He said he understood how much I saw and how wise I was to keep quiet about it. 'You miss nothing,' he said. 'You know me better than I know myself. You understand what is happening. You don't know where it will lead – none of us do. But somehow you are ready for whatever eventuality arises. Sadly, I have made you so. I have taught you how not to live your life, giving you inexhaustible examples all along the way that we have travelled together.' These are not his exact words, and I am probably wrong in suggesting that it happened on one occasion. It was a regular speech of defence, made in the dock before his most fearful judge, myself. He made it in different forms and on different occasions. Some of them were occasionally happy, in a self-mocking way, meant kindly, perhaps ameliorating some actual or supposed hurt he had inflicted on me. But mostly the occasions were ineffably sad. They expressed his own defeat and the fact that he stood on trial before me, undoubtedly guilty of most of the things with which I loyally refused to charge him. I could not bring myself to blame him, to accuse him of neglect or failure. Somehow his love for me, emotionally declared but unrealistically delivered, transformed our life together as it always had done and certainly did at this time as Barbara was drawn into that life, transforming it with the excitement I am trying to record. Does it deserve the description? Was it *excitement*? Or was it just the life of this middle-class English family into whose mixture of happiness and sadness, success and failure, we had been drawn? The question is posed for only one reason: it shows how my life as a boy since my mother's death had been distorted to the point where what was negotiated by these two adults promised a transformation of incalculable importance to me. I had lived on the strange, unique sustenance of my father's love. Now settlement, security and a different life was on offer through his love for another. Would it happen?

My father's anxiety about his future with Barbara took a dramatic turn that January of 1953. He became jealous of another man who had become increasingly interested in Barbara, though no detail emerges in the letters of any actual approaches he had made to her. This was a Dr Norman, who owned a toyshop called Pringles in Knightsbridge. He employed Barbara's friend and ex-WAAF colleague, Sheila Stewart, to run the shop. Sheila was a laconic creature and probably quite lazy. She moved with a relaxed and easy pace, wore tweed skirts and twinsets, had sandy-coloured hair curly in a slightly 'frizzed' way, a freckled complexion and front teeth that very slightly protruded and faintly touched on her lower lip – this in an attractive way. Sheila was a part-time teacher at the junior school in Plymouth House where the lion's share of the work was borne by a very dynamic and rather glamorous woman called Joan Trembath Carpenter. Others who taught us were Miss Anwyl, whose knowledge of botany was impressive, and Miss Attlee, whose brother was the prime minister. Sheila left teaching and moved to London. During the summer of the previous year, 1952, she had come to Steyning to join in our holiday and she is in photographs with Barbara and with Georgiana, Charmian and Ulick. My father met Barbara through Sheila; while he worked at the London Bedding Centre, he would have been only a short distance from Pringles.

Pringles was a fashionable Knightsbridge shop. It was small and had no stock room. Sheila worked there with another woman who wanted to leave, and my father records in one of the letters a conference in January about the future of Pringles and Sheila's role in it. Ever practical, he was ready to help in making room for the stock and improving the layout with better shelves. He had a talent for that kind of organisational work.

He wrote to Barbara: 'I phoned Sheila before phoning you and offered my services for any indoor work like putting up shelves, work that would come in handy on a wet day or in dark hours.' This would all seem mundane information, perhaps, were it not for the next phase in that letter where he adds: 'Also I would like to meet this formidable Norman.'

Norman was a doctor. He emerges out of the blank shadows that letters always cast. They always tell just part of the story. George saw Dr Norman as a threat, a cause of worry, and he now provoked a new emotion in my father: jealousy. He had returned to London from the south coast, missing Barbara very much. And in the very first letter he writes: 'I kid myself at times that if anything happened I should get on just as well.' But this was clearly not so. He goes on: 'Which brings me to the Doctor Norman – He has been worrying me quite a lot and I can see pretty plainly what he is after – He has advantages and money is one. I get frightfully het up and wonder if you are keeping anything from me – Has Sheila written again? And have you arranged another meeting? You see darling you don't tell these people that you are supposed to be getting married so they don't restrain themselves, and I should think this doctor is a slow but steady mover in the direction he wants – you may think I'm silly sweetheart, [but] I'm right in many things…'. Indeed this was true. But was he right in this as well? I think perhaps not.

The weather was cold. It snowed over London and this affected my father's work. He was on his own. He must have been brooding about Dr Norman. Whatever the reason, he represented a real threat to my father, whose resources were, as ever, precarious. In his nervous state, he ended the 6 January letter: 'I must go out now into the snow – And let me have a letter by return and let me know anything that you have not told me – Don't forget and always remember that I worship you … Things have not been too happy – the work has been bad because of the weather and now it has changed I am going hard to pick up what I have lost. Worked at Caldwells today and tomorrow, Sunday, I am going to her brother-in-law at

Park Royal to prune fruit trees. Monday Monros and I hope the weather will hold good.'

Thinking of what he did in winter, and of the difficulty of it, I wonder: did their love cope with what he seemed to be facing? He always said that gardening suited him best. My father loved being out of doors, loved gardens and plants. He loved the freedom and the independence, the ability to dictate or suggest or persuade his clients about what he should do for them. But he was dependent on the weather as well as on them, and the pay was poor. Only by working hard and for several clients could he make ends meet. I am sure they put him under stress. He was careful in the way he handled his clients, persuasive rather than argumentative, but from quite a young age I witnessed him in many encounters with those he gardened for. I do recall, above all, the innate charm that underlay any discussion or debate. But I also remember the frustrations he felt and sometimes the anger boiling over and leading to a breach. When he said in that letter 'things have not been too happy', I saw that he was referring to much more than what he did so well, even in difficult weather: tending the gardens of others.

I cannot remember the state of mind I found him in when I did arrive back on 8 January, the day before he posted that second letter. Reading his account of what was going on and of his fears about Dr Norman reminds me of Pringles and of Sheila. I am sure I went there with messages for Sheila from my father or from Barbara and I recall how Sheila's laconic style suited so well the smart women who came there to buy toys for their children. Of course I knew nothing of the distress that Norman caused my father. I came back to a cold, rationed city, its lighting then meagre, its shop fronts making brave displays of the economies and privations that affected everyone.

I think, together with her letter, I lifted his troubled heart when I came back to him after Christmas. But I was in no position to assuage his anxious feelings about Dr Norman. If, in return, he did touch upon his own worries, the touch would have been a light one, a quizzical glance, perhaps a forefinger to his lips meaning 'Keep mum' and possibly a wry look of apprehension. He was of a stoic disposition, particularly when he told me things, and he covered up any anguish he felt by making some joke about 'time healing all', or 'what would it matter in a thousand years?' Norman would not have been mentioned. Nor would my father have said to me that his naval pension had been cut at the beginning of January, or that work was difficult because of the weather and stopped early in the evening because of winter nightfall.

But I *was* drawn into a closer involvement with Sheila Stewart. Two days after my return from the south coast, my father and I called on her and she gave us supper. 'Sheila did most of the talking on various subjects,' he said in his subsequent letter to Barbara, and the evening was clearly a success. 'Sheila has been very sweet indeed and I retract anything I have said against her. She naturally feels for me and can guess what my feelings are like. Norman will know about me and will then no doubt keep away, but it's no good, Barbara darling, telling me that I have not the right to do this or that – the ties of marriage are not more binding than the ties that bind you and I together now, and I have every right to act as I think – '

Sheila was fond of my father. He charmed her, as he did all women, and she was quite relaxed in his company, knowing, as they both did, that she was an attendant party on the passionate relationship between two of her friends. She held his charm in check with a fey and relaxed charm of her own.

PART TWO

I was fond of her and, though it may seem strange over a period of fifty years, I do remember that evening and particularly the way she seemed to steer him through troubled waters. I had always remembered the evening in question for some reason, perhaps tension, and this had been the case long before the letters came to light. Something was in the air; his uncertainty, his suspicion, his jealousy. Aware of it, she sought to assuage it. At one point I remember being asked to sit and read in one room while they talked in another. The net effect was that when we left, he walked with a lighter step.

I was quite interested in Pringles. I asked Sheila about the shop and what sort of people came to buy presents. One of its patrons was Queen Mary. She gave me her description of a royal car arriving with chauffeur and servant in attendance and Queen Mary, grandmother to the new Queen, stepping down from it. She wore a full-length coat with high fur collar, cuffs and a toque. Her purchases had to be delivered, or so Sheila said. I think they were furnishings for a royal dolls' house. I looked differently upon Sheila after this revelation, and thought how proper to its circumstance was her relaxed and unconventional manner. She would not have danced attention on anyone, not even a dowager queen. She was playful with my father. She coaxed him towards being more relaxed about Norman. I was not privy to the more private, serious conversation, presumably about Norman, and did not even know at the time that she was more than just a friend, being also a guardian of Barbara's life. Only the photographs, which came so many years later with the letters, tell me that she was with myself, Barbara and the children on holiday the previous summer, either in Steyning or St Leonards-on-Sea. And those same photographs tell me how youthful I was, a slightly gawky, bespectacled youth, only on the earliest fringes of manhood and uncertain of my place between these adults deciding great issues about their own futures, and the children in the same photographs all younger than me.

There is a wealth of episode in the letters, and still today they cannot be fully untangled. They cover just a few days in early January 1953. Yet I see in them portents both for him and for me as I try to decipher the language of love in which, in their strangely troubled way, they are so firmly delivered. It is a language carrying the darker seeds of jealousy, as well as the haunting odour of nostalgia.

The first letter after his return, and containing the reference to getting 'frightfully het up' was followed the next day with a much longer letter, warning Barbara, 'You've told me when I feel like writing to you to do so, so here goes.'

> It's 11 p.m. and I walked through Sydney Street tonight and, as before when you've been out of London, it's almost as sad as walking in a graveyard looking for something you've lost – London is absolutely hopeless without you in it – I looked up at the windows and wondered if by some miracle the lights would be on, the curtains suddenly pulled back and your face peering out looking for me – It all really happened in my imagination and I suppose I shall do it again and again when you're away and hope one day you and I will never be parted. The thrill and love of Sydney Street was as strong as ever and you've no idea, my darling, how much I love and miss you. Don't, my sweet, ever let me down because you know by now that whatever happens that love will last to the end of my life.

And so it did. I would love the letter to have ended there and not to have gone on to contain the attempted unravelling of the Norman episode. But my father was deeply troubled by it and had to confront the demons that were threatening his happiness. He believed that Sheila was in some way conspiring with Norman to further her own ends which involved a male friend of hers called Tom. My father believed that Sheila had put to Dr Norman the simple proposition that they help each other: 'You help me with Tom and I'll help you with Barbara.' He put it in the letter, just like that. Wisely or not, it was like a declaration. It was of course wrong. Then, after these words, he paused and left the letter overnight.

When my father wrote letters, he always read them over. I can see him in my mind's eye holding up the pale blue paper on which generally he wrote and surveying with his stern inimitable gaze the words he had so carefully set down. And I wonder now: did he pause at all over the strangely disturbing suggestion about Sheila and Tom and Dr Norman? Evidently the setting down of this thought passed his critical gaze. Not alone that: having posted the letter, he began another even longer letter the next day, returning to the theme of Dr Norman.

The visit that my father and I had paid to Sheila, together with a phone call on that Saturday evening, had dispelled any thought of her being involved in intrigue or of intrigue altogether. But, in a letter to Barbara, he then goes on to deal at some length with 'the Norman incident'. The starting point was for him to say that it made him even more determined to marry her. The conversation, obviously on his side from a phone box and restricted to three minutes which he described as 'silly', was not the best of exchanges to have at that time. And so the letter is a more forceful summary of his thoughts on the whole affair:

> When you say I have no right to discuss that or that with Sheila (or anybody else), I think I have every right to act as I

think proper to safeguard my interests in my life with you and to prevent anything parting us and therefore I naturally act on my own intuition when I know it may be right. I know you laugh at me so much and think I am a fool, but at least I do know how gullible you are and can be led up the garden path by men as well as women – I am telling you what Sheila and I talked about and of course you won't phone or talk to her about it until after I have seen you on Monday – Sheila and I both agree that Norman may have fallen in love with you and as he is of that age when he wants a companion (in more ways than one) I naturally object that he should become friendly with you. He is sexually incompetent because he has had his prostate gland removed but the desire is the same without satisfaction and men in those circumstances sometimes become a pest – He has the advantage over me in that he has cash but I am hanged if I'm going to lose you on that account and you're certainly not going out with him – in fact, Barbara darling, it would be better if you faced up to the fact and said to people 'I am going to marry a gardener!' It would certainly create a fuller character in you. I should feel differently, too, that I am not being slung in the background when you've got something better to do or somebody better to meet – Don't say I have not the right – I have the right and that is enough about the Norman incident.

Dr Norman passed out of the picture. He was never again a figure in Barbara's life and there is no further mention of him. Calm was restored to my father's relationship with Sheila and the letter ends with a flurry of phrasing which to me is as exquisite as the soft ending of a Schubert impromptu. He adds in *my* love to her; and then he says 'he wants me to marry you'. Did I so dare? To say that? It must be so. He passes on my love to the children and to Barbara's sister and her mother. And then he concludes: 'And now I am going to bed – Don't forget how much I am longing to see you and how much I love you – Love from George.'

I had lunch with Barbara's other sister, Roberta, and it also is referred to in the letter. The three children had stayed on in her grandmother's house and were due in London a day or two later. I think I went along to that lunch – it was in the flat in Cadogan Gardens – happily enough. We were considering some post-Christmas outing. James, Roberta's husband, was there briefly. I think he did no more than acknowledge my presence and then hurried off to his business, leaving the two of us together.

I think it took no time at all to decide what we might do about the outing and who would be included. There was the question of Barbara coming and whether or not my father would come as well, and I asked if James would be with us. Roberta must have shaken her head, probably an instant reaction and possibly accompanied with a sad expression. She would not have explained.

But I think I realised about Roberta – and it must have been at about that time – that she was no longer certain over well-defined things in her life. All that was sure was her love for her children and their love for her. About her love for James and his for her there was doubt, which I came to know about only much later. My father may have hinted at it to me. He had spotted the tension, sensed the disenchantment and had concluded that all was not well. To me this knowledge was a heavy burden. It added to my own anxiety about what I most wanted in the world at that time.

Roberta would certainly have known of my wish for my father to marry Barbara, but we did not really enter this entirely new territory. While everyone who flowed in and out of the changing pattern of encounter, which was focused mainly on the house on the south coast, had views and concerns about Barbara and George, it was not discussed in a way that involved the younger participants. I belonged with them. I may have been the eldest among them, but this gave me neither adult status nor the privileges to accompany such a position. Like my father, I was an observer of the family rather than part of it, and this intensified the anxieties I felt when with other members of the family. I remind myself, in the light of the known story – still not, by any means, the whole story – that I was no more than a sixteen-year-old. Even my stature was still quite small. I existed in the firm, dependable glow of my father's love for me. That was all I was certain about. It mattered not at all that he was what he was. His substance in the world was overridden entirely by the force and strength of his personality and by the passionate feelings he expressed. Like a shower of golden sunbeams, the effulgence bathed me.

I know what he wanted so desperately from Barbara and this was in absolute accord with what I wanted from the rest of her family. So the tiny notes of doubt were fearful things to me and I covered them over with the temporal reality. The outing was there for us. The return to London of the children was imminent. On Monday evening I would stand a little shyly beside my father at Victoria Station when the train from Hastings drew in to the platform and Barbara, with her easy relaxed way of walking, would approach, ready to ease the doubts in both our hearts.

In the second week in January I returned to school. Whatever I had known, or not known, of the turmoil during those days that began the new year, all was resolved as best it could have been in the circumstances. This is not intended as an evasion, but to express the lack of knowledge I had then and the degree to which I depended on an uncertain hope carefully cherished, but vain. George had passed through a crisis over Dr Norman, a crisis that had pushed him again to the edge of desperation. As at the outset of his love for Barbara, expressed so forcefully in the first letters written in 1951, he had again grappled with the stark issues of his impoverished life. For a time they were set in the jealous contrast presented by a supposed rival, but he then turned out to be no rival at all.

Dr Norman had status in the world. He had money and the modest influence that goes with it. My father, free spirit though he was and determined on expressing his right to fight for the woman he loved, was like the character in Bunyan's poem, which surely is Bunyan himself. Unlike Bunyan, George did not have the Christian spirit to sustain him, but he did have spirit of a different kind and it did lead on to a pilgrimage in which I shared for many years to come.

Up until that time my father and I had always been hand in hand, our adversary the world. Into it Barbara had brought another presence. Her hand, softer and gentler, reached out to both of us. I am gratified to find my own presence in all the letters. There is a natural expression of the fact that I belonged there with them. I knew it by instinct at the time. Half a century later I came to know it within the prospect of my being accepted as part of a family. Perhaps it was tentative, cautious. I judged the family to be a loving one. Its members of course cared for Barbara. Collectively, it was no doubt nervous of my father's role. Undoubtedly, or so I felt, there was a more relaxed view of a place in it for me.

My father was a proud man. He was handsome and stood with his broad shoulders squared against the world. He had been battered by drink and there were red lines in his face. Regularly enough, his visage took on a florid, flushed appearance. At one time, in the distant past, he had engaged in some fight or other in which his nose had been broken. It had mended unevenly, giving a slightly crooked, hawk-like appearance to his face. Together with his stern grey eyes and fine, overhanging forehead, it made him formidable. He was a warrior. He was at war with the world, or with his own destiny, or simply with the modest jobs in which he became engaged in those years. There is a raw and ragged movement to his days and he records the modest toil in little, off-hand paragraphs that chart his financial struggle.

There was certainly no poverty of spirit, no failure in defending himself. In the letter in which he presents his idyllic rendering of the appeal of Sydney Street and of how hopeless it was without Barbara in it, he gives some flavour of his work:

> I've been to Munro's today, cleaning the car and their silver (plenty of it) as they have only just got back – Outside work is practically dead and if this weather is going on I shall definitely have to think hard. Tomorrow, if the weather is the same as today I can go to the 'Battle Axe', because I have a good deal of pruning to do and also a certain amount of indoor work she can give me.

Which particular 'Battle Axe' this was cannot be recovered from memory. As later letters will show, and as I knew at the time from first-hand experience, there were always 'Battle Axes' looming over my father, demanding more than he could give, presenting him with difficult judgements about what he might do next or when and where he should choose to move on.

Among his few papers he kept two or three work 'references'. Those who wrote them cannot easily be traced. How can the piecemeal life of an itinerant servant be traced when everyone is dead? From the envelope marked 'References', I choose one simply because I remember the place, which on occasion I went to as a servant boy during a school holiday. He worked just at that time – the winter of 1952/53 – for Sir Edward and Lady Hulton. She was perhaps the 'Battle Axe', though I remember he always saw her as a benign figure, the centre-pin of his working life for a time. There were, after all, things to choose from and he told Barbara about them all. But Lady Hulton employed him for two years and later, when he asked her, she gave him the reference. For whatever reason, he kept it in the envelope so marked until his death.

I went away to school with hope in my heart. I *did* want them to marry. I *did* think it would happen. And if the settlement of his life which was so much on his mind in the earlier letters was to be realised, then this was the right time for it.

By St Patrick's Day of that Coronation Year he had moved to new lodgings in Oakley Street, Chelsea. It was close to Sydney Street. The 31 bus passed down both these streets and was on his way to work, and on mine to all the engaging things I sought to do when I came home for the Easter holiday. A letter records his move to the new lodgings:

> I worked till two o'clock this morning putting things in order and I am now all shipshape – I hope we shall be quite comfortable here – I am writing this in front of the window – open – watching the traffic and buses – I think I shall like it here, notwithstanding the snobs and of course if work remains good so that I can afford it.

There is a sad note also in that letter. He missed by accident a meeting with Barbara; it was over some confusion about time, he arriving at her flat early the previous evening but too late nonetheless. He had intended to carry her suitcase to the station to see her off, but she had already departed. She was going to a convent school in Essex on a teaching job. I suspect it was a reluctant journey. I think part of the desperation that lay between them, hidden as best it could be lest it should frighten them into parting, was the potential difficulty of their marriage being viable as far as work was concerned.

Barbara needed her family and her family home. She had grown up in some comfort and security, and while her mother was alive and her eldest sister, Marg, at home, there was a way of life open to her as well which allowed a reasonably leisurely and discursive approach to work. She did 'this and that'. She did not quite know what to do if 'this and that' proved insufficient in marriage to a man who was engaged in such a raw and painful struggle as my father was. On missing her, he said in the letter 'So disappointing, so I sat down in the armchair for a while –'. I see him there now, the expression on his face vexed and forlorn. He was so easily put out. When he was like that, his slack hands hung down over the arms of that chair and his grey eyes would be looking at nothing material. They would range over the haunt of his happiness. 'I shall be thinking of you, my darling sweet, all the while – If possible I will meet you at Sloane Square – if not I will be at the flat –'

He moved to Chelsea for my sake, but also to be nearer to her. He made a temporary home for that holiday, to which I came and for which provision was included. He did it in part, I think, because it was required of him. There was, or there had been, some monitoring of his capacity to be in charge of a child at that time. I remember earlier periods, when I had first rejoined him in his itinerant existence and, when he was working, I was consigned to regimes I never really enjoyed. I remember there was an organisation called 'Universal Aunts' available to take charge of the child whose parent, usually a single parent, had to work. It happened only in the early days after the war and I never liked it. I remember the irksome reality it represented, of being in someone's charge and inevitably deprived of various freedoms. By this stage, with Barbara, my father sought to establish conventions and proprieties. He was a man for decorum, strange though this may seem. He followed a protocol in possessing me as a son, ensuring that I saw nothing of the intimate side of his relationship with Barbara. He protected me from the full weight of the troubles that at times oppressed him, never fully revealing his despair.

One other fragment survives from that time. Written on Post Office telegram paper, it records a weekend, possibly that Easter, when I was away and my brother Hugh visited from his army duties and was with them both on the south coast. There are photographs with the letter, of my father and brother rowing in the sea, my father wearing a bandanna handkerchief, pirate fashion, and looking so handsome and relaxed. It is a scribbled note, undated, without an envelope, probably left for Barbara in the flat. It reads:

> Saw Hugh off at 1 a.m. He so enjoyed the weekend – I think I shall have to leave 102. Hultons I think is OK. Am seeing Mrs Thomas on Thursday – No news yet of Hultons' return. Give my love to Mother and Marg. Love, my darling, from George.

He did leave 102 Oakley Street. Where he then went to live, I do not know. He got his divorce not too long after that, but he and Barbara did not marry. There are no more letters from that year and only one from the next, making a gap in their correspondence of eighteen months. The letters they did exchange up to this point indicate many things. There is the uncertain nature of his existence; the need he had for her, at times frantic, at times fearful that she would let him down and it would all fall apart. The jealousy he felt about Dr Norman that was clearly groundless. The nostalgia he felt about Sydney Street is for me particularly moving because I so vividly shared in it. There is the enjoyment and pleasure they had together, in each other's company and in each other's arms. There is the wider enjoyment of the Young family and my father's real affection for Marg, the unmarried sister, whom I loved too.

All this breathes out from the correspondence. Details can be pieced together and from my own memory I can add with advantage to the packet of information and share in a recollection of all our lives more than fifty years ago. But when there is nothing, nothing can be added. At a time of change and challenge in my own life, looking forward to my last year or so at school, shouldering responsibilities, coming to terms with the meaning of work and the forming and training of my own mind, I began to lose him. I lost him as the all-powerful father figure who had embraced me, protected me, looked over my actions and judged them and responded to my half-developed understanding of what I wanted to be.

He became diminished in my eyes. I do not mean this cruelly. I was never dismissive of him. I always loved him and still do. But in understanding him better as a human being and in recognising his star-crossed vulnerability and the inevitable defeat he faced, I loosened deliberately the hold he had so powerfully exercised over me. He became less of a presence in my heart, less of a force imposing itself on my mind.

VI

I TRAVELLED ABROAD for the first time in 1953. My first passport was issued in March, and I went by way of Ostend and the Hook of Holland to a small town called Viersen on the border between Germany and Holland. I stayed there with the family of Hartmut Schultz, the friend I had made at camp on the Norfolk Broads the previous summer. The trip itself was suggested and then organised by Geoff Rocke. He was acting, with caution, *in loco parentis*. It was a self-appointed status and he was always careful to ensure that I discussed such events or proposals with my father, which of course I did, getting his approval for this act of generosity, one of so many that were influencing my life at this time. Hartmut lived with his parents and his elder brother, Dieter, in a small house. I crossed the border by train at midnight, falling asleep and missing my connection, so that I arrived late and was deeply relieved that he had waited patiently all that time. He brought me back to his home where I slept on a camp bed in a downstairs room. Hartmut's father practising at the piano woke me. He sang with a fine bass voice and was a member of a choir in the town. I listened silently to the careful exercise of scales and then to familiar passages from the last movement of Beethoven's Ninth Symphony, to the words of

Schiller's 'Ode to Joy'. I knew the work from family enthusiasm for the composer. We regularly went to the Promenade concerts in the summer and bought tickets for the highest gallery in the Royal Albert Hall, Hugh and I hurrying ahead up the broad staircases to reserve places where we could sit close in by the rail and see the musicians a long way below, Father following behind us. I was never sure of the degree of his enthusiasm. Friday night was Beethoven night and that was how I first came to know the symphonies.

Lying there that early April morning listening to Beethoven was a reassuring experience. Hartmut's family in Viersen lived very modestly, their house only large enough for the parents and the two boys. It was in a suburban area towards the edge of the town. I recall no traces of the warfare that had swept through the region less than ten years earlier and nothing much was said about it. Only Hartmut and Dieter spoke English; which they did with me, politely and with an interest in my life, which was not all that easy to satisfy. Meanwhile their parents looked on.

Breakfast was early and frugal. I had been advised about gifts and brought them tea and coffee which seemed to be precious, the latter being taken on Sunday before going to church. Herr Schultz sang in the choir. The music was impressive, the Lutheran service in its form familiar, though I did not understand the words, and I sat, during the sermon in particular, overwhelmed by the very idea of this language so forcefully expressing complicated and reverential expositions of God's love and purpose.

German was not studied at my own school. If we thought of it at all, it was to parody the guttural sounds – part-invented, part-imitated – from the films of that strange era. In post-war Britain, at least in the early years, Germany was looked on with distrust and sometimes with loathing as the seemingly unending disclosures of atrocities followed one after another. It was therefore a revelation to see at first-hand a different aspect of the people of a country which, under Hitler, had devastated most of Europe.

The Schultz family were socially the most unassuming of those I visited. At a slightly later period I came to know Dieter when he visited England, as Hartmut had done. He was tall, quite thin, and both he and Hartmut spoke good English. Apart from acquiring a few isolated words and phrases, I learned no German. It was not the purpose of my visit. Christian fellowship was much more the reason, though this was lightly explored and experienced. The Schultz family were good and natural people. Viersen was a dull town. I drank in the atmosphere and survived whatever tedium there was, coming to a relaxed and youthful first-hand knowledge of post-war Europe.

After five days I travelled down to Bonn. I stayed with another friend of Hartmut's, called Peter. Together we climbed in the Drachenfels, the steep and picturesque hills on the east bank of the Rhine. I bought a small cap and then little badges which I attached all over it, a record of places I had visited. The spring weather was dry, bright and sunny. We tramped in easy friendship up steep, cobbled streets among colourful crowds of Eastertime visitors. The town, which was then the seat of government, though Germany was still under a form of evolving administration monitored by the Four Powers, was far more interesting than Viersen, though I remember less of it. Peter lived with his mother, a kind and jolly woman. I stayed with them for a shorter time and then went on south to Wuppertal to stay with the Bernings. They came from the eastern part of Germany where they owned a successful camera business, making in particular a small 35-mm camera not unlike the Leica, called the Robot. It had impressive features and I longed for one. The Bernings had been fugitives from the East and had left property behind. Yet in the nature of business and of banking, they must have rescued or recovered some wealth, for they lived in a far more comfortable style than either of the other two families and drove a large pre-war BMW saloon.

A reader might ask, what this has to do with the subject of my story? And the writer will always answer, whatever the story, at its heart there resides the soul and purpose of the one who tells it. In short, I was separating myself from my father; I was disentangling our two lives. In part the things I decided on doing at that time, helped by others, represented instructive acts of self-protection. He was, as I came slowly to understand things, losing his way; I could not afford to lose mine. I would go on being a witness of his life as all children are, but the conclusion had been drawn, between Christmas and Easter of that year, that his love for Barbara, wherever it might go in future years, was not going to lead to marriage. The family that mattered to me, the generation within it that was *my* generation, would move away and become remote. I was facing that sad reality and acting in response to it. And I think others around me saw the implications of this.

The theory of comfort in stories is often linked to the threat of loss or danger. What was happening to me was a common change in what I believe were uncommon circumstances. In breaking away to pursue a life of my own, I was not leaving my father, nor in the emotional sense severing any connection. I was just seeing him differently, and behaving differently as a result. The change was in me, not in him. He would, as I recognised, tumble along from crisis to crisis. In the time immediately ahead, he would fall in and out of my life at the dictate of his emotional needs, his passions, and his downward fall from grace, which was an increasingly regular part of him. But he acknowledged, I think, that I had to determine my own future, and would do so in a more rational, considered way. I faced the challenge of my first 'external' exams. On the horizon were two inescapable objectives: university, for which I had to begin working that year, and National Service, which in advance haunted young men of my age at that time.

The trip to Germany, brief though it was, helped me in this process of asserting my independence. My father had nothing whatsoever to do with it. In a quiet but persistent way, Geoff Rocke had become, unofficially, an ever-stronger guardian. He made himself aware of the precarious circumstances surrounding and affecting me, and he offered choices. He held out to me the equivalent of 'Hidden Hands' and became a lifelong friend.

Other 'Hidden Hands' – though of course they were not hidden – helped as well. Infrequently, but with the best of intentions and motivated by real affection, Christine Mohan, the wife of the clergyman in Beckenham with whom I had stayed after my mother's death and who had wanted to adopt me, would write and ask me how I was. I visited her. She gave me hand-me-down clothes that had belonged to her son, including my first suit with long trousers; she appraised me in it and decided on the colour of the right shirt and tie. No one had done that before, certainly not Barbara or Irene, who saw it as my father's prerogative, one that he was careless in fulfilling. Christine had an eye for me, saw me growing up in circumstances she thought strange, and intervened in them, but not obtrusively. She was a plump woman, not terribly tall.

I would have been the same height at that stage. I suppose in a way she indulged me and I certainly enjoyed our occasional encounters. I remember how much she laughed at my seriousness and the slightly puzzled pride I had in my appearance as a result of these wardrobe changes that came out of the blue.

Did I outgrow my father at that time, shifting the way his guardianship had worked? I think perhaps this is what happened, helped in the oddest ways by my own friendships. It had been always an emotional protection, rooted in his love for me. Yet it was not a very well-organised love. It seems odd to speak of love like that, yet love has to have a design and shape to it. I wonder, looking back, what was it that lay behind the great capacity in him to inspire affection? He managed to appear so rocklike and dependable. In fact, so much of the dependability lay elsewhere or derived from other sources, while he himself was anything but dependable. I do not mean to disparage him, but in those years when we were so close and I was growing up so much under his shadow, the resources that a loving relationship has to provide were wafer-thin. I was taken care of at school, and it cost him nothing. I was taken into a loosely framed guardianship that had emerged out of an accidental encounter and that also cost him nothing. The woman who had been frustrated from adopting me was yet another form of accidental help. I began to do things, like travelling to Germany, which again were a denial of his role and the assertion of someone else's.

This is the theme of my second novel, *The Song of the Nightingale*. Where the central events of the first are really about the relationship of the character 'George' with Ursula, the second is more clearly focused on the adolescent emergence of his son. None of the events from which the story derives took place while I was at school. They belonged to a later period in real time. But they suited the main theme of this second novel, which is about what I recount here, the substance of that question: 'Did I outgrow my father at that time, shifting the way his guardianship had worked?' And of course I did. It was in the nature of things. It is what one does at sixteen.

So the main thrust of the novel's narrative is a school story. The narrative is of school friends and schoolboy adventures, beginning with a night walk by three boys accompanied by two girls, and, as they start out, a nightingale is singing in the trees. There are experiments in adolescent love and the erotic exploration of sexuality, as well as spiritual love. George is otherwise made quite marginal in order to allow the narrator to take centre stage.

Part of the book is a portrait of a marriage that does not work, and at the heart of it there is the claim, 'Laurie was the first who really took him away from me.' Laurie is a character who actually says to the narrator and George when they are together, a few pages earlier, 'I'll not come between you.' Yet this is precisely what she does, in the novel. Laurie? Another woman? Ah, yes. Laurie was indeed another woman, modelled on a Chelsea widow who had a house in Tite Street. She let rooms there and lived in the basement. In effect, looking at what really happened and how it was used as fiction, two quite different time frames are overlaid; one of them – related to the narrator's life at school – roughly as given here, the other drawn back from real events that lay in the future. The reality was that Barbara still occupied a significant place in my father's life and this is what the letters tell me.

What Barbara had brought, in those years so far covered, was an entirely different set of relationships. All of them derived from another way of looking at the workings of family love and sexual love. What I had lost, in the dispersal of our own family, after the death of my mother, I had found for a time in another family, through Barbara. Despite that dispersal, what I had always been familiar with, in respect of my father, was the passionate declaration of his own love for me. To this, when it manifested itself, was added, in the most natural and acceptable way, his love of Barbara and hers for me. That was how I saw it from the start, a quite different construction from the one he was grappling with; in my eyes his relationship with Barbara seemed to transform and even ennoble him, and this was what I wanted. And so I built on it, and told him how I felt about it and how much it all meant to me. Here was a family that absorbed both of us. It had depth and structure and design. Between us all, in that period that began with the uncertain and rather chilly letter of February 1951, no less than twelve lives became entwined in what I like to think of as a dance, a kind of stately, well-performed pavane where formality was important. This was certainly the character of it in the visits paid to Chapel Park Road in St Leonards-on-Sea. Some of the time it was more carefree and spirited, as when we were on holiday in Steyning. Other times it was loving and intimate, the two of them, the three of us. Yet it had a sustained pattern, and the music to which we danced was a sweet sound, and I thought it would never end, perhaps because it was the music of love. But of course it did end.

I believe in love as a magic currency. The more we spend, the more we have. But the way of the spending, and the desire to exhaust it, can distort its power and change the magic nature, perhaps darkening it. My father spent it as though there were no tomorrow. He was prodigal, carefree, and everyone whose lives he touched believed in his powerful, passionate nature. But love has other measures applied to it. If love is a currency, it is also a weapon of trade. It buys more love certainly. Spend it like a prodigal and more flows into the marketplace. But it is so diverse, it buys many other things too. Love has to be traded in, if it is to work as a currency, for things like security and certainty, for the wider issue of what will be there each week, of what will be stored up each month, of what we harvest from it as one year succeeds another. And it is when these things are considered that the flaws in my father's life are laid bare by the chronology of that time.

He had declared to Barbara, at the outset, 'I want to make some sort of show of my life without the eternal worry of hoping against hope'. Two years on and that situation had not really advanced at all, nor had the dance, nor had the widening needs that love was generating. Even if it is a currency that grows with spending, it still has to be spent wisely and there are investment portfolios watched over by many witnesses. Perhaps for him it was not like that. Perhaps the prodigality of his spending was of a kind and nature that I still fail to understand. Whatever it had developed into, in the later months of 1953, after the letters ceased – thus depriving me of any guidance about how things were during that time – Barbara and George were just lovers in a comfortable and accepting way. It was fleeting as well, as it turned out. Their lives were well suited to the bohemian drift of life in the early 1950s. It is inescapably associated in my mind with the King's Road in Chelsea. I think of the pubs my father frequented, the figures, the 'characters' who enlivened the life of that area, and George and Barbara themselves at home in that changing world.

At first, on looking at the letters, I misinterpreted the way things happened and what they meant. For me, the two years 1953 and 1954 were radically different. The first was an uncertain period in my life. In contrast with that, 1954 was defined and absolute. The differences could not have been greater and were clear-cut. Before coming to them, however, I must try and explain more of how the two years were for my father. I do so from a paucity of evidence.

He was, as I have said, resident in Chelsea, his presence established there; perhaps he was even by way of being a 'character'. I know, from the reference Lady Hulton wrote for him, that he worked for her between 1952 and 1954. He worked for others. The 1953 letters, long, detailed and of critical importance, since they dealt with 'Norman', have already been covered. They had ceased in the early part of the year, suggesting, as before, that George and Barbara were then together. What is described in those letters had led to a resolution in their love and the epistolary silence of the rest of 1953 is a mark of comfort for them both, since they appear to have settled into a loving but unstressed relationship, living together but with the idea of marriage unresolved and set aside. I still saw Barbara, but the opportunities were fewer than before.

The bright star that had led us all in a well-defined direction faded. Though I think I may have kept up some tentative contacts with Roberta and her family, this too changed. Being older, I moved on. Earlier, when I had first been drawn into close and loving friendships with the family, and with the Lorings in particular, my need had been great. What I had wanted from them, in 1951 – ill-defined, unclear, but of course related to my father and Barbara – had not materialised. Nor did it in 1952. At some stage in 1953 I must have realised it would not happen. Was I perhaps a little embarrassed at more youthful adolescent needs? Did I now see with a harder gaze the reality of those things that do not happen when we want them to? For a time this makes us unhappy with the perverse sense of losses that are unpredicted or unexpected. But then we get over that and we move on.

PART TWO

Perhaps this was the case and perhaps other opportunities and friends closer to my own age crowded out the earlier set of experiences. It did not end the friendships, or the very real love I had for Barbara, for her sisters, for the family. It introduced changes first of all with the children. The pattern altered. The relationships began to be different. Each of the three of them, Georgiana, Charmian and Ulick – always distinctive characters, determined and independent – grew in difference as they grew in age. The collective simplicity, that had perhaps been at its most appealing because it responded to a direct and clear need during that brief summer holiday in Steyning, was never entirely recaptured.

I love them still. I don't really understand quite what I mean by that. How can I reach back more than half a century and reclaim so emphatically those feelings that belong there? The feelings have not been reinforced by much. Of the three of the children I have since met only the youngest, Ulick, when I was given the letters. I then corresponded with him, read more reminiscences that he had written and we visited each other. He came to my home in Dublin, and I visited him in his priest's house in Twickenham. After that I corresponded with Georgiana, also briefly to begin with, but then visited her as well. This was on a return visit to St Leonards-on-Sea to look at the places there, including the house in Chapel Park Road where we had spent Christmases together. The third of them, Charmian, has corresponded about those days, again with the same affection and strong memories. We have yet to meet.

So how can I say I love them still? Yet I do. And I know that I will always. Nothing has to happen either to reinforce this or to lessen it. Love can be as fixed as the stars in the sky. It is delineated in the little twisting streets of Steyning, which recently I revisited – almost by accident, on an afternoon walk in November – realising where I was and trying, unsuccessfully, to recover memories. We once traced those streets together, their small hands reaching for mine. My hands, only slightly larger, were still the hands of a boy exploring the possibilities of a new family life that seemed so decidedly possible in the warm sunshine of those youthful days.

I think I was troubled by these changes and affected by them in my work at school, making 1953 a rather difficult year. I believed that I worked hard that summer, but others thought differently. Kingham Hill was a small school. The most senior form had just five or six of us, and the school had only in recent years adjusted to the higher level of examinations. The 'O' and 'A' level exams had replaced the 'School Certificate' and 'Higher School Certificates' taken by a small percentage of the earlier generations of boys. For the school year of Michaelmas 1952 to summer 1953 we doubled up, preparing for O levels that summer and embarking on the first year of a two-year curriculum for A levels. But it was still an uncertain period.

The year 1953 was different for a number of reasons. It was much more the end of a cycle of time in my life. This put it quite at odds with the sense in which, academically, the two years represent a coherent preparation for what I had set my heart on. This was university entrance, whether it came before or after National Service. There must have been anxiety about achieving this goal, not only in my own mind but in the judgement of many of my teachers at the end of the summer term.

It went deeper than that. I fell out with the school warden. The relationships he had with many boys could be uncertain and volatile. He had favourites. Many of his favourites were members of the school's Pony Club which the warden ran from his house. This was beside meadows that were part of the extensive school estate, and his house itself had sufficient room to accommodate horses. He rode himself. One of the trustees, in my own early days there, Colonel Tom Roche, rode to hounds with the Heythrop Hunt. In the school hall there was a photograph or an oil painting of him, on horseback and looking particularly dashing. He had been wounded in the Great War and had a scar on his face, adding to the authority he naturally assumed. It was a different thing for the school warden to ride to hounds and an even more marked departure from the school's earlier characterisation in the local community when he arranged for the boys, first to go cubbing and then to ride in a hunt. I was one of those and eventually hunted with the Heythrop, which began to meet regularly at the school from 1948, and with the North Cotswold hunt.

They were heady days, giving the boys concerned an unfair privilege that was protected additionally by favouritism. Senior staff did not approve. One teacher in particular – and he was my housemaster – was strongly opposed to the Pony Club, but had to accept its existence and the membership in it of boys from his house. Ray Metcalfe was an able teacher of science and mathematics and had come to the school from Merchant Taylors' School in Manchester. He was a strong character, formal and determined, considered quite conventional. He was, for example, critical of the school warden for entering the staffroom unannounced, thinking that this breached school protocol. If it were necessary, he believed, permission could and should be sought for staffroom meetings with the warden. They should not be imposed. Metcalfe felt in general that the warden was involved too closely with the boys and was involved in a selective way that was bad for overall discipline. In retrospect, though I was myself favoured, I think he was right. John Woollan's style as warden was idiosyncratic, the subject not just of staff criticism but of disaffection among many of the boys.

For me that aura of favour ended during the summer of 1953. There was a possible reason behind it, and that was my own growing association with Geoff Rocke. It was, in its way, an echo of what was happening with the warden and his Pony Club favourites. My inescapable if partial disconnection from the Pony Club as a result of the growing burden of work, and my trip to Germany the previous Easter, paid for and arranged by Geoff Rocke, coincided with yet another more painful event which broke trust forever with the warden.

I was accused – inconceivably, as it seemed then, and now – of having removed some female underwear from a clothesline used by one of the housemaster's wives. The offence had occurred during a 'free' period when it was shown that I *could* have been responsible. I was severely beaten by the warden, notwithstanding my strong denials. The warden invited me to reconsider what I had said to him and to tell the truth at an encounter later in the day. I boiled with indignation at not having been believed before, which itself was a serious breach of trust since I was one of his school prefects and since he did not intend publicly removing me from that post. When I once more repeated my claim of innocence, I was *again* beaten.

This happened early in the summer term of 1953. In due course the culprit was found and I was exonerated, the amelioration for the earlier humiliating experience coming from the housemaster rather than the warden. Nothing with John Woollan was ever the same again. I saw him thereafter as unbalanced in his attitude to me and therefore an alien figure, exercising an authority I resented.

At the end of that summer Woollen left the school without much ceremony. Later still, when my school report for that term arrived, the section reserved for his judgement on my performance was written by another unsigned hand, though I presumed the words were his and were dictated. They are his last on me, a rather chilling valedictory. The paragraph says: 'I hope a change of warden will help him. Whenever we meet he seems to be trying to find a short cut to success and to be hopefully giving orders without realising that boys only obey those who set an example. He undoubtedly has talents but unless he really goes to work and unless the new warden thinks very highly of his character he has no hope of reaching Oxford. I wish him every success and still think he could make the grade if he tried.'

My housemaster was slightly more positive. He said I was very reliable and conscientious in the House. 'I am sure he has the grit and determination to do well in his school subjects.' My form master was less sure of this, feeling I was underestimating the task ahead of me, and this was the view of the two teachers in my main subjects. It seems I had mountains to climb.

Tom Worrall, who taught English, and Jim Lund, the senior history teacher, were the core figures making judgements upon me and I acknowledge, with a recall that is crystal clear, the justice and fairness of what they said about this sixteen-and-a-half-year-old schoolboy whose way forward into life they were attempting to guide. I weighed ten stone and was five foot eight, and still growing. There was praise for my music, for science, maths and French, and the elderly retired clergyman, C. S. Donald, who had arrived to give grinds in Latin for two of us in preparation for university, wrote 'He knows the sort of stuff it is. He can make no progress unless he learns the elements. He must do this. Very kind to me.'

C. S. Donald was a friend, possibly a relation of the

outgoing warden. He was a schoolmaster like James Hilton's unforgettable character Mr Chips, full of age and and bathed in the affection of the boys, who always found with him a willing ear for their stories and problems. He had lived at the school for some years. He wore a black clerical suit with a waistcoat, and sat in it even in the warm summer sun of the later part of that term, enjoying the contentment life seemed to have brought. His hand shook a little. He often spilled food and the severe colour of his waistcoat was patched with grease stains and spots. The kindness to which he refers must include my own readiness to sit and imbibe more detail of the ablative absolute or the understanding of gerunds. He was then in his eighties; as a young clergyman he had worked in the London missions. That would have started around the time of Queen Victoria's jubilee, just when my grandfather was emerging from the wild turmoil of being a child in the urban jungle, to which C. S. Donald, the 'C.S.D.' on my school reports, believed he had been sent by God.

Despite all this, the year 1953 – at least, the academic year – had its moments. Following the celebration of Queen Elizabeth's coronation, the school put on a musical event entitled 'From Elizabeth I to Elizabeth II'. I opened the event with a recitation of King Henry V's speech before Agincourt, the lines beginning 'This day is called the feast of Crispian.' There is a change of tone that stirs the heart in those words 'We few, we happy few, we band of brothers'. I remember the stillness among the three hundred or so people gathered in the hall on that July afternoon. The decorations included great bowls and vases of flowers in front of the stage. The scent of the stately white Madonna lilies filled the air with exotic magic as they still do in my fond memory of that time.

We sang the Agincourt song, and madrigals including 'The

Silver Swan' and 'Fair Phyllis I Saw Sitting all Alone'. A master who was a trumpeter, Gordon Curl, played Jeremiah Clarke's Trumpet Tune and Air. There were other recitations, orchestral works and an epilogue written by the English master and recited by John Hunt, a friend from my earliest days at Kingham Hill, when we were juniors in Plymouth House. I like to think that what had been a difficult year for me ended on the right note with this warm summer occasion in the soft daze of a July afternoon, and not in the other setbacks that made me realise something of the challenges that still lay ahead.

VII

I was uncertain, at the end of that summer term. My father, in contrast, was stable and settled in his work. I was looking towards that first great passage of arms – the proof of intelligence, the passing of examinations, the entry into the world – with some misgivings that needed ironing out. George, despite his often-expressed uncertainty, was settled in London and living in Chelsea. I think, perhaps for the last time, I needed him. He did not need me, as on occasion he had done before.

Though I have since thought his employment with Lady Hulton was part of his work as a jobbing gardener, it was more comprehensive than that. Her reference, written five years after he had left her employment, suggests he was a member of staff. So, too, would the place and circumstance. The Hultons lived then at Cleeve Lodge in Hyde Park Gate with enough garden to keep him busy and enough money to pay for it.

Lady Hulton was a Russian princess called Nika Yuryevich. Her father was a sculptor who had been a chamberlain in the court of the Tsar. She was Edward Hulton's second Russian wife. He first married the daughter of a general in the Imperial Russian Army. That marriage was dissolved in 1932. The second marriage, to my father's employer, took place in 1941 and there were three children. Eventually they moved from Hyde Park Gate to Carlton Gardens in St James's, and this may have been the reason for my father ceasing his employment with the princess.

Lady Hulton's flowers were arranged by Constance Spry, and at some stage in 1954 George took employment with her in South Audley Street, at the premises that had been the centre of her business since the 1930s. Constance Spry was to flowers what Elizabeth David was to food, an innovative, even a revolutionary, force.

My father had employees under him, and for the first time since his representation of the London Bedding Centre at the Daily Mail Ideal Homes Exhibition two years before, he was in a position to exercise his not inconsiderable abilities as an organiser and his natural aptitude for authority.

Professionally, this was a good period for him. Emotionally it appears to have been a stable time, his love for Barbara relaxed, balanced and even-tempered. It seems that during the late summer or autumn of 1953 it passed beyond the prospect of marriage. As a result, their love became unaffected by the strain and stress of wanting this particular end. I do not know when the idea of this, so emphatically expressed in the earlier letters, was abandoned, nor do I know why. Years later, her nephew mentioned the fact that occasionally Barbara called for help from his father because of George's drinking, but I think this may have been at a later stage. Such evidence as there is suggests that at this time in his life he was engaged on a reasonably prosperous voyage in seas that were calm.

That summer marked the end of my childhood. At the end of term, instead of going to stay with my father, I went to stay with Geoff Rocke, who shared with a cousin a large and comfortable apartment in St Thomas's Mansions, just over the bridge from Big Ben. Geoff had become increasingly concerned that my father's life, fascinating to me as spectator, was not really the best background for a relatively innocent youth coming to the end of his sixteenth year. I was grateful for the judgement he made, giving me relief from the obsessive claustrophobia of sharing a bed-sitting room and providing a different life during that summer holiday. The kindness was exercised with tact and discretion. It changed – in a way forever – the uncertainty. Geoff became more effective as my unofficial guardian, accepted by George, possibly with relief, and welcomed by me. I readily accepted the offer and what it entailed, a series of holiday tasks much as I had done for him before.

Geoff and his cousin were, for the time being anyway, confirmed bachelors. Notwithstanding this, he subsequently married, although his cousin remained single. They had both been at Charterhouse, and neither of them went to university. Geoff entered the family business, while his cousin became an accountant. Both men were in their late forties and financially well off, and I also did some work for the cousin. A daily woman looked after them, shopped and prepared food. Geoff Rocke was 'my friend' (my father came to describe him as 'your friend', thus avoiding mention of his name and therefore too close a reflection of what he now represented). I was translated to a new life entirely and transformed in my view of myself.

I think, even as I write, of Bunyan's 'Shepherd Boy'. The words of that poem served both my father and me well enough for a time. For me the privations were over; good fortune and endeavour would see to that. The social circumstances in England in those underrated years of the early 1950s would help as well. So I choose easily, and with particular emphasis, the words 'I am content with what I have, little be it or much'.

What I remember most about this change in my fortune

was the care with which both Geoff and my father handled it. I had come to call him Geoff, dropping the more distant formality of 'Mr Rocke', which had seemed necessary with a school trustee up to and including my penultimate year. He had suggested it, and, it seemed, even in those long-distant days so noted for strict behaviour, as well as deference and formality, it had been natural enough. In our conversations he referred little to my father's status or circumstances. He knew enough from me of Irene Spindlo's emotional and financial entanglements with George not to want anything similar for himself. Otherwise, I think he was impressed by my father's jobs during this period, even if they did change. What he found more difficult were the moral questions that arose on account of my father's love life. This was hard enough for me to understand, even though I had been an intimate part of it all since my mother's death. Relaying it to another, as I did in answer to questions that were motivated by compassion, led inevitably to misunderstandings. My father's unconventional existence, his love for Barbara, the fact that nothing had come of the marriage I had so longed for, and the way in which all this had drifted into a Chelsea life, weighed on Geoff's Christian conscience. His judgements were undoubtedly more severe than mine, despite his much greater age and experience. He could not read through my continued love for my father and see beyond it the monogamous reality of the so-called bohemian atmosphere surrounding and compromising my father's still strong desire to make something of his life. All he could go on, I suspect, was the faint odour of sexual and moral liberality that hung over Chelsea in those years, so different from other parts of London.

Both men were sensitive about my increasingly divided loyalties. My father would inquire about 'my friend'. He would listen to the things I did, the people I met, the places I went to. Wearing John Mohan's hand-me-down tweed suit and a tie that Irene had given my father, I would, on rare occasions, accompany Geoff to Boodle's, more often to the RAC Club in Pall Mall, or sometimes, on a summer's evening, down to the RAC country club outside Epsom, on the edge of the Downs.

My father would caution me about not getting flooded with self-importance or developing a taste for a life that had little to do with his life or what I might expect for myself in the future. But he valued and welcomed what had happened. Barbara dealt with it differently. She was concerned about him and must have detected, when I was not about, at least a hint of sadness or of fear that he was losing me. And of course he was, though not because of Geoff Rocke. I was not being taken away from him; I was just moving on. It was happening at the dictates of time, of growing up, of not wanting to be held in the charmed but outdated happiness of the ending of childhood.

I think, for me, it was a very complicated process. The intensity of deprivation and uncertainty, ameliorated happily by my father's love for me, nevertheless rendered my childhood something that I wanted to leave behind. With him I suppose I always felt that I was a child, and this decided the nature of school holidays until the breakaway of which I now write. With it came a new intensity in the way I responded to my own growing up. And the account I give now, both of how I spent my holidays and also the energy with which I undertook activities at school, are, in a deeper sense, dictated by what had gone before.

That summer passed in a cloud of mixed experiences. I came to know and love London better than ever before. I visited my Aunt Peg, my cousin Pan, my Great Aunt Bertha in

Wyndham Street and even met with school friends. I did the work and the reading that had been set, and came to an understanding of European history, of Bismarck and his period. I wrote several essays, one of them on Jane Austen, another on Walter Scott. Thus it was that when I went back to school at the end of the holidays, I was a determined and toughened individual, ready for the final phase in my school education.

I was just seventeen at the beginning of that Christmas term of 1953. A half-dozen boys made up the sixth form, all of us working for A-levels, myself and two others doing History and English. We did Scripture as well and, though I had the obvious difficulties of coming late to the study of Latin, I reportedly worked away steadily enough. We took no other classes. This meant unfettered attention to our reading and lessons in English and History that extended into lengthy debates. The air was charged with the energy of our perpetual inquiry. We were guided by two men, Tom Worrall and Jim Lund. They were quite different from each other, never together much in our presence, but bonded by their commitment to our many intellectual needs.

Jim Lund was a recent arrival at the school, a dark, good-looking man, sharp, energetic and well spoken. He had the build of a rugby player, sharing with Tom Worrall an enthusiasm for the sport. Tom Worrall taught English. He was older than Lund, a housemaster, and he had been at the school much longer. Indeed he was something of an institution, a man of mixed emotions who could display quite sharp anger, mediated by a good sense of humour. What hair he had left was reddish in colour, but he was essentially bald. He dressed as we expected our teachers to dress, which is to say he followed the classic style of the 1950s: brogues, cavalry twill trousers, tweed tie, tweed jacket, check shirt and usually a waistcoat, quite colourful; at other times he sported a cardigan or pullover. The essential colours were brown, sand, beige; the ties blue, yellow, red. The cut of his clothes indicated the hand of a tailor. I was always envious of the generous fall of the pocket part of his jacket since he stood to teach us, when he did, with his hand or hands in his pockets sweeping back the skirted tweed below the button at his waist. In that later time, of course, when we were only a very small class at the sixth form table, he was vitally present with his hands, like ours, expressing the flow of words and ideas. I think in my mind at that time, and as circumstance permitted in my dress as well, I modelled myself on Worrall and it was part of the strange patchwork of growing up, seeking to be independent and discovering the strange and varied ways in which youth asserts aspects of style to define both separation and direction.

Sartorially, Jim Lund was like him in the dress he wore. His colour scheme was less sandy, more dark brown. It suited his saturnine appearance. Though clean-shaven, Lund carried at all times the heavy shadow of dark hair, close-shaved yet bluish, around his chin and jaws. He had a slight indentation in the chin, and clear, direct eyes. He seemed to lean into the table at the start of our lessons, pregnant with a host of points to make and arguments to pursue. And as the debate took on life and direction, he used his hands to steer it forward. I remember the astonishment we felt at his knowledge. He brought notes with him and they were open on the table, as were ours with the textbooks we were using. These included the standard history books at the time, one by Grant and Temperley, the other H.A.L. Fisher's *History of Europe*. But in Lund's presence they ended up being incidental.

I run together the two men because that is how they were for us; they represented the overriding force in our lives at that time. They drew us out, stretched us, made us discover ourselves. Also, they became examples to us. When I think back to those days and the fullness of our final terms, I see both the people and the events as separating me from my father. It was not that he might fail to understand; it was more that he would feel himself alien from the vitality and the sense of direction. He could not join in my pleasure without somehow feeling a sense of shame about the dwindling attraction of the life he offered me and from which I was in the process of escaping.

He would not have understood fully the importance of these two men directing my mind in my last year at school. And if he did, his thoughts would, in part, have been either nostalgic or jealous speculations. Blea Tarn, in its Wordsworthian way, had shown me two things: the overwhelming vastness of nature and the logicality of practical knowledge, how to divide the known from the unknown in the world and change the balance of that knowledge by practical investigation. Jim Lund taught us a quite different form of investigation, into the past and into the nature of men's actions. We looked, as many had done before, at the motives behind human power and conflict and the elements that shaped those motives. For Tom Worrall, critical judgement of the effectiveness of creativity on ourselves and on others was central. It was quite different. There *was* a historical dimension; Wordsworth in his time, his impact on his contemporaries, how he was shaped by childhood and early experiences as a student and then in France, all this mattered. But none of it equalled the soaring wonder of his vision of experience, and the beautiful haunting language in which he set it down. I realise now, on account of his solipsistic nature and the bizarre self-obsession that governed his life, how little my father would have been able to share with me the intellectual adventure of learning to use my mind to analyse people and literature.

We surged on. I think now that maybe we thought that all literature was at our fingertips. Chaucer's *Canterbury Tales*, and in particular the tale of Patient Griselda, started us; Shakespeare was a continuation of something we had all known from junior forms. Had I not declaimed, before the whole school, the speech before Agincourt, Hamlet's soliloquy about settling man's quietus with a bare bodkin, and other passages that remain with me in clear and exact detail and ready for instant recall half a century later? 'How sweet the moonlight sleeps upon this bank', or the words that Jaques utters, 'that one man in his time plays many parts, his acts being seven ages', defined me by declaration. I delivered, in public, those gems, as I had memorised them, and I did so with joy and assurance and a revelling in the greatest of all art's glories. We handled Milton differently. He seemed then a cold figure and the debate in Heaven which, from book two of *Paradise Lost*, was for a time to haunt us, with its subtle arguments on the direction of spiritual disaffection, was heavy-going.

What was most exciting of all was the harmonious and well-tempered presentation of an era in literature which exactly conveyed the period we studied in European and English history. While Jim Lund sought to explain to us the tide of blood that engulfed France after the fall of the Bastille in 1789, Tom Worrall led us through the contrasting worlds of Walter Scott and of Jane Austen, with the Romantic poets revelling in between.

If we were young again, now, in a new century, it would all be different. We had, in the mid-1950s, that precise presentation of greatness in human destiny in the way we were taught and in the books and writers brought before us. In literature, there were these magical discoveries to be made. Can one ever match again the discovery of Keats's odes, have oneself be carried along by Byron's presentation of the ocean rolling on, or be soothed in the needle-sharp observation of domestic life so truly lived in the pages of *Emma*? That was the wonder of it all. If I dwell more on literature than on history, it is because, even at that time, the subconscious construction of the future direction I would take as a writer was being built within me.

Kenneth Bowman was my form master. He taught French. Having taken, and passed, the subject as an O-level subject, I gave it up in the Christmas term of 1953. He nevertheless presided, in a general way, over my studies and wrote of me, that December, 'He, and his work, are maturing steadily'. I don't know what my father made of that, nor of my housemaster's comments, that I was 'a most willing and helpful house prefect, always most reliable' and that I maintained 'a much better attitude towards the smaller boys'. The acting warden, Denys Wood, filling an interim term between the departure of John Woollan and the arrival of Teddy Cooper as the new Warden, expressed his satisfaction in what he described as 'the great help' I had been to him as a school prefect, conscientious in all my duties.

My father should have been part of that. Yet I found it difficult to tell him about my life and work at school. Looking back, I feel that my success made him more conscious of his failure. The later discovery of the man revealed in the letters to Barbara, and later still the man I discovered from his few diaries, would support this view.

Though far from unruly, the school at that time was tough to run and required a good deal of tact, energy and patience. Denys Wood had been a housemaster since 1948. In age he was probably the most senior member of staff, though not perhaps experience. As warden he was perhaps a harbinger of changed times ahead, the more ameliorative, Socratic and less authoritarian period for the school under E. C. Cooper. Denys Wood was white-haired and quite elderly, a man of small stature and precise manner in speech and gesture. He needed his prefects to give weight and vigour to the code of discipline which was followed.

By the time we came to the carol service at the end of that term I felt immensely more confident of myself. I sang bass in the choir. We copied the King's College Chapel service of nine lessons and carols done each year in Cambridge and possibly familiar from early recordings, though I do not remember this. Stewart Brindley, our choirmaster and music teacher, had fashioned the school choir into an instrument of great quality during the years from around 1950. He recalled to me, many years later, that before 1950 the choir would not have been of a high enough standard to sing at a society wedding with anthem and solo, which is what we did. The year in fact had been 1952 and the time of it some six weeks or so before Christmas, as already recorded earlier. But the quality reached then led on to greater feats and to an approach that attempted many exacting works, none more so than 'The Silver Swan', the madrigal by Orlando Gibbons of less than a minute's duration and sung in the concert the previous summer. Musically, it is as perfect as Keats's 'Ode to Autumn' and shorter in length, but a difficult piece to get right. 'The Silver Swan' dates from the closing years of a golden age of musical creativity and the words are thought to express this. Because of George VI's death and the accession of Queen Elizabeth II, and then the Coronation, there was an association of the first Queen Elizabeth with the second, and in our singing of madrigals it was on this we focused our minds. In quality our treble voices expressed a certain brief invincibility that is as much the prerogative of the well-trained and well-timed singer as it is of any display of sporting excellence. One did not punch the air at the sad concluding notes that accompany the line 'more geese than swans now live, more fools than wise', and yet one is completing a work of symphonic magnitude. In any case sportsmen did not then do so either. But the inner sense of triumph and of supreme achievement was a joy then of unprecedented and unparalleled power.

What of the romance engendered by the sense we then developed of our growing independence, our curiosity? What of love? Had I not been schooled at close quarters in the art and agony of love? Had I not felt for Barbara an imitative passion drawn from the energy and vitality of my father's feelings for her? Was I not, like Turgenev, in a curious, bewildered and modest fashion, seeking and finding objects of desire to serve as patterns for love's erratic but undeniable force within the heart? I come now to that, but first a note of poetic introduction.

It was in November of that year that Dylan Thomas died. He was a favourite of Tom Worrall's, though not a poet he could easily introduce into his teaching; his love of the Welsh master was a private enthusiasm. However, on the day after his death in New York, Tom Worrall brought in Thomas's *Collected Poems*. He was moved by the undoubtedly tragic way in which the poet, in mid-flight as it were, on a lecture tour in America, had been taken from us. He was, even then, a national possession, with a voice as fresh and lyrical as Robert Burns's had been in his day, and possibly Keats's in his. Whatever it was, the combination perhaps of visible grief with the robust and infinitely rich language of passionate authority, the event lingered as long as the lines from 'Do not go gentle into that good night'. Thomas, it seemed, belonged to our generation; 'Poem in October' was an accessible icon. His death at that sensitive point in our growing up, coupled with the widespread images of his rebel nature, his bohemianism, his indulgence in drink, caught our imaginations. For me there was more to the story, since my own life had at its fringes, through George and Barbara, through Chelsea, through the growing impact of poetry, added fusions with the event and how it had shocked the otherwise reserved Tom Worrall.

Poetry was an expression of love, an explainer of love, a key to defining it as a prelude to actually exploring it. The secret heart of it, in that crowded year, was experienced in several different ways. There was pure love and impure love. There was intense eroticism, idealised passion and, from the most unlikely quarter of all, a balanced and intensely felt love which I recall as having been on a grand scale, though in truth it was on no scale at all. It existed in my own mind and heart. It was largely inexpressible, inhibited by convention and by a limited understanding of where it came from and where it might lead.

At quite another level, erotic desire burst upon some of us in the shape of Jennifer, the elder daughter of our housemaster, Francis Meerendonck, and his wife, Gladys. Jennifer was fifteen or so when she came to the school. She was very pretty, well developed, and with sultry eyes. I marvel now at the close proximity in which we all lived. Her bedroom was a short distance along the landing from our dormitory and she was not averse to invitations for chosen boys to visit her for fumbled embraces and experiments in the art of kissing. In night attire, on creaking pine floorboards, at high risk and in a mood of intense excitement, one made one's way to her bed and enjoyed there a kind of love-making, perhaps mercifully now enshrined in veiled recollections that enhance and perhaps exaggerate reality. Her disposition was liberal, her body a map for the future, her own desire for love a form of heady encouragement, itself an aphrodisiac.

How time enhances those particular memories of discovering the physicality of desire, the eroticism of touch, the uncontrollable force of lust, an instinct without which romantic love could not possibly come to life. It did not with Jennifer, though other more earthy affections did. She was a willing leader in our inexpert experiments with her and ourselves. She had a friend, Elizabeth, for whom I conceived an affection and who in her turn felt, and shyly expressed, her love for me. There were kisses and embraces, but the romance had a more limited life and prospects, since she came from another house and was the daughter of one of my teachers.

If the intellectual life we lead at school was difficult to convey to my father, when I saw him at holiday time, the growing up sexually and emotionally was even more complicated. Without really being able to analyse it, the process was the entirely normal one of adolescence leading into early manhood. What was not so easy was negotiating this as my father's son. This passage in life has its difficulties for everyone. I can but describe my own and leave to the reader a judgement on the commonality of it all.

The Christmas of 1953 was the last one my father and I spent together, the last on the south coast of England, in St Leonards-on-Sea. Though I did not know of this in advance, it was to be another point of change of considerable moment. It was a contented rather than a happy occasion. I did not fully understand what was going on, but probably sensed that the high hopes of two years previously were slowly disintegrating. Barbara and my father still loved each other; they always would. There was never, in the whole cycle of letters, evidence of disaffection. And the same remained the case with Barbara's sister Marg and with other members of the family. But James, Barbara's brother-in-law, married to her sister Roberta, and father of the three children, had by then experienced something of my father's waywardness, his drinking and his potential, when drunk, for violence. I never heard of George being violent with Barbara, but I did hear of her being frightened of the possibility of it and I amended my own expectations at this time.

I enjoyed again being the oldest of the young people, not least because of the lasting affection I felt for Roberta's children. But I was no longer to be seen as an older child to mind the others. I was now a youth, casting my eyes in other directions.

That effectively was the end of St Leonards-on-Sea. My father and I travelled back to London on the train. The train from the south coast up to London had been the monotonous and unresponsive witness to both high and low points in my own emotional experience. For my father there was acceptance that, for me anyway, it was over in any respect embracing *my* needs. As to his, which included his yearning search for a more stable life, for belonging in a place and with a family, these aspirations too, I think, were on the point of dissolving. It would have been characteristic of him to convey this to me, perhaps with little more than the lifting of an eyebrow. There would have been the sigh of resignation that yet another passage in his turbulent life had not worked out.

We had one outing before our departure, on 27 December. It was a concert in the White Rock Pavilion, in Hastings, by the London Philharmonic Orchestra under their conductor, George Weldon. I still have the programme. Iris Loveridge played the Grieg piano concerto. It was a 'popular' programme, opening with Roger Quilter's Children's Overture. Dvorak's symphony 'From the New World' filled the second half of the cold winter afternoon, with the grey light low across the foreshore. Though my ears had not really been opened to Wagner's music, I was moved by the seamless and silken texture of the Prelude and Liebestod from *Tristan and Isolde*.

I am still haunted by the sadness of those actual compositions; music that has become so familiar in the intervening years, so often heard, and yet still redolent of that time. I treasure the programme, a casual printed memento of a winter's afternoon – the concert was at three o'clock – and of the likely party to attend: Barbara, my father and myself, Roberta and her three children, possibly Marg and maybe their mother. The faint mist by which memory becomes flawed was like the grey light across the calm winter sea of that distant afternoon, tinged by a low sun touching with dull red the grey flat water and the faint line of the eternal horizon. It was for all of us, though all of us know it only in part, a farewell as attenuated yet as inescapable as the piece of Wagner's music we had heard.

VIII

*I*F THE RICHER LIFE for which I had so passionately hoped during the three previous years was not to be, it did not end George's loving relationship with Barbara. She was with him during 1954, perhaps closer in a way as a result of their acceptance that living together was as much as they could hope for. If true, then I know it only in the light of later correspondence. The year 1954 is remarkably free of letters. Since he was in settled and reasonably happy employment, as well as living close to her or with her, in Chelsea, I assume that all was well between them.

I went on seeing Barbara from time to time, but from a more distant perspective. If I chose to see her, it was *my* decision. It only occurred during school holidays, and it usually coincided with my visits to him. These were now less frequent. I had a form of independence from him framed out of a new dependence on Geoff Rocke. And I no longer saw Barbara's nieces or nephew.

Whatever his relationship with Barbara may have been, I knew less of it than had been the case up to that point. There are many reasons for this. Some of them sound like excuses, as though in some strange and biologically confused way I had taken over responsibility for him and was not doing my duty by him. I was letting him down by allowing him to slip away from my love.

The women who had loved him looked to me to care for him at times. When that failed to provoke a response, they got on with the job themselves. This was never burdensome for Barbara, whose easy style of life and, on the whole, relaxed handling of him, made life easy for us. It was a different case with Irene, and she found it difficult that this teenage boy, who had once been so faithfully at his side, now began to move away. I was present in either case less frequently and less faithfully. The women went on as they had done before, addressing me almost as an adult. They had reason for this, since over the years I had shown the necessary capacity to play my part in the monitoring of my father's erratic and turbulent existence.

But I could no longer do it. It had induced in me a partial response which, at one level, did add up to looking after him or at least keeping an eye on him. I did exercise power over him – the power of that wonderful currency I call love. I loved him into a strange form of submission or obedience.

My father had a fundamentally moral nature, deeply flawed in its execution and at times disrupted by what amounted almost to psychotic behaviour. But with me he was faithful to an ideal of fatherhood that was loving and dutiful, in ways that may seem frugal and inadequate, but he did ensure that my dependence on him was never seriously betrayed. It was different for my siblings. My two sisters, now adopted, saw nothing of him. Guy, four years my senior, had made a deliberate decision not to see him. Hugh, who was the eldest, six years older than me, had long since gone through what I was experiencing and at that time was serving a short-term commission in the Royal Irish Fusiliers, first in Armagh, then Berlin, then Korea and finally in Kenya, during what he described as the 'war' against Mau Mau. When he could, he visited Father in London, stayed with him on occasions and they got on well.

I was wrestling with the need to become independent of George. I could not go on doing what the women asked me to do, and Barbara was one who recognised this and probably said it to him. I can hear her. They are imagined words, but they represent things she later said to me, even as late as the years after his death. She would have told him, 'Ease off, Georgie. Let him have his life and you get on with yours. You have me to care for and to care for you. Your son must make his own way.'

I had to make my way in my own fashion, deciding on the direction and on what I should do. I did not want my father's advice. He would have set his sights too low for my great expectations. Through all the vicissitudes in my life up to that time, I had harboured a great sense of what was due to me from the stars that shaped my life, the destiny prepared by 'Hidden Hands' which I believed to include those of a Divine Being. My father occupied less and less of this blessed territory.

He was good on generalities. He talked with authority about ordinary life, about behaviour towards people, about hard work and standing up for oneself and finishing the job. But he had no comprehension of what I dreamed of becoming, how I saw myself, what aspirations were moving me, with delicate, uncertain steps, across the ice fields and mined land of creative purpose. I had started to write. I addressed poems to people; sometimes showed them or gave them. They were expressions of love and need and loneliness. I shiver physically as I write these words, remembering the tense feelings with which they were created. We were bathed in the effusions of Keats and Wordsworth and Byron, from studying them at school, but not free, individually, from the acute lack of confidence or uncertainty.

PART TWO

And so my last year at school became a time of separation. George and Barbara were in Chelsea together. There were no letters during the Easter and summer terms. He wrote to me of course and what he told me was essentially reassuring, but I am unable to fill in any details. We had become separated. This was the case even in holidays. Our paths had diverged, with him living in Chelsea and me on the south side of the Thames, opposite the Houses of Parliament. More than that, yet another aspect of division was there to reinforce the sense in which our lives were moving independently; the pace at which we were living had altered appreciably for us both. He had resigned himself to the fact that stated achievements, however nebulous, had not been reached, and that his happiness had not really been fulfilled. By contrast, in everything I did or tried to do I was accelerating, and this meant accelerating away from him. How many times, in my mind over the years, have I heard his voice echoing and re-echoing with the deeply frustrating force of his failure, as he told me to be guided about what I should *not* do as a result of watching his many mistakes? The lessons, though sad, were real enough. I followed them.

I returned to school for the Easter term with no sense of regret at parting from him. I looked forward to everything and once again plunged into all the complications of seniority and responsibility, work and recreation. The advent of a new warden, Teddy Cooper, made a big impact. Above all else there was the very real pleasure of an ambitious piece of school theatre, a production of Oliver Goldsmith's *She Stoops to Conquer*. Details of this had been worked out the term before, and I had been chosen to play the romantic lead part of Marlow. I think I may even have worked on the lines during the holiday.

Tom Worrall directed the play with Jim Lund as his

assistant producer. The scenery was done by Reg Durrant, who had been a senior housemaster but had then taken charge of the junior school to which I had come as a child of seven, ten years earlier. My housemaster, Francis Meerendonck, was stage manager, and of course the music for the evening and Tony Lumpkin's song, 'The Three Jolly Pigeons', were under Stewart Brindley's direction.

Nigel Tanner was a suitably slow and contemplative Hardcastle and John Glover a prickly and vituperative Mrs Hardcastle. Paul Millard was a relaxed and easy-going Tony Lumpkin; he was the star of the show. My friend and partner in the play, Hastings, was acted by Tony Norton who, with Nigel Tanner, shared the teaching table in the very pared-down occupation of the sixth form during that last year. Martin Bee was Sir Charles Marlow and David Perryman was Constance Neville. The prodigality of school casting involved several others as servants and ale-house characters. The task of learning lines and movements on stage, the gathering momentum that brought staff and boys together in stage design, the making of props and costumes and the refining of the production as best we could, seemed also to invigorate our school work.

I leave to the last David Dann, who played Kate. Quite small in stature, he was at the time the leading treble in the choir, following in my own and Carl Browning's footsteps. He was quite delectable and I was very much in love with him, far more so, I have to say, than with either Jennifer or Elizabeth. He was a wonderful younger boy, playful, irreverent, cheeky, clever, witty, and he had a beautiful voice. He was not in my house. Our friendship was noticeably close, entirely innocent and of the utmost importance to me in the stress and strain of those last two terms. It was to him that I wrote poems. I went always to rehearsal in the winter evenings of February and

PART TWO

March with a happy heart, knowing that he would be there. And the make-believe of our playing of the parts of the two main lovers in the play reflected, certainly for me, an unexplained yet deep affection for him.

She Stoops to Conquer was put on for two nights at that Easter term's end. It was a triumph. What else might I have been expected to say about it? We loved ourselves, loved what we had done, loved each other. I was sad that the proximity with David would end, and that the coming holiday would part us still further.

David was fourteen years old. For the school magazine he wrote a rather good essay entitled 'First Appearance' about how playing in *She Stoops to Conquer* 'was the event of the year for me'. It reminds me how we were gathered together in the library before the end of the winter term with 'little red copies' of the play. (I still have mine.) David ignored the demands to learn the part he was allotted before we left on holiday and then, when he returned, having lost his copy of the play, was reassigned to play Kate Hardcastle. Then he got a sore throat and was in the sanatorium for what he described as 'two completely lonely weeks. 'I said my part as best I could to empty beds and deaf walls.' Then he gives an account of his return and the intense rehearsal that went on and on until the dress rehearsal and the two nights playing to audiences. He wrote in the piece, 'Friday, 27th March, was a very great day for me, and will stay in my memory for many years.' That pleasure, which I have often enjoyed myself, was denied him. David Dann became head boy of Sheffield House and then Head of School. He joined the Royal Navy, was awarded his 'wings' and saw action in the Far East flying helicopters. The 1963 *School Magazine* describes him 'leading a boarding party which captured a Chinese pirate vessel during anti-piracy patrols';

and he was briefly nicknamed 'Desperate' Dan after the comic hero. But shortly afterwards David Dann died in an air crash.

There is a natural enough unwritten code for such affections and it was worked out between us and accepted by others. It was friendship of a particular kind, and however one wants to interpret it, there was, within the liaison, love of an overwhelming kind as well. When I had been his age, I had experienced no less than three such friendships in which boys a good deal older than me had singled me out for special kindness or protection. They wanted to be in my company and simple, protective gestures reinforced the obvious choice they had made. One of them had written me poems. One kept up a correspondence after he had left school. The earliest of them, very senior when I had just moved up from the junior school, had been the least communicative. And yet he was tenderly caring of my safety as a very small, very new boy in a rough and at times unsympathetic house. Such affections exercised or expressed a balancing force against bullying or victimisation, or the intolerable loneliness of newly arrived boys in a house at boarding school. All of these friendships were innocent, both theirs and mine. All of them were immensely important and remain memorable, even crowded with detail.

I surged ahead with my work. Historical fact and theory fell into place. We came to 'know', in a deeper, more effective way, the literature we studied and the place it occupied in the context of history, just as history was being enriched by a widening understanding of social and artistic life.

I went to London, lived again across the river from Westminster, and saw my father from time to time. I worked at my studies during the holiday, yet returned to school for my last term with a sense of foreboding. Had I done enough? Would I be found wanting?

PART TWO

I returned also to an unforeseen development. That Easter the wife of Geoffrey Phelps, housemaster of Sheffield House, left him. She had fallen in love with our history teacher, Jim Lund. Some of us had known about it. Secrets are not easily concealed in the close community of a boarding school in the remote countryside, particularly in the 1950s when few of the staff had cars. But this development – of her leaving – created something of a crisis and certainly devastated Phelps.

He was much older than her. There might well have been twenty years between them. The story was that he had flown out to Czechoslovakia in 1938 to help bring Jewish children to England and Marrietta was one of them. It was thought he was teaching at Bedford School at the time, but was in the RAF reserve. He had come to the school as a housemaster shortly after World War II. He was already married to Marrietta. A version of the story, even then, among us schoolboys, was that he had indeed 'rescued' her; also, that he had sent her to school and only later married her.

Phelps was an interesting figure, a 'character' even. Against the universal practice among staff, of walking from place on the school estate, he was the first to show an interest in motorised transport, using a Vespa moped on which he rode about. He came on it to the staffroom to take his classes – he was the geography master – and used it for all other travel while others walked or cycled. He was the first housemaster to introduce television to his house, though it was in his own quarters, and to allow boys to view events through the snow showers of poor reception which constantly obscured whatever was on. The screen was the size of a dinner plate and ten boys watching around the set had the obsessive absurdity of the early television comedies which we were so obviously unable to see.

He That Is Down Need Fear No Fall

I took on and managed the difficult role of joining Phelps in leadership of the house in which things had not been going well in the two previous terms. The sad little tragedy had been working itself out, and he had suffered. So had house discipline.

Among the boys I remember, there was one in particular on whom I had to focus attention; his name was Michael Singer. He was big for his age, good at sport, very noisy and essentially unruly. He had a mass of red hair and the freckled, sensitive skin that usually goes with the redhead. If I were going to be faced with conflict, then he would be the source of it. After a couple of skirmishes, I began to work round him, bringing him into line, not always successfully, but on the grounds that he was pivotal; clumsy but good at sport, aggressive but not malevolent, he needed a role that involved him on the side of the house. Unexpected help came from the fact that David Dann was also a boy in this house. Out of sympathy for me, he understood the strange predicament I was in, focused, as such situations usually are, on one potentially difficult customer. David Dann, two years younger than Michael Singer, had a strange effect on him, making him dutiful. And on this basis we went forward. Also in the house was Carl Browning. He was probably the most gifted boy, musically, at Kingham when I was there, a good pianist and an exceptional treble voice.

I think my time as head boy of Sheffield House, which lasted one term only, was a success. The house went forward, recovered its spirit. Self-confidence inspired good sporting achievement. We did well in the inter-house cricket and particularly well in athletics. Not only was Michael Singer a powerful runner, but I also had become one, and the two of us proved to be stars. In the sports finals I won the 100-yard sprint, the 220- and

440-yard races and the long jump. In that summer my father was very much in the background of my life. I was happy to have a house and be head of it, happy to be in close proximity to David Dann, to share with him the joys of music, to see my own work progressing towards the ultimate school challenge of those final examinations. I took them, and in due course heard that I had passed. I took the Oxford College entrance but did not get a place. My way forward was in part defined by this; I would put off university for the present and instead go into the army for National Service.

And so the summer ran its course and I saw before me the end of more than ten years at school in that attractive countryside deep in the Cotswolds. It was inevitable that this period in George's life, and in my own, would furnish me with the material for another novel. And indeed it did. *The Muted Swan* was the result.

Like the first two books in 'The Coppinger Chronicle', *The Muted Swan* is a school story. It is about adolescent friendship and growing up. In it the changing nature of the relationship between the narrator and the main character, George, is explored with the greater involvement of the narrator's brother, Francis. Both he and his Oxford friend, Philpotts, who in the story is an art historian working on a doctorate, become significant figures. Philpotts is modelled on Michael Flinn, a school contemporary of my brother's, who later became a friend of us both and took an interest in my writing. Through Francis, the narrator's sister Melanie is also drawn in, so that the family of George, up to this period in the novels both shadowy and marginal, now plays a part that is deliberately concerned with reconciliation.

The title of the book is derived from the words of Orlando Gibbons's madrigal 'The Silver Swan'. It is a favourite piece of music, hard for any madrigal group to sing well. As I have said, it is a valedictory on the age, its last line a dismissal of present superficiality in favour of a remembered time of perfection. This was why I later chose it for title and theme. 'More geese than Swans now live, more fools than wise.' For a swan to be muted, it must first sing and swans sing only when death approaches. That is the belief presented by Orlando Gibbons.

The swan in the novel is the younger boy loved by the narrator. He suffers from epilepsy. Through a tragic sequence of mishaps, the boy drowns, and the catastrophe of this forms the climax of the book. There is a coroner's inquest into which, in highly charged circumstances as a result of reading newspaper reports, George intrudes. He literally barges in, only to be dismissed by his son, whose concern is focused elsewhere. It is a cold moment. It fits the penultimate line in Gibbons, 'Farewell all joys. O death come close mine eyes'.

The main theme throughout all three novels up to that point is of the healing forces of different loves. In each of the books there has been a series of breaks and departures. The final one of all is the departure from the school, with the narrator telling his housemaster that his father has gone missing and that he must go and find him. The finding is pursued in the last of that quartet of books, *Running to Paradise*. But it a quest that takes the narrator in two directions, back in time and forward in a final series of events that are drawn from eight years later, what I call here 'A Time of Crisis'.

Early in August 1954, with a party of boys and staff, I sailed from Lowestoft to Bergen and took a coastal steamer up through the Norwegian fjords to Stavangar and beyond. We went on north to another fjord fed by a glacier and for a fortnight carried out an exploration which was designed to measure the movement of the glacier. Even during that very brief period, it was measurable. By making holes in the ice across the four or five hundred feet between the two rock walls and inserting bamboo poles, we were able to measure the movement and give some mapped detail of the slight curve produced in the line. There was a medial moraine; two separate ice flows joined farther up the valley so that between the two rocky banks, somewhere in the middle, was the lesser debris picked up by the side ice of each branch of the glacier.

The brooding recollections of William Wordsworth were wholly absent from the snow-capped mountains distantly visible, and from the ice floor along which we climbed each morning from our base camp beside the river that flowed out from the end of the glacier. It was appropriate that only the natural order, and our slight impact on it as fledgling explorers, should have occupied our minds in the way that it did. We were in remote territory. It was chilly by day, cold but not freezing at night. Towards the end of the month we returned by steamer to Bergen and sailed back to England.

The summer was drawing to an end. School was behind me, and with it my childhood uncertainty, my peripatetic life with my father, all security of place. In mid-September, responding to a call from the War Office, I handed in an army travel warrant and took a train to Catterick Camp in Yorkshire. A new and very different life lay ahead.

PART THREE

A Time of Crisis

IX

*T*HERE WAS A SINGLE LETTER from my father to Barbara in 1954. It was written at the end of October. Following my departure from school, I was well and truly in the army. I was having a hard time at Catterick Camp, being bawled at by loathsome lance corporals. One was of such diminished stature that he seemed to bury his nose among the buttons of one's khaki tunic in order to scream out obscenities. The Yorkshires moors, which bordered the camp, were a solace at times. The rough country represented a sanctuary in which one could walk at dusk, recovering from the raw experiences that punctuated each day. Catterick at that time was notorious for its brutality. Suicides were frequent and provoked questions in parliament and newspaper stories. Basic training at Catterick Camp in 1954 was bleak and harsh; we strove to survive.

George, in that very brief message to Barbara, had scribbled the words rapidly on a 'lettercard', a pale yellow, single-page fold-over card bought, already franked, with red printed images of the required stamp. In this case, though King George VI had been dead for two and a half years, it is his head that adorns the front. The only date is the postmark. He gives no address.

> Darling – I may not be able to phone so am just sending this to let you know I am always thinking of you – we go at six o'clock unless anything happens. All my love, George.

He sent it to her in Sydney Street, posting it in Chelsea. When I think of him at that time, and look at the simple message, I fail to fathom the suddenness of his expression of love, just at that moment. All his letters had an urgency about them. He wrote with passionate intensity and with an essential economy of statement. But this occasion was different. There is something that borders on the desperate hovering behind each detail. The handwriting is large, filling in just ten lines, none of more than four words, the whole space. He spared no time for date or address. He left blank the space on the back marked 'name and address of sender'. She obviously knew whom he was with and where he was going. He posted it shortly after noon on that day, a Friday, and yet the journey, 'unless anything happens', was six hours later. What was it? Did it involve another member of our family or of hers? Why, above all, the need to say that he is letting her know that he is always thinking of her?

I am tempted strongly to think of it as a pilgrimage. Why this should be so I cannot explain. He was no Christian setting out from the City of Destruction. And I cannot think that he was with a companion named 'Faithful' who strode beside Christian at a later stage in Bunyan's story, and was destroyed in Vanity Fair where faith has no remit. So with whom did he set out? And did they in fact go, or was the journey aborted? And where were they going? And why was he not able to phone? And why was he compelled by his beleaguered heart to tell her what she had been told so many times before, that he was always thinking of her? 'Here little, and hereafter bliss.' Did he so hope?

He had existed in her life, resting there as a butterfly might or a bird of passage, touching her in passing if only by the few tender words designed to make her recollect him before the strange portent of a timed departure which seems overshadowed by the threat of interruption.

There is afterwards another gap of three months. And then Barbara left England to live for a time in Cyprus and in Egypt. George's life meanwhile remained stable. I am not entirely sure where he was, but I think in Chelsea.

The idea of marriage was clearly over for them. The family connection had, to all intents and purposes, come to an end as well. We had enjoyed our last Christmas in St Leonards-on-Sea and it had become a place of memory, the source of the intense nostalgia that my father both suffered from and welcomed, as he did the many scents of the garden. There were times when he seemed to devour the smell of flowering shrubs like privet, buddleia, lilac, as though they were a potent and an immediately effective drug.

While Barbara was living abroad, George wrote her four letters. They are completely different in tone from the tense missive of the previous October. There is no hint of the meaning of that strange journey, even whether it was taken or not. Yet there is a further mystery. The four letters all date from the month of February. They are all are written on 'Air Letters' with the red printed sixpenny stamp. King George had at last been replaced by a portrait of the young Queen, the design of it elaborate, the portrait in a central oval flanked by two crowns and two maces. What is odd about all the letters is that my father puts no address, and in one of the letters he writes, bizarrely, 'Am not putting an address in case it goes astray'. Whom did he think might send any 'lost' letter back, and to what place?

He was still working for Constance Spry. Had the letter

come back there, it would have been handed to him, and the likelihood of this happening was remote. I wonder where he was now staying in Chelsea and if this might give me a clue of the great tide of trouble building up for him. But time enough for that. He records his work and the weather.

At that stage I was an officer cadet. I had come down from Catterick to Aldershot and was at Mons Barracks, being 'proved' in various ways as 'officer material'. It involved hard days and nights. I remember the infantry training at night, in the cold and wet, across ground traversed by countless soldiers before me, during which decades it had been a major military training ground.

I met my father on the last Sunday in January, on a 48-hour leave, and we had tea together in the Grosvenor Hotel, near Victoria Station, a strangely formal encounter. He mentioned it in his letter to Barbara four days later, adding 'Victoria Station is my favourite station and it reminds me of you.'

The salutations in those letters are loving ones. The mood he expresses is relaxed and, as far as his work was going, confident. He mentions Barbara's sister Margaret, who had lived on with their mother, Edith Young, in Chapel Park Road. Edith had died the previous year and that meant the end of the magnetism exercised by that family home, which was sold. This place, above the seafront and the railway, had been a wondrous component of my own late childhood during the early 1950s. Barbara bought a home for herself in Hastings. It must have made it easier for her to give up Sydney Street, though things now were tougher for George. He had no home with her, and the sense of this parting, a gentle severance of the stricter binding of passion I had witnessed and loved, is like a hidden message in code underneath the texture of those letters.

PART THREE

It is clear that he and I were writing to each other and meeting as well. I am mentioned in each of the four letters: going through strict training, recovering from a brief spell in hospital for gastric flu, and then working hard for my passing out. For this I was back in Catterick. We wore the white flashes of officer cadets on our collars and we knew where we were going.

There are other illuminating passages in those letters that I have striven to understand. Sheila, one of Barbara's friends since WAAF days, was with her. Joyce, another friend of Barbara's, was in London. George and Joyce passed each other in Bond Street, Joyce with her nose in the air, ignoring him. He thought she looked funny, deliberately trying to cut him. Barbara was having an exciting time. Cyprus was a tense and difficult place, the British Army keeping the peace between the increasingly volatile Greek and Turkish communities; it would erupt later in the year. In the third letter he wrote, 'I would not be surprised if you did not stay out there in some job or perhaps marry someone.' Barbara did not stay out there. She did not marry. She returned home and took a new flat in Chelsea, in Mulberry Close, and lived there and had her home on the south coast in Hastings from then on.

That was the last letter for three years and four months. Less than a month later, in April 1955, I was commissioned a second lieutenant in the Royal Signals and ordered to report to the Officer Training Wing at Catterick. I opened my first bank account, at the Cox's and King's branch of Lloyds Bank. I also opened an account with Flights, the tailoring firm for the armed forces, and bought the initial accoutrement, judged as fitting for the exalted station to which I had been elevated. I was posted to Germany, a Westphalian town called Bünde, famous for its cigar-making, but also the headquarters of the

Sixth Armoured Division. I joined the Royal Signals Regiment there.

My father was living now at 40 Tite Street, Chelsea, a house facing the Royal Hospital. The landlady was Leslie Alison. On 14 December of that year, George married her. On leave from the army early in 1956, I stayed with them for a few days. I was not immediately enamoured of Leslie nor she of me. Neither then nor later did I understand what chemistry created the attraction between them. Her interesting story does not impinge on that of Barbara and George. In so far as it concerned the letters, and his love for Barbara, the marriage was an interruption, though not one that lasted. But it was protracted, and it became increasingly bitter and unstable, eventually ending in his second divorce. Well before the marriage was finally dissolved, in March 1962, it was over. But it did last, at first for a couple of years, and then, with angry interruptions, for further periods of which I knew very little.

I did like Tite Street. They were only a couple of doors down from the house where Oscar Wilde had lived. That district of Chelsea, from the river up through Tedworth Square to the King's Road, was quiet and stable, unlike the more raffish parts of the borough. The other area of Chelsea I had come to know in much happier circumstances lay on the other side of the King's Road towards Brompton Road. Now I was discovering the Chelsea of Tite Street, luckily associating it with more than just the unhappy marriage with Leslie. For my father, they were the two sides of a doubtful coin that he seemed perpetually to toss, 'hoping against hope'.

George was adrift from the mid-1950s until he left Leslie, and left Chelsea and London as well. I was distant from him, positively enjoying myself to begin with as a young officer in a front-line armoured division in Germany. He and I met on rare occasions, once or twice a year, but the Tite Street house was never home to me. His manner was quite debonair. He was a Chelsea character. We drank occasionally in the White Hart, in the King's Road, a place to which other Chelsea 'characters' came, greeting him, being introduced to me.

I was invariably ill at ease with him and his friends and he knew it. Resentment no longer flickered in my eyes as once it had when, as a boy, he collected me from outside some pub or other in which he had drunk for an hour or two, or indeed the whole evening until his money ran out, and took me home. We were equals now, and the feelings I had, not always concealed from him, were of boredom with a touch of disdain. We had climbed together out of troubles long before; we had made something very modest of our joint life. We had come close to the stability of a family existence involving Barbara, her mother and her sisters, and then that had faded. Gradually, all else seemed to have been taken away: his pride in work, his capacity to love, his charm attracting love, and he had been rendered into a figure inviting pity.

I did not like to be the witness of this reduction in his self-esteem. I was ashamed. From the soft but well-cut tweed cap on my head, to the cavalry-twill trousers and brogue shoes, I was indelibly marked by the characteristics and appearance of the tribe I had joined. I had become so transparently different, transformed into what was then defined as 'an officer and a gentleman'. I suppose I felt that I was somehow compromised in my father's company. I was not just ashamed of him – on many of these occasions, and in the encounters we had in public places, he was a caricature of himself, almost laughably so – I was ashamed of being ashamed. I was what he had wanted me to be. I was, modestly enough, but also clearly enough, the 'success' he had wanted me to be. I was an echo of what he had been, many years before, in 1914, starting out as a midshipman in the Royal Navy. But I was also now recast out of witnessing his many failures, through which he had instructed me. Nevertheless, he did not seem to like that very much.

I still looked on my father with love. He was the fountain of my life. From him flowed wisdom that I envied, judgements that I admired, affection that moved me and love that won my heart, but it seemed now to be surrounded by a sordid and baleful atmosphere. His home life with Leslie was precarious and uncertain. They raged at each other, there were growing differences, and from time to time the police were involved. He became truculent in drink, and abusive. His life with tedious and pretentious companions seemed to me superficial and unworthy. One of the things he had taught me was intolerance. I am distressed by the thought of it, since it has remained part of me. I paid it back to him and am now sorry that I did. Others were kinder, including women friends and his sister Peggy. My eldest brother was more tolerant than me. George's neglect of those he had let down – most of his family – rendered him a sad figure, no matter how endearing he managed still to be.

My heart floods with regret both for him and for myself. On those rare occasions when I had to obey the stern dictates of military service and head back at the end of my leave to Westphalia, I was glad to say goodbye to him. My farewells were not from the Tite Street house. After only a couple of early visits, I did not like to go there, nor did I see any more of his wife. I did have short periods of leave, but I sought other encounters so that those with him were brief and increasingly intermittent. When I eventually left the army, in September 1956, I went to teach for a year in a school in Kent. This meant that relations with him were infrequent.

PART THREE

I went up to London to see others. I stayed with my brother Guy, then working in London. He had a quite challenging job, concerned with Africa, overseas aid programmes, then in their infancy, and with an equally new phenomenon: the involvement of young people in voluntary work overseas. Mystery and excitement surrounded Guy's life and he let me be part of it. He was also, in his own forgiving way and in response to my father's growing admiration for him, interested more in the occasional encounters, so that from time to time we ventured together into Chelsea, a bit like explorers of a domain that was fascinating but never entirely comfortable. It was not Guy's habitat and never had been. He preferred Marylebone, Marble Arch, the Edgeware Road, and even farther east. As for me, the Chelsea I had known and loved, a place located in the heart and not within any geographical frame, was gone forever. What I went back to find were memories.

Leaving aside our forays into the King's Road, there was a positive value in time spent with my brother. I took to staying with him in another flat he had in quite a different part of London, Putney. I think I benefited from the fact that Guy had deliberately detached himself from my father some years before. This had meant him spending his time with other relations. For a good period of time Guy never really saw George at all. In changing this, in part I think because I still made visits to George in Chelsea, Guy opened up a different set of circumstances between us and the exploration of yet another territory. This, too, was located within the grey and misty boundaries of nostalgia. Deliberately, I led Guy into discussions about the early life of the family. I plied him with questions concerning my infant years, when, because he was four years older, and Hugh was six, they had experienced and witnessed what seemed to be a wholly different past from the one I recollected. I longed to know of it, even though the knowledge was one of privation and hardship. Whatever I have recounted, of the period during which my father was in love with Barbara, was a guidebook to how things might have been with my mother, only more intense, more unrelenting.

I wanted to know how this man, with all the faults that had brought grief and uncertainty to the years I had known him and grown up in his company, had managed with five children, his violently fluctuating financial fortunes, and the drink he enjoyed. How had it been? I had been too young to know. I had also been much favoured by my father, his pet child in the family, and therefore guarded from the waves of envy, fury and uncertainty which affected my siblings.

It puzzles and pleases me that Guy divulged so much. Out of the sessions we forged a new brotherly affection, an interdependency that I found enriching. He told me of how the early life had been with Hugh and our mother. It was an account rather than the recreation of experience. I like to think that I remembered some of the episodes he outlined, and indeed there were some that evoked true nostalgia. But to many others I listened enthralled, enjoying the wonderful recall he at times had of the life of our family in the late 1930s and then during the war.

We had lived near Croydon Airport. We suffered bombing, the life in the bomb shelters and other hardships and catastrophes. Houses were destroyed nearby, the windows of our own house blown out, neighbours were injured, occasionally killed by explosions. My father took against the life in the shelters which followed sirens announcing a bombing raid. He preferred to be at home and he made a crude form of shelter in the basement of the house, stacking the beds so that we could all be there. So we deserted the upper rooms at night and slept downstairs, all of us together. No doubt in the event of a direct hit, our lives would have been forfeit to his peculiar view of what was safe. But the worst we suffered consisted of the crashing in of glass – from which we were partly protected by sticky paper stuck across windowpanes – and of plaster ceilings. White chunks of chalky debris and clouds of fine dust rained down through the house. I had no more than dim memories of this time, but Guy's remembering it for me brought me closer to him.

At this time, I met again my two sisters, Marion and Lena. I had not seen Marion since my early schooldays when my father had brought her once to Kingham Hill School. I had not seen Lena since our mother's death. Marion was in various jobs and happy about her occasional encounters with her brothers. She had met a Jamaican called Paul in the autumn of 1957 and had become pregnant. Their baby girl, called Diana, was born in July 1958. Our reunion was emotionally unsure. This pretty and mature sister, less than two years younger than me, was a puzzle. We were curious about each other but found bridging the differences between us, which filled ten crucial years of our growing up, difficult.

In the case of my sister Lena, it was more complex. Having been adopted and brought up as part of a family, the problem she faced, of adjusting to an alternative family containing three grown-up brothers she had not seen since she was three years old, raised enormous complications for her. On the other hand, she was younger and more innocent than Marion, and had an attractive strength and directness. We took a particular liking to each other and got on. She was in the full flush of enthusiasm about literature, having just successfully completed her O-level examinations. I was filled with a parallel enthusiasm, being about to embark on university studies in Dublin. We talked about poetry, compared views on T.S. Eliot, went to the theatre together and turned otherwise halcyon days into a ferment of mutual discovery and examination. The idyll was brief but exciting. I remember particularly a day spent in Kew Gardens, with Marion too, sitting or lying on the grass in warm sunshine. We were a 'new' family. It could not and did not last; there are inevitable and sad regrets that this was so.

Lena's story is a sad one. After our mother's death, and through the 'good' offices of Aunt Dorothy, my mother's elder sister – why she did not keep them I shall never fully know, though 'blood' was part of it – Marion and Lena were sent to boarding school in Uckfield, north-east of Brighton. It was run by two women, Miss Lindsay, who was sweet and nice, and Miss Gordon-Jones, who was stern. Marion, then five, was too much for them and was sent 'home' to Dorothy.

At some stage – and if Lena's memory is correct it would have been in 1947 and therefore when Father was working in the Cotswolds – Kathleen proposed that Lena should go to friends she knew called the Knapps. Her motive was more in the Knapps's interest than in Lena's: they had lost their eldest son, Francis. He had been a navigator on Lancaster Bombers in the war and was lost in circumstances that Lena never knew. A younger brother, Peter, was ready to leave home, and Lena gave Mrs Knapp, whose name was May Florence, a new interest. Mrs Knapp was born in 1889 and was fifty-eight at the time of this 'arranged' adoption.

Her husband was a company secretary to a Swiss manufacturing business in Enfield. He was younger than May Florence and was from Somerset; she was from London. Because of this, she had relations around her, and perhaps because she was older, May Florence was the dominant parent.

PART THREE

Mr Knapp had a sister called Winnie who was married to William. They shared Kathleen's flat and when Mr Knapp – at his wife's insistence – went to call on his sister, taking Lena along, she would spend time with Kathleen. They got on well together. In addition to Winnie Knapp, there was another sister, but the brother could not stand her.

They always drove up to London in a car, and Lena invariably looked forward to it since she enjoyed meeting Kathleen. She would even sneak off to be with her while Knapp talked to Winnie. She never knew of the friendship between Kathleen and our mother.

William was an Anglican and went to church near to Kathleen in St James's Gardens. He got to know a couple who also worshipped there and, after Winnie's death, when Kathleen no longer wanted or needed him living in her flat, this couple took him in. The husband was a dumpy little man, while his wife was enormous, tall and buxom like a sergeant major.

The first brother Lena met was Guy, when she was sixteen years old. At that time, every Sunday, they used to drive out, buy the Sunday papers, park and the Knapps would read them. 'Sundays were awful,' Lena has told me. She was bored and was not really getting on well with her adoptive parents. Lena had done well in her O-levels and this was a headache for the Knapps. They realised they would have to send her to university when they wanted something much less complicated, like her becoming a nurse – which is what happened – or going to work in a bank. The Knapps responded wrongly and badly to Lena's undoubted success at school and her considerable abilities.

One Sunday they said they were going to visit Aunt Dorothy, and Guy was there. There was no warning. Aunt Dorothy had been preparing her usual colossal Sunday lunch and then Lena was told 'Your brother Guy is here'. They were the spitting image of each other, with blonde hair and clear-cut features. Lena was greatly troubled by what she describes as Guy's 'ghastly cut-glass accent'.

Dorothy got out family albums and, under the concentrated and collective gaze of Chris and Caroline, Dorothy's adopted children, Guy, the Knapps and Dorothy herself, Lena was put through the bizarre rigours of rediscovering a whole family, over three or four generations. For the first time she saw pictures of our mother, of Grandfather's fine house in its own grounds, of evidence of money and class, one sister being a debutante. She went out of the room and wept. Dorothy found her and told her, 'Pull yourself together and wash your face.' Lena cried and cried. 'You should be grateful,' she told Lena, not knowing what for.

Then she met me. With all these bewildering encounters – with Marion, Guy, myself, and then later Hugh and my father – the Knapps told Lena to describe us as 'distant cousins'. Those were preposterous times, deeply disturbing, often because of the behaviour of those who were meant to be the closest and most loving of all. Perhaps her meeting with Hugh, which came after the rest of us, was the least fortuitous; he told her, unwisely, 'You are just ripe to have an affair with the wrong man.' Lena promptly did just that and fell in love with Roy, the man she later married. She was left emotionally marooned, and overwhelmed.

I was about to go to university and went to Chelsea to visit my father before leaving, and Guy was about to emigrate to Canada. He had a job teaching in a school not far from Toronto. During the time before he left, at the end of the summer of 1957, I was staying with him. It was a happy time for both of us, embarking on new directions in our lives and,

PART THREE

though we probably talked about Lena and Marion among the many other subjects we covered, I don't believe we could possibly have recognised or understood what their lives were like, and what Lena in particular had gone through at that time.

I departed before he did and travelled in the early autumn of that year to Ireland, where I had a place at Dublin University to study English. Guy and I struggled with my luggage down the stairs of the Putney house, and I was into a taxi and away. It would be more than three years before I saw him again. I had with me my army trunk – a heavy metal box, still with my name, rank and army number painted on the lid. I had no sense of this possibly provoking interest to the Customs Officers in the Republic of Ireland, nor did it happen.

My father wrote to me in Ireland, but I hardly saw him out of term time. In December 1957 I went to London and worked in Simpson's in Piccadilly, selling ski-ing clothes and living in one room in Islington with Michael Flinn. It was a spartan, even sordid situation; two mattresses on the floor of the room and a gas stove in the corner where we made tea and toasted bread.

X

*G*EORGE WROTE to Barbara from East Tytherley, midway between Salisbury and Winchester, on 25 June 1958.

Up early and not a sound to be heard except the birds. Things have improved and I feel happier about the job than I did when I came yesterday – there is a certain amount of vagueness about people who live in the country which I suppose one gets used to in time – I arrived here at 2.30 having changed at Salisbury and got a train to Dean. No one here at all until 4.30 when Mrs M.W. came back and we had a cup of tea and then Tina came in – the housekeeper has gone and they are looking for another and it is not quite certain whether I am going to be in the bungalow or the house. Anyhow I am not worrying and have established myself in the bungalow at the moment. Nice dinner last night with them and a glass of Beaujolais. I left your flat yesterday very sadly and much too early of course and got to Waterloo at 10 a.m. and had to wait an hour – Had a drink on the train and when I got to Salisbury wandered about the town until my train went to Dean. Tina is making the breakfast and then a day's gardening. I shall be seeing you soon. Goodbye darling. Love from George.

He did see her again soon, promising to come up to town,

which he had to anyway. Following his stormy departure from Tite Street, his wife sought a maintenance order against him and this led to a court appearance. Leslie was awarded a nominal amount of one shilling a week, together with a non-cohabitation order. He explained in a letter on 10 July that this 'means a judicial separation and I shall now try and get a divorce'. He said that one of the three magistrates had tried to make it a shilling a month. 'I don't think Leslie went down very well with them.' She was in court, 'all dolled-up – new hair perm – with one of the tenants and Michael the rat.'

I knew about this episode from other letters. I believed, with some relief, that it was all over, the life with Leslie in the Tite Street house. There is no mention of me in either of the two letters he wrote to Barbara, but we had been in touch. He had renewed with these letters his love for Barbara after a break of three years and four months, the first period of his stormy marriage with Leslie. The former intimacy and trust is immediately re-established, including the happy visit to her and the promise that he would come again.

The 'Mrs M.W.' of the letter was Judy Munkhouse Wilson who had two daughters, Tina and Anne. My father felt secure enough with his new employer to be able to invite me down. I must have looked on this phenomenon – a strange one, at the very least – in a mood of innocent encouragement of something that might work for him and fulfil his eternal wish for settlement of his own future. That view, of course, marked my acceptance that there was no practical future with Barbara. On the strength of his confidence, which he must have expressed in his usual positive way, I crossed from Dublin and travelled down to see him.

He seemed happy in the new job, relieved at his departure from London and full of praise for Judy, who was a widow, and affection for her two daughters. He had a large garden to look after, together with some indoor work. He told me what he had been through with Leslie and how relieved he was to be away from Chelsea and out of London altogether. As was characteristic of him, he performed a volte-face. Having been a habitué of Chelsea and a familiar figure among the characters who drank in the King's Road – Leslie was one of the few women in his life who drank with him – he now rejected that life with a moral fervour that was comical. He saw this and laughed about it and then immediately afterwards became rueful and sorry for himself. 'I've made a bit of a mess of things, haven't I?' was the gist of his argument. And I did not deny it.

I had not seen him for some time, in part because I now lived abroad as a student and had no reason to 'come home' to England since no real home existed. We had been growing apart and I suppose both of us were resigned to that fact. But he wanted some gesture, some endorsement. I gave it. I don't remember what I said, but I felt a surge of love for him and was warmly encouraging about what he was doing, hoping it would last, but fearing, rightly, that it would not. I stayed for a few days.

My father did not really understand what I was at university for, and offered me the possibility of working with him and abandoning my studies. His suggestion made no sense; it was just a casual reflection of the recovered closeness between us of former years. I was amused and touched by it. I am sure he told me, perhaps with some bitterness, of the wasted years in Chelsea when he was unhappily married to the waspish Leslie. He had, I think, abandoned hope of a life with Barbara. And he must have told me of Barbara as well, his resumed relationship with her, his love and his longing to be with her more often.

PART THREE

I did not believe in his emotional certainty any more. I did not see any future with 'M.W.' nor, as it happened, with Barbara. But I did leave him reassured that he was, as he would have said himself, 'on an even keel'. I went off to France by boat from Southampton and hitch-hiked through the valley of the Loire, sleeping, at least some of the time, under apple trees or in vineyards. I would often wake to the sound of French farmers harvesting fruit. I learned very little French.

I visited 'M.W.' and her two daughters again on my return from France, and was drawn into the family atmosphere that prevailed, coming to believe in my father's characteristic confidence and self-assurance. I had grown a beard while tramping the roads of the Loire valley. He ordered me to shave it off, which I did. I was sunburnt and relaxed, easygoing about everything and doubtless full of myself. George's relationship with the Wilson family does appear to have blossomed as the year went on. I was at first off-hand about it, perhaps sceptical about this new start. It had painful echoes of previous experiences in his and my own life, but the household seemed to be a happy one.

I was having a wonderful time at university. My first year had included a good deal of theatre, and I was writing for several student publications. It had a decided effect on both Tina and Anne, both of them becoming romantically inclined towards me, Anne, the elder, in particular. I enjoyed this, went out with them both to parties and on trips and had a nice time with my father who seemed happy in their mother Judy's company.

My father went on working in East Tytherley through that summer of 1958, and this raises quite a different possibility for the split with Barbara. In any case, what he referred to afterwards as 'the Munkhouse Wilson job' – Munkhouse also being the name of the place – did not, in the end, work out. He went up to London from time to time, it seems, to see Barbara, and then much later in the year he returned to London. But the dates and letters do not square satisfactorily and I think there must have been a break in their lives, possibly caused by her meeting another man. Her nephew Ulick tells me this was possibly so, but is unable to put a date on the event. Much earlier she had met someone in Belgium and this may have been the man.

In the spring of that year I had directed James Joyce's only play, *Exiles*, in its first full Dublin production. It ran, with some critical success, for a fortnight, and was then, I think, the Trinity College entry in the Universities Drama Festival in 1958. Terence Brady played Richard Rowan, and Juliet Tatlow played his wife Bertha. I had fallen for her and we had seen much of each other during the earlier part of the summer. But I was heading back into the arms of yet another woman and my stay at Munkhouse was cut short.

I fell in love with Mavis Cleave later that summer on a visit to her home in Sligo. I had met her in my first term at Trinity when we acted together in Players, the university drama society. The play was *Jim Dandy* by William Saroyan, a work of American surrealism ably directed by Louis Lentin. Mavis played the part of Little Johnny and was dressed in a tunic made of sacking. I was Jim Smithers and spent much of the play behind bars in a cell at the back of the stage. Between Acts Two and Three I died or was executed and returned in the final act to the same cell as a new and younger character called Jack Adams. Terry Brady played Fishkin and Juliet Tatlow was Molly. Many of us were new students that autumn and we thought of ourselves as talented and innovative. Certainly the play was, with its setting in a transparent eggshell broken and open along one side and filled with ruins. Everybody in the play has survived the worst that can have happened – famine, torture, crime and madness. As a result they have been filled with dignity, humour and simplicity, or so Saroyan said. We played with our hearts full of excitement, and love was in the air.

True love did not run smooth. Mavis had decided on me, but I had other thoughts for a time and she then left to take up a job in Derbyshire as a psychiatric social worker, committing mentally ill patients to hospitals and travelling the dales in a smart little Morris Minor. Our lives are recorded in a series of love letters in which each of us tells the other what we were doing and why and how it was affecting us. There is little or anything about my father. I saw no wish or need to see him. I have no letters from him from that time and think that if there had been any, they would have been fringed by the dark black burden of despair that surrounded his return, later that year, to live with Leslie. Circumstance is a proof of this and in due course plunged him into crisis. But I was not a party to his circumstance at that time. I was writing poetry, acting in plays, engaged in college journalism and editing *Icarus* and *T.C.D.*, two student publications at Trinity.

Mavis and I wrote many letters which are a record of our lives at that time. Searching them for some detail of my father, I came across a brief enough entry recording the end of the East Tytherley idyll. 'My father has walked out,' I told Mavis, 'and I no longer have a house and two half sisters and Judy, etc., etc., etc.' The date of the letter was 26 October 1958. There had clearly been a romantic dimension to his involvement with 'M.W.' and it had not worked out. That was how I must have seen it and it suggests much more than a job; it was a hopeless and ill-considered attempt by him to create yet another workable way of life, even attempting to acquire a new family;

but it was based on an impossible set of hopes and aspirations. Clearly I was bitter about it, but not in any sustained way. He was just becoming something of a trial to me if I became involved. And the wish not to be involved was strengthened as a result. I had always half-feared his return to Chelsea and characterised it in dark perceptions, including the view I expressed in one letter that 'my father is back in Chelsea getting drunk with all the bums there and cadging money and food'.

This was not the truth, but it became so early the following spring. But that autumn, when he returned to the city, it was to live with Barbara. She had left Sydney Street at this stage and was renting a flat in Mulberry Close. He lived with her there through the autumn and part of the winter, paying for his share of gas and electricity. This is carefully detailed in a letter to Barbara early in the new year, after the bills had come in. He must also have paid a share of the rent. I don't know what work he did, but he could easily have resumed the jobbing gardening of previous times, settling once more into Chelsea, though with a different and almost certainly more subdued approach, avoiding the pubs and companions of earlier periods. Barbara would have seen to that.

He went to the country again, in January 1959, this time to a place called Broad Oak Farm, near Lewes in Sussex. He gives in his first letter an account of the journey and a brief description of the people employing him. In this case his boss was a Mr Fordham, who met him at Lewes Station and brought him back for tea and cake. He had a room in the wing of the farmhouse and a set of duties that put them together side by side on daily tasks. 'The first week is over,' George wrote in his second letter to Barbara, on 25 January. 'All is well and I am still liking it – Mr Fordham is a pleasant old man and we get on well together – He and I are still outside most of the day on different jobs – the food is terrific and I shall certainly be getting fat soon.'

Still liking it, after a week? How vulnerable had he become? He was a creature of routine and he reported, almost obsessively, on his day's work: what he ate, trips in to Lewes, the health of Mr Fordham and slight rows with Mrs Fordham. They ate together, a cooked breakfast at nine o'clock – by which time my father had been up working for two hours – porridge with cream, bacon, egg, sausage, toast. The main meal was in the middle of the day at one o'clock, 'soup, joint or pie & sweet & cheese'. There was a cup of tea at four o'clock and television, though it seems that work went on into the evening.

He wrote to me about the new job and I reported to Mavis on 'a splendid' letter from my father. Yet again, I said, he had found his feet in no uncertain manner and was on a farm. 'He promises to send me eggs, butter, cheese – the lovable old reprobate.' I told her, in that letter, that I was writing back to him directly. I was pleased and relieved that he was once more in the country, once more working on the land.

For the first time, he wrote to Barbara about his own health. He was in bed with a bad dose of flu for five days and was understandably annoyed when Mrs Fordham sought to deduct from his pay the money for the days he was ill. These included a Saturday and Sunday. 'I had a slight up and down and considering I've worked every day since I've been here up to the illness including Saturdays and Sundays it was a bit much and of course I got my full money – I simply cannot understand the mentality of some people – .' All was well, however, and the work, he said, was going smoothly. It was hard. Broad Oak farm was, he said, run down. At the beginning of his third week, in early February, he told Barbara: 'I have to pull myself up sometime as to put the place in order would mean 24 hours a day.'

Milking the cows was part of the job. George, who was good with all animals and with children, except his own, having a natural and relaxed disposition, loved milking. It was a contract between man and animal, each beast to be milked a different challenge. A new cow arrived, 'a docile Guernsey but very small teats and difficult to milk – I have only been getting one and a quarter gallons down so far but it will improve.' He had made a conquest. There was a black cat not unlike Barbara's, called Ming, though much younger. Ming was coming to the end of his days and died within the year. The new cat, which George called Ming II, had been half-wild, and nobody had been able to go near it except Mr Fordham, who was now ill with rheumatism. 'I soon got it under my wing and we are now great friends – it's got a swelling on its face which I shall have to doctor if it does not go. How is Ming I?' He invited Barbara to stay at Broad Oak and suggested that she should bring her cat. In a few weeks the new Guernsey cow was giving wonderful milk and Ming II sat and watched it all. 'We have plenty of cream – porridge and cream for breakfast and cream on all puddings – and Ming II has some as well. He is getting quite big.'

My father often talked to me of the people for whom he worked as being 'a lifeline' or as giving him 'a lifeline'. Between the two of us it became a source of humour. We laughed about it and I would tease him when things went wrong: 'She not being "a lifeline", Dad?' He would laugh and shrug off what in effect could often represent the impending catastrophe of the lifeline being drawn in or severed, leaving him to drift on down the uncharted waters of what was no more than a form of itinerant employment. Yet he never saw it like that. He

PART THREE

addressed himself to each of the places he worked in with remarkable energy, helped by his great organisational ability. By engaging the engine of his mind and the strength and ability of his body, he grappled with other people's woes and problems. His sharp eye and innate wisdom were also engaged. In the beginning he trusted his employers, though was quite quick to see the cracks in their trust for him.

But the real lifeline was Barbara. She did not let him down. And being able to write and tell her *everything*, and by so doing make her a loving witness of his endeavour, kept him going.

The Fordhams were all right to begin with, and the life he enjoyed at Broad Oak Farm in the early months of 1959 satisfied his modest needs. He lived in, and clearly was fed very well. He was part of the family. He watched television a good deal. It was, he said, 'a boon in a place like this and I get my eyes glued to it about 6.30 and finish from 9 to 10 according to what's on when I go to bed.' There was a risk, he said, of his becoming 'a TV maniac'. He was particularly addicted to a serial thriller called *The Scarf*.

And so he poured out his heart, as best he could, describing the many simple acts that made up his life on the farm. Being able to tell her everything was the all-important channel for his strong and passionate instincts about her and himself. His 'darling Barbara' to whom he gave 'Good Night' salutations – charging her, 'See nobody does you down' – was his world, his audience, the anchor holding him secure from the drifting that had been so often his fate, blighting his past and any possibility of permanency in the future.

Mrs Fordham was not entirely satisfactory, nor was the job. The attack of flu had shown George this; it did so again later. 'Mrs Fordham was scared stiff of catching it so I was left completely alone except for Dillon the old waiter who brought me tea – sometimes forgot it, so the answer is not to get sick here.' He became feverish, ran a high temperature 'with everything that goes with it' and felt weak and light-headed. He told Barbara of a persistent dream:

> When I slept or dozed I had the same sort of dream *every* time and although I can't remember all the details it was some extraordinary method of mixing soil so that you could always get what sort of soil, sand, gravel or anything you wanted without moving – I had been mixing soil before going to bed and as I couldn't move when I was in bed. I suppose it was a fairly reasonable dream – It got too much though.

As well as Broad Oak Farm having cows to milk and chickens and ducks, it took in guests. That was why there was an old Irish waiter tottering about irregularly like Fears in *The Cherry Orchard*. Clapham, the comedian of Clapham and Dwyer, who had lived at Hastings, was a paying guest; so too was a woman called Mrs Howes, who owned a bookshop in Hastings, knew Barbara's family and remembered sharing a gardener with the Young family in St Leonards-on-Sea. Another guest hunted with the South Down. 'Yesterday I broke off at 11 o'clock to see the South Down meet at Golden Cross – not a very big field but a fair percentage of pink coats and quite a nice sight. You could hear them all day around here in the woodland – Jimmy Edwards [the well-known radio comedian] hunts with them but unfortunately he did not turn out as I went up especially to see him. I must get the right jargon – bays, greys, hounds, etc – otherwise I shall be hounded out of the country!'

That year Guy published his first book. He had led an expedition to Sarawak in Borneo after leaving Oxford, and his account of it, in *Longhouse and Jungle*, published in time for

Christmas, was reviewed in *The Observer* on 25 January 1959. He was then living and working at Pickering College in Canada, and Father, who was very proud of the event, gathered copies of the review to send to people, including Hugh, who was then also abroad. Barbara's niece Georgiana, working in publishing for Dent, also helped spread the word.

For the first three months of 1959, George was happy in himself and poured out the details of his life to Barbara in long and chatty letters. He was worried about me. I was in hospital in Dublin for a time, ill through over-stress and a suspected fracture of my spine. It seems that all three of his sons were corresponding with him and this was a source of pleasure and reassurance which he passed on to Barbara.

George worked very hard. Being meticulous, he liked the idea of 'getting the place in order', perhaps an impossible task with a farm. He wrote to her, 'it is not appreciated as much as it would be in some places I've been in – It is not 100% satisfactory here which is just as well perhaps – quite pleasant but definitely a business deal and Mrs F. likes full measure.'

The weather was warm enough in early March to work without a shirt. He wanted Barbara to visit him, to stay at Broad Oak Farm as his guest for two nights and then go on to Cranleigh which she had reason to visit. He wrote to her: 'I've taken the cow over & she gives me plenty of good milk and I'm getting very attached to her – Plenty of work and its quite interesting shaping things up to my liking and am enjoying life at the moment.'

His last letter opened with the sentence: 'You sound as if you have been unhappy about something that it had to take my letter to keep you in a good mood – what's wrong?' Usually she wrote on the envelopes of the letters when she had answered them a simple 'Yes'. On this one she wrote 'Yes, by telephone'. After that, there was nothing. The 'nothing' lasted for nineteen months. He did not return to her. He did not live with her.

When Mavis and I married, in August 1959, my father did not come to the wedding in the west of Ireland; Guy was in Canada and my other brother at sea. My sister Marion came. Many friends attended, and I found thereafter the happiness that had eluded me for so many years. The loneliness ended. With the prodigality and energy of youth, living on half-nothing, we mixed work and study and began a family. We were part of one as well, not mine but Mavis's. She must have been puzzled at her own sense of security compared with my insecurity. But it lay in the past and, wisely and lovingly, she always looked to the future.

XI

*I*N OCTOBER 1960 my father tried to commit suicide. He took an overdose of pills. He was back at 40 Tite Street with Leslie and was brought to St Stephen's Hospital where his stomach was pumped out. The police interviewed him at his hospital bed. Suicide was a felony, the taking of life, and questions had to be answered. No charge was laid. The questioning was by then little more than a formality, though still on the Statute Book. The police, he later told me, conducted their investigation without really knowing what to ask him. His was an act of insanity, wilful, inept and fortunately not fatal. The attempt to do away with himself and end a troubled and troublesome life was made on 11 October. Less than a week later, he was moved to Banstead Hospital in Surrey and, on the following Saturday, he wrote to Barbara. He was in surprisingly ebullient form and due out in a day or so. The letter reads:

> My Dear Barbara,
> Have been here since last Monday and previous to that I was at St Stephens from Tuesday Oct. 11th. So I am having quite a good rest – Nothing wrong with me now & I shall be coming out the end of the week – Took too many pills and they had to pump them out – Finished with No. 40 Tite Street and have been served with injunction and divorce

papers – my solicitor visited me yesterday to discuss tactics – The appearance re injunction has been adjourned until next Thursday week – My wife's petition was one pack of lies which of course I answered pretty thoroughly in my A.I. form – The solicitor yesterday helped me add all the mud I could remember about her – Its quite interesting how the proceedings have started – In the meantime I have answered some of the letters I have had in reply to my advert in *The Lady*, because I want to get out of London. Irene comes tomorrow and my eldest son comes today from Rochester – It's quite interesting here after one has got over the first shock and one finds more intellect and intelligence amongst the patients here than you would in an ordinary hospital – Some have been here 21, 30 & 40 years – The food of course is appalling and badly served, but one even gets used to that. And now I must get some billiard practice in – We have a foursome and I am improving quite a lot.

    Goodbye now. Love from George.

He meant Chips, my half-brother, when he referred to his 'eldest son'. Chips was going into the Church and was then at Rochester Theological College.

The suicide attempt was the direct result of George's return to Chelsea and to Leslie. For reasons that will forever remain unfathomable, he went back to his wife some time between the summer of 1959 and the middle of the following year. She was still in Tite Street and she accepted him. On her side, there had been the non-cohabitation order and the maintenance order, for one shilling a week. On his, there had been the determination to try and get a divorce. Along with that, he had expressed against Leslie a bitterness and rancour from which otherwise his letters to Barbara are free. After that, he went back to his own, self-made slough of despond, seeking then to escape from it by suicide.

PART THREE

When seen in this context, the somewhat jaunty view he took of Banstead Hospital for the mentally ill, with some of its patients being lifelong inhabitants and others sparkling with intellectual skills and intelligence, is a reassuring expression of his powers of recovery from yet another setback in his life. And whatever loving sustenance he was given as he worked out his recovery, from Chips coming over from Rochester, and Irene from Cheniston Gardens, it was to Barbara he turned with his simple scheme for life expressed in that journal of perpetual salvation for him, *The Lady*.

He got out of London, which is what he wanted to do, going far away from the city to the West Country – to Wookey, near Wells, in Somerset. Mellifont Abbey was for him almost a place of pilgrimage. He had worked there before – not at a time when he was corresponding with Barbara, so there are no letters – and was remembered. Even the dog, Troy, remembered him and stayed beside him in his room while he unpacked. The Abbey was a retirement home for the elderly run by a Mrs Pritchard. He told Barbara in his first letter, written on 29 November 1960, that Mrs Pritchard had made his bedroom 'very comfortable – Incidentally she is 75, a bit older than I thought and she certainly doesn't look it & her daughter went to school with the Mitfords or some of them – '

My father was very keen on the Mitfords at the time. Irene had given him a copy of *Don't Tell Alfred* by Nancy Mitford, for Christmas. He wrote to Barbara: 'Seems that the Mitford relations are as mad as the Mitfords themselves.'

He was relaxed and happy, planning his gardening at that time of year, the late autumn, when all the aspirations and ideas for the following spring and summer stir the heart of the true gardener and set him at the soil and the plants with loving energy. He recovered himself. His self-confidence returned.

He That Is Down Need Fear No Fall

He battled against the gardener's great enemy, appalling weather, and in the meantime laboured at other tasks around the house, helping 'the old ones' and telling Barbara 'I would like a few younger people about'.

He was then sixty-two. Barbara was fifty. She celebrated her birthday on 12 December and George sent her a present – probably photographs enclosed in a letter. He sat at mealtimes beside a Miss Stead. She was eighty and very concerned about him. 'She is the one who keeps on about eating, saying that I'm wasting away, after I've had double the amount of anybody else – '. He was beginning to suffer quite a bit from asthma, but Miss Stead watched over him like a hawk. She kept three cats in her room and they came down for meals and were given choice morsels off her plate. There was a Miss Spinks, who sang in the Wells Cathedral choir and he went with two of the Mellifont guests to Bach's Christmas Oratorio there. He was there for Christmas, looking forward to the festivities and, it seemed, quite contented. On Christmas Eve he wrote to Barbara to say how much he liked writing to her and telling her, 'Must go into Wells again this afternoon and then settle down for a quiet Christmas.'

My father was habitually vexed by small things. Some 'gear' of mine in a suitcase had been left in London in Barbara's care. He felt he had to sort this out – mainly because of my failure to collect it: 'of course it has not been collected' – and he gives her instructions for sending it down to Somerset and from there he said he would post it to Dublin. On that note of quiet Christmas enjoyment and the dispersal of odds and ends, which give evidence of my limited contact with him, the correspondence with Barbara concludes for some four months.

But I went to see him in the new year, having spent Christmas in Sligo. I met both my brothers. I stayed also with my

PART THREE

Aunt Dorothy, in Banstead as it happened, and he phoned me there. I said I would travel down to see him over the weekend. He had not been well at the beginning of the year, in bed with a sore throat and being visited and cared for by women. There was another woman he was seeing before my visit called Edna, to whom he wrote. He phoned her and then travelled to Taunton to meet her. The weather was cold and raw, no garden work was possible and he was travelling across country by bus. Mrs Pritchard had retired to bed with a bad chest.

Father got drunk on the weekend of my visit. He wrote unusually long entries in his diary over those days, crossing out everything and then crossing and scribbling over the words so that they are difficult, though not impossible, to decipher. They seem not important enough to untangle, accounts of going into Wells, buying tea, and eventually, on the Saturday, meeting me. 'So pleased to see Bruce. Have had a slight relapse. E[dna]. L. sees me as I am. She reproaches me with her eyes. Bruce likes her.'

I confess I do not remember liking E.L. since I do not remember her at all, and, apart from meeting her on the day of my arrival, my father and I spent the time together. On the Tuesday we went to Bath. He travelled on to London and I went to Cheltenham and from there by coach to Liverpool to catch the boat back to Dublin.

George read voraciously at this time, mostly books by Nancy Mitford. He read all her novels, Irene keeping him supplied, and when that failed he turned to the local library, taking out *Voltaire in Love*. He seems to have resumed correspondence with the mysterious Edna and also with Isabel, a name that was familiar from years before in London, a woman younger than he was and a good skater, who used the rink at Queensway off the Bayswater Road. Whether it was the same person or not I could not be sure, but for a short time, from the frequent references in his diary, Isabel mattered to him. Though I do not remember Edna, I do remember Isabel, a friend rediscovered, since I had met her some years before, when still a schoolboy. She was not unlike Barbara in appearance and character, easy and relaxed, instinctively fond of me, and she was friendly. But the encounter at that time was a brief one.

At the end of February 1961, there is an entry in my father's diary, heavily scored out, in which he says, 'Feeling rather depressed – Hoping against Hope – God help every one of us –'. The following day, there is an even more cryptic reference: 'A letter from ———. All is well'. The name is scored out repeatedly and is illegible. There are no other clues and no further entries until late April. I wonder if this was some reference to a possible pregnancy?

Life in Wookey ended. He said farewell to his friends in Mellifont Abbey, to dear Miss Stead with her three cats and her fear that George might starve, to Miss Spinks singing music that glorified worship in Wells Cathedral, and to Miss Pritchard, who had welcomed him on arrival, probably knowing well in advance that he was a transient soul.

On 25 April 1961, George wrote a rapid note to Barbara from the country club at Fleet in Hampshire. He told her he was 'fixed up' there and 'pushing ahead' in order to be ready by 1 May when the 'season' for country clubs appears to have started in that part of the world. I came to know the Fleet Country Club at first-hand later in the summer of that fateful year. But in April this was a distant prospect, touched on in a letter, but no more. To Barbara he wrote more letters in this year than in any other. He wrote to her thirteen times from April to the end of July, in his last letter promising to meet her on a visit she was to make to Fleet in August.

PART THREE

Barbara was living in France. She went there to her sister in the spring of 1961, and was with Ursula and Bernard in Paris during April and May of that year. Then she moved to Nantes where she lived with a Madame Cherhal and taught there. Apart from the visit she paid my father while he was still in the Fleet County Club, in August 1961, she seems to have lived out of England for close on two years. It was a settled and an agreeable time for her. Her sister Marg missed her and my father recorded this. There is no mention in any of the letters of Roberta or James. Ulick was still at school. Georgiana was married, Charmian was at art school.

I followed my father's affairs from a distance. I had more or less detached myself from him and was firmly resident in Dublin. Though I was still a student, marriage had determined our life and work, and in the background was a tacit decision that we would, if possible, stay on in Ireland.

Mavis recorded the birth of our first child in my pocket diary, 23 March 1961 with the words '6.15 p.m., Emma Isabel arrived safe and well.' I was doing part-time teaching as well as studying during my final year. My teaching term at Sutton Park School, on the south-west slopes of Howth Head facing towards Dublin city, had ended the previous day, and the lecture term at Trinity College had ended a fortnight earlier. As well as studying and teaching English at the school, I was also busy giving grinds. But we managed to take a holiday in the west of Ireland with my mother-in-law and I remember stopping on the car journey and taking photographs of Emma while she was being fed. I sent one to my father, who wrote to Barbara and told her: 'Emma the baby is thriving and looks very cute and pretty by the snap.'

It was a very happy time for us. Looking now at the crowded diary entries, I am amazed at the amount of work I planned for the few crowded months remaining before my finals. I seemed to have packed in so much more than strict requirement demanded for my degree. We did a play reading of *The Importance of Being Earnest*. At Sutton Park School my two pupils, Caro and Chloe, were doing 'A' Level English and I was teaching them what I was learning myself – T.S. Eliot, Chaucer, Conrad and Trollope. I read my first Anthony Powell novel, *Venusberg*, and laughed at his light, humorous touch. I was reading widely anyway, and we read aloud to each other in the evenings.

Then my last term at Trinity College started. We were living in Wilton Place, off Baggot Street, our flat at the top of the house having lower rooms than the others but with the best views, north at the back towards Howth, and to the south across the canal to the purple undulating outline of the Dublin Mountains. The trees were in full leaf, the green of them fresh in tone, and we could see the gently flowing water of the Grand Canal as it spilled into the lock and on down to the sea at Ringsend. It looked eternally cool, dark and inviting. A Guinness barge was moored there. It briefly inspired thoughts of buying and converting it as a home; thoughts that were soon abandoned as we considered Emma as a crawling baby on a boat.

What foolish summer dreams we engaged in, what busy hope-filled days rushed by us. I stand again in that room and look down at the dark water or across the treetops and houses on the other side of the canal at the mountains in whose shadow I have now lived for the greater part of my life. I remember our carefree innocence and the simplicity of our self-assurance. Did we think we were invulnerable? Did we consider that this world was ours? Were we fortune's fools?

On 5 June 1961, Emma was admitted to Harcourt Street Children's Hospital. She had gastroenteritis and was running a temperature. Dr Steen, a kindly man with white-grey hair, reassured us, but said that she was dehydrated. We were frantic. We went in and out to see her, not knowing what to say or think. It seemed that an eternity of time was punishing us, but in fact it was not so. At five o'clock the following afternoon Emma died.

Our world fell apart entirely, and it was never, ever to be reconstructed in the way we had known it. No one had warned us of this possibility. No one had helped us to prepare for it. That is never the way in life. The unimaginable does not happen in advance and the warnings of crisis or tragedy are in the end only warnings that the human spirit chooses to ignore. We confronted a loss that could not ever be redeemed. We did so together but yet alone. We were surrounded by loving people. They flew to our protection. They took care of the event, arranged for Emma's funeral, tried in vain to comfort us. But they knew no more than we did of how we were to negotiate the black valley of death. It had no gleam of light whatsoever at the end of it. We did not know how to grieve. We were bewildered by the condolences that flooded in. We fled to Sligo.

Later we learned more of the sweet acts of kindness that reached out to protect us in our grief. Ronnie Wathen, who had been best man at our wedding, took charge. A student, a year ahead of me, he had married Eliza Collins and they had taken a flat below us in Wilton Place. The funeral took place the next day, in our absence. The coffin bearer was Teddy Figgis, carrying on his own that tiny little scrap of mortal remains on which our love had been so totally focused. Now, in our desolation, that focus became a terrible burden. Alec and Beatrice Reid, Bill and Ann Staunton, David Laing, Penny Gibbon, Brendan Kennelly were at St Stephen's Church.

Teddy wrote to us later that day from his office in the Hodges Figgis bookshop: 'You will wish to know that everything was just right this morning. About twenty of your close friends were there and Rev. Poyntz conducted the beautiful little service with a right note of hopefulness. The flowers were lovely and your own kept perfectly fresh. Ronnie and Liza have certainly done their best and I hope that your trouble may have helped them in a way. Everywhere in college yesterday there was a wave of sympathy for you.'

Teddy was very practical as well. I had my finals to work for, but he offered Mavis a job in his bookshop.

Our flight to Sligo brought us no comfort. Time does not heal. From Sligo we were invited to go and stay with friends in Wales. It did no good. From there we went on to stay with my father. That was even worse.

I find it very difficult writing of my father's part in these events. Both Mavis and I had one parent. Both seemed to a degree to be uncomprehending, at least in the expression and exercise of help or guidance. George wrote to us, of course, his letter containing the highly charged solipsism: 'this must have been a terrible blow for you and I can feel what you must be feeling – it has given me a bad blow too. She now rests in peace and quietness.' For him it was a solution to the problem of explaining the nature of our knowledge of the external world. He wrote again the day after the funeral, hoping to hear from us and repeating that 'it has been a bad blow for me as well'.

His numerous letters to Barbara at this time did not coincide with the death and it was Irene who went down to see him the following Sunday, 11 June, for the day. When he did eventually write to Barbara, on 17 June, it is clear he had already told her about Emma, possibly by telephone or in a letter that may have been lost subsequently. He wrote of me being 'cut up' about Emma's death, and crying on the phone to him. We were with him shortly after this letter.

Father had tried hard in his way. He had been sending ten shillings a week for Emma since her birth, so we had been regularly in touch. Yet the letters from him at this time, both to us and to Barbara, emphasise, if anything, the growing gulf, and sadly the visit turned out to be a mistake. A country club in the heat of summer, with children boating on a lake or swimming, was a bizarre, almost nightmarish place in which two young people might try to mend their shattered lives. We stayed for about ten days. My diary is entirely blank at that time; the empty pages tell only of desolation. We may have gone to London once or twice, but no memories have survived of what we can possibly have done in what was socially such an exposed and alien situation. Again, it is a mark of my father's solipsistic attitude that he could have written to Barbara on 29 June, the day after we left to return in mortal trepidation to our flat in Dublin, now so empty, and tell her 'their stay was a great success'.

He was at the time preoccupied with the awful circumstances in which he worked. Despite praising his employer, Mrs Broadhurst, for her kindness in having us to stay, the picture he gives is of unrelenting work for a poor return. Again self-centredness is in play. Her husband, who had been a tea planter, was dying of cancer.. Father helped to nurse him and observed in an earlier letter, on 12 May, after he had been there just over a fortnight, 'I have never seen such a deterioration in such a short time.' Mr Broadhurst was moved into hospital five days later, a Wednesday, and died the following Sunday. In the midst of this there is the description of 'Mrs B's slogan: "We play hard and we work hard", but there is no play and I presume that comes with the work.'

George was optimistic to start with and settled for the job, against other possible respondents to the advertisement in *The Lady* which had attracted the Broadhursts. One of these was a Mr Witton. He told my father that he was pleased on his behalf, but to ring him if it did not turn out to be as successful as it seemed at the beginning. Another was a woman: 'I had a heartbreaking letter from the lady from Broadstairs, telling me to write in a week's time if not satisfied – when she got my letter she drank three ports to drown her sorrows and then got the "Navy Sway" – .'

He engaged yet again in the difficult process of getting his divorce from Leslie, though it seemed that the initiative came from her side. 'My wife's solicitors are pressing for something or other,' he told Barbara. 'I hope I shall be free soon and you had better come back to England quickly darling.' He went so far as to tell her that Mrs Broadhurst was looking for someone to cook 'in the rush periods' and that if she didn't like her present job, she should consider a move to Fleet.

Barbara replied with frequent letters, two in two days in the middle of May. Perhaps she was lonely, teaching in Nantes and living 'chez Madame Cherhal'. Her work, like his, was hard, with long hours, and she was having money problems; something had gone wrong with her promised expenses. It seems from his advice to her – to send an account and not be squeamish – would indicate some failure on her part, and this would be consistent with the rather vague, fey side to her character.

More letters came from the lady in Broadstairs, whose name was Blanche. 'The old dame who replied to my advert – she still writes and I think she must be a little off her rocker – the one bit of French she has got into her head is "au-pair" and puts it in all the wrong places and does not know what she is talking about.'

PART THREE

There were small signs of tension; people were brought in to work at weekends, on a voluntary basis, and this annoyed him, as did Mrs Broadhurst's tactlessness, though examples are not given. He simply said in a later letter, 'I cannot get on with her', but he took action as well, writing out draft letters and saying that he would send one to the RAC country club at Epsom. He did not see his job at the Fleet Country Club lasting through the winter and was edgy about his future and rather forlorn that Barbara was in distant Nantes. 'Marry me,' he wrote, 'when the divorce is through and then we would advertise in *The Lady*. Hurry up and make up your mind my sweet because I can't keep on waiting and the divorce will be through before the end of July when the Hilary Term ends.'

It was warm and sunny that June and the crowds flocked into the Fleet Country Club, the children boating and swimming, the bar full and my father run off his feet. Barbara did return to England on holiday in July and promised to come down and see him. But the bad news was that she had relet her flat and was talking about him coming to see *her* in France, financially an impossibility.

The thirteenth and last letter to Barbara of that year, 1961, he sent on 24 July. In it he recorded 'the excitement of meeting my daughter Lena after 17 years – she is now married and going to have a baby and always wanted to see her father – we are united and she is a lovely girl and will come down when you are here.'

My Aunt Dorothy, my mother's eldest sibling, together with my elder brother Guy, had been nervous about the effect any encounter with my father might have on his youngest child. By the time this took place, Lena had already been to stay with us in Dublin. That visit was a happy one. Now she was married and pregnant. She met George a second time, promising to visit when Barbara came down to the country club in Fleet.

That year's last letter to Barbara ends with the words 'Looking forward to the 9th darling, and will do my best to meet you'. The correspondence with Barbara concludes there and does not resume again until February 1962. They did not meet on 9 August. If she came home from France, as planned, it was to visit her sisters Marg and Roberta, and possibly Roberta's children.

What then happened to my father derives from a mixture of sources, mainly letters to me, not only from him but also from Lena. In addition, I have taken further details from the diary he kept for the rest of that year, 1961. It is the first of several, spanning most, but not all, the remaining years of his life. The entries are mainly in the form of brief notes, letters received and written, work done and payments made to him. Later they contained many references to racing tips and bets he placed. He became almost addictive about the turf, not only recording details, but telling of them in his correspondence. Apart from that, later diaries are brief indeed. But in 1961 and in 1962 there are fragments of self-examination, small confessions about loving and being loved; they are still painful to read in the light of what happened.

Lena visited George with her husband, Roy, on 22 July. She detected on that visit to the country club that things were not going well. She wrote and told me of her doubts as to whether or not he would stick out the full season, 'But he may not, I feel. I think he's beginning to get a bit desperate.' Her baby was due in November, and she and Roy had found a flat in Wimbledon, into which they were moving in late September.

Then came George's abrupt departure from Fleet. 'Finished country club', he wrote in his large, clear and most flamboyant hand across the space for 29 July. He put in figures for what he was paid and recorded letters written to me and

Barbara. Lena wrote to me on 31 July, 'At five o'clock on Saturday Dad arrived on the doorstep.' She reported that he had had his final row with Mrs Broadhurst.

He had been in London the previous night, meeting Lena and Roy. Then, that Saturday night of his arrival from Fleet, his visit turned into a supper party for four, with the arrival of Irene. 'Dad and Roy went out and came back with a bottle of red wine. Dad gave Roy a lesson in buying wine.' This was the first occasion on which Lena had met Irene. She liked her 'very much' and observed the obvious – that Irene was in love with Father. Irene observed about Roy, 'He's a perfect pet'. Lena cooked. There were not enough lamb chops to go round and she shared one with Irene. At some stage Father divulged that Lena was pregnant. In that same letter Lena said that she and Irene exchanged 'addresses and sisterly hugs'.

They had persuaded the landlord to let George have a room in the house where they had a flat. It was not well furnished and he slept on the floor. He was unwell. His time at the Fleet Country Club had ended with him getting bad flu and he was wheezing and had chest trouble.

Lena and Father went to visit his Aunt Bertha, who lived in Wyndham Street. She was my grandmother's sister and Father's favourite among a large family, mainly of aunts, though there was a formidable Uncle Leonard Croft, a successful barrister who was as addicted to the bottle as my father but far more capable of pursuing his addiction as well as his legal practice, the latter with considerable success.

Father was disappointed in the visit to Aunt Bertha. He wrote in his diary, 'Met Aunt Bert – same as ever – 30 and 40 years ago – rather boring.' Lena recorded in her letter to me, 'Dad was rather disappointed with her – too respectable and sophisticated. He told her how she used to be in the old days.'

They brought her presents, ginger and grapes, stayed to tea and left at about eight. His visits to Aunt Bert – and I remember many I made as a child – were for comfort. They usually occurred during a drinking bout. They often included touching her for ten shillings. She was a soft touch, which might explain the irregular visits, motivated by trouble, depression or despair. He tried to do the same with Uncle Len, who lived with Aunt Dora, with less success. My brother Guy and I once made such a visit. Leonard declined Father's request and then, rather pointedly, gave each of us a half-crown and said we should keep it for ourselves.

Lena and I corresponded a great deal at that time, loving each other's letters, she giving me news of George and I telling her about our life in Dublin. Despite Teddy Figgis's hope that our tragedy over the death of Emma might help my best man, Ronnie and his wife, Liza, they decided to divorce. Lena commiserated over this. Father fitted into her and Roy's household well enough. When he did the washing up, Lena wrote, 'Isn't he super?!!' He soon thought rather differently about them. The rapture of meeting his youngest child for the first time in seventeen years wore off. It was replaced by his criticisms of her as frivolous in letters he wrote to me. He grew anxious to move out.

My father stayed with Lena for almost a month. He had advertised yet again in *The Lady* and records several possibilities and secured interviews in Daventry, Shropshire, Canterbury and Worthing. Also, he was now seeing a good deal of Irene. She was then at 22 Cheniston Gardens, willing as ever to help him and to take over her role as his 'port in a storm'. He was drinking, as his diary records: 'Slight Head', and then 'Feel ill' and 'Went to bed early'.

Irene was retired and was thinking of buying a small house

PART THREE

for herself in the south-east. She went to look at a small cottage and stayed in Canterbury. Father, who had been at King's School, travelled down to join her. He recorded: 'Nice hotel Irene is in but dead boring', and he meant her, not the hotel. The next day he wrote in his diary, 'Feel very depressed – No outlook, no hope.' The day after that, he accepted the job in Shrewsbury and travelled there the following morning.

The work was much as it had been in other places. It was a lovely Adam house with fine furniture to match. He scythed the lower lawns which stretched down to the banks of the Severn. The house was in the Crescent along the town walls and there was a Boat House Hotel to which he repaired with his employer, Mr Brodie, who involved George within the family, taking him out on one occasion to Much Wenlock to dine.

It was early September and there were days of warm sun in which he gardened happily. He even thought of a trip to Dublin and found out and recorded the return fare, only £4 10s. He listed rhododendrons, azaleas, hydrangeas and spiraea to be bought. A garden was there to be made and he also suggested genista, berberis, potentilla, veronica. Suddenly he seemed happy and optimistic, gardening for Mr Brodie and shopping for Mrs Brodie, both of whom seemed to want his company in the evening. But then on 11 September he wrote, 'The job is finished – informed they are going to Italy.' He worked that week quite contentedly and spent time in Shrewsbury, putting into his diary descriptions of the narrow cobbled street, the innumerable passages between them and the old houses; he thought the population 'polite, unfriendly and prosperous'. And that was the full measure of his time in Shropshire.

My father went next to a school near Northampton where he settled in immediately to his general duties and was ready with other staff to receive the boarders who were to come back to school the following day. The school would have been his first choice, but he was worried that the work would be too hard, even more worried that his up-to-date insurance card would be demanded and this might lead to a heavy bill for social welfare arrears. He was always a bit like the Harold Pinter character Daviess, wanting to get to Sidcup for his papers. As a child, I went on many (often inconclusive or abortive) excursions to sort out papers, and had come to understand his preference for jobs within the hidden economy where records received scant regard.

He was detached from Barbara now, for a time anyway. There were no letters after the end of July and it seems the break was by mutual, unrecorded agreement, since there are no diary references and they did not meet on her visit home. He was seeing a good deal of Irene and I suspect receiving some financial help from her. And he was writing fairly regularly to me.

My father came to stay with us in November. I met him off the boat from Holyhead on 3 November. He knew the town by another name, as he wrote in his diary: 'Arrived Kingstown 7 a.m. after 42 years.' He had last been there on board *HMS Verdun* in 1920 to patrol the seas around Ireland. We took him to Ibsen's *Ghosts* at the Gate Theatre on the Saturday and went out to lunch with Mavis's aunt and uncle in Delgany. It was a happy visit. He left us on his birthday, 7 November, and wrote two days later: 'Thank you both for such a lovely holiday – There are very few events in my life that have stuck in my memory for happiness, but this five days in Dublin will always be remembered.'

XII

*G*EORGE FELL IN LOVE with Brigid, whom he called Biddie, in the autumn of 1961. She was half his age. She had three children, but had parted from her husband. George and Biddie had a passionate love affair and he set the greatest store by it. She lived in the village near the Northampton school where he had gone to work, and she herself worked in some capacity on the staff. In terms of his life and the over-arching presence of Barbara in the story – to be resumed again all too soon – this was a brief, tempestuous and, in its way, wonderful interlude. He thought the world of Biddie. She loved him more deeply than she had thought was possible between a man and a woman and later told me so. And from the quieter, more settled circumstance of our lives in Dublin, where we were still struggling to recover from Emma's death and trying to have another baby, we looked upon the events as they unfolded with affection and compassion, hoping – as he hoped – for the impossible.

His happiness was expressed in everything he did. He gardened, mowed the playing fields, took cuttings of gera-niums and carnations and, with the help of an assistant in the garden, worked on the vegetable plot. He got himself a provisional licence and drove the small school bus. He helped Biddie to look after the children, taking them to places, and they all went to visit my brother Hugh and his family who were then living in Corby. When he came to stay with us in Dublin, letters from Biddie followed him, three of them in five days, and he told us repeatedly how much in love he was.

We could only express the wonder that we felt, together with encouragement and enthusiasm. Our emotions were heartfelt. Here was this man of sixty-three, in love with a woman of thirty-three, who loved him with just as much passion as he felt. We were swept up in what seemed to be heaven-sent and were rewarded by it. His love for Barbara had been superseded by this more focused love for Biddie.

He engaged once more with lawyers. Previous efforts at getting his second divorce from Leslie Alison had failed. This was probably on account of Barbara's reluctance, even her downright refusal, to make a commitment. Now, once again, there was motive for action. We had the sense that he had torn himself from a hopeless situation to engage in one that was infinitely precarious. We could only await the outcome. In his diary he records occasional minor hints of trouble looming. At the end of his letter to us on 9 November, after his Dublin visit, he added: 'Nothing to report from here except that Biddie and I have had a row – Clears the air and we are on firm footing again.'

His diary for that month of November is peppered with elusive comments such as 'bad weekend', with him spending Monday morning in bed – a hint that he had had a bout of drinking. Then he writes about a fine late November day which he spent putting up a 'run' for ducklings: 'Biddie had atmosphere with Miss Welsh. She is slightly depressed.' Miss Welsh was a senior member of staff. Prize days, junior and

PART THREE

senior, came and went. More than once, in letters, remembering happy visits he had paid to my brothers and me at school, he compared the strong attraction Kingham Hill School had exerted on him with what he now felt.

At the same time he seemed to sense that things were not going well, and that the rather odd *ménage à trois* – himself, Biddie and the school – could not survive the radiant fire of their passion. There were, in addition, her children, and, in the background, Irene, with whom he was corresponding; and then Barbara, who is mentioned as having written on 13 December.

I am not quite sure of the sequence of events that followed. There is mention in his diary of a doctor, of an injection, of him being reminded – of what I am not certain. And then, boldly across the top of a right-hand diary page in the space for 21 December, he wrote 'Exeunt Omnes' and immediately below it, on the next day: 'Came down to London. Phoned B.' And on the day following: 'Saw Barbara. Phoned Biddie.'

There were no further diary entries for that year, but in the surplus pages at the end, dated for the first week in 1962, he wrote out Rudyard Kipling's poem 'If'. I read the poem now with tears in my eyes. So many of the lines seem so well fitted to his condition at that time. Of course there is the obvious idea – of meeting with triumph and disaster, and treating these two imposters just the same. There are the entirely appropriate injunctions: to trust yourself when all men doubt you, or start again at your beginnings, never breathe a word about your loss. But of all the lines, from that impossibly wonderful and inspiring poem, I choose in the end the simplest, and also for his story the saddest: 'If you can wait and not be tired of waiting'. He had written to me in a letter in late summer, before these events began to unfold, 'I feel I must get cracking again as soon as possible – get dug in somewhere, always hoping it will be permanent.'

Nothing had ever been permanent for him. He left the school at the end of term to spend Christmas in London. He had taken a room at his most familiar port of comfort, the Fremantle Hotel in West Cromwell Road. He saw Barbara the next day. She must have been home from France for Christmas and on her way to St Leonards-on-Sea and to her sister Marg, who was still living there, though their mother was now dead.

The departure from the school, the dramatic 'Exeunt Omnes' had not been final. In the New Year he returned to the school job and wrote to us from there on 2 January 1962. He seems to have been in good spirits. Biddie, however, was not so well. She was pregnant, though he did not tell us at that point. He wrote encouragingly about our plans at the time to buy a house. He warned us about taking on somewhere too far from Dublin and cautioned us about buying anywhere that needed repair. Our taste at the time and later was for old buildings. Mavis was pregnant. We were looking at all sorts of houses. The place we lived in, where he had visited us the previous autumn, was a converted dairy. This attractive building had a huge upstairs sitting room with a bow window looking out on great forty-acre fields which are now covered in part of the Darndale housing development. There was a small octagonal dining room, once a saddle store. The owner, whose child was taking grinds from me in English – the main reason he had offered us the tenancy, so that I became a part-time tutor-in-residence – lived beside us. The early eighteenth-century house was called Belcamp. The ruin of it still stands.

I wrote an article, I think for *The Irish Times* where I was working as a sub-editor, though it may have been for *The Guardian* (I was the Irish correspondent of the paper at the time). I sent it to him, and in his reply he praised it, declared he would send it on to my half-brother, Chips. Then, in the middle of that letter, out of the blue one might say, came the surprising announcement: 'I told Irene about Biddie and the balloon went up.' The comment he then made was rather cruel, 'I can't help feeling that I bet she enjoyed her supper that evening after I had gone.'

His lack of understanding, or of any feeling for Irene, was staggering. Did he have any compassion at all towards her? The astonishment was compounded by the next off-hand observation: 'Biddie would like to meet her.' He was waiting for Biddie even as he wrote the letter; she was driving back from Yorkshire with her three children. Both of them were unaware that the axe was about to fall. Some time in early January, before the pupils returned, George was asked to leave the school.

He had treated Irene badly. She remained faithful to him, as she always did. And at that time, as in the past, I looked on with a mixture of relief and incomprehension at her care and concern for him which so eased my life and lessened my responsibilities, such as they were. Once more, they came into play.

Worse was to follow. On 20 January Biddie had a miscarriage and went into hospital. The situation was aggravated by my father's inability to cope. The miscarriage was on a Saturday, and Biddie left hospital the following Wednesday. On the Thursday he wrote to Irene: 'This has smashed everything – I've got to leave and Biddie is going away for a holiday – We shall separate and I shall come to London, but will let you know later when – for God's sake help me because I am just about at the end of my tether. Love, George.'

Irene sent me the letter with a full account of everything that had happened. He had asked her in an earlier letter for money – 'the incidental expenses are £1 a time to go and see her' – and explained his impoverished state, no doubt brought on and then exacerbated by the drinking that always accompanied such moments of crises.

She considered all that he told her and sent him £10. She gave me her reasons, one of which was that 'I don't want to have it on my conscience that I have been callous at this unhappy time and that he has not been able to get to the hospital through having no money for the taxi fares.' In what she described as 'a somewhat formal letter', she told him it was over as far as she was concerned.

In her letter to me she summarised both her feelings and what she had said to my father:

> No one can help falling in love, and if he and B. wish to make their lives together, well and good. But I fail to see why things should be any different for her than they have been for me – in other words why *she* should not have to spend her money on looking after him and coping with his constant money troubles, just as I have had to do in the past. To be asked for money – even on a loan basis – in existing circumstances, has made me furious. Your father seems to think that he can do just what he likes, and he has only to ask for money, and it will be forthcoming. So it has been, for something like 15 years, but the time does eventually come when one simply cannot stand up to any more – and that is the state I am in at the moment. I really feel quite ill with it all.

She left the letter overnight. The following morning the daily help brought up my father's letter, already quoted. It increased her fury that Biddie was going away, leaving him, as Irene saw it, in her charge. She sent me a telegram telling me she would pay for his fare to Dublin, but do nothing more, and she apologised if anything she had said about him was hurtful to me.

PART THREE

We were alarmed at the prospect, but he had no intention whatever of coming to us, though he did write and ask me for the fare money to Dublin 'as it will help me to live and pay the rent here'. I sent him five pounds and suggested more modest accommodation than the Gloucester Road hotel from which he wrote to me. I said he would be welcome to come and stay but preferably after our child – expected in May – had been born, adding that of course he was to come in the event of the crisis worsening. I had no idea of how this might be.

Irene solved the material side of his crisis as she had done so many times in the past. She helped him with the immediate problem of where he would live and supplied him with the money to pay the rent. My father survived during the month of February 1962 largely because of her help in finding him a job. Sending him to Ireland, sensible in theory, was impracticable since he simply refused to go. It was more than justified, in terms of making me share the burden of caring for him, but that was not what he wanted and everyone recognised the fact.

As she had done in the past, on so many occasions, Irene took charge. She was practised in the art of looking after my father. She did it because she loved him. It was a hopeless love; it always had been. She got such a poor return, but her dedication to him went on, undimmed. It seems she was overwhelmed by his despair and self-pity. But she loved him for his passion, his energy and his charm. This shone through on the blackest of days.

I have often wondered what really took place in the unspoken parts of conversation between them when she had issued the edicts and conditions under which she would help and he had accepted them in order to go on with his life. She controlled him because she cared for him and, notwithstanding her statements to the contrary, her feelings would not change. This was so patently evident to him, in every word and gesture between them witnessed by me since 1947, that he could and did rest secure at all times in the knowledge that her help would be forthcoming. It underlined the fact that he would always come back to her. She knew that, too. She had been there in the second half of the 1940s, when he was on his own. She had been there during the long love affair with Barbara. She helped when required to do so during his tempestuous marriage to Leslie Alison. She supplied his needs in the short but passionate relationship with Biddie. Always, the ultimate controlling figure in his life was Irene.

She wrote me two long letters at this time, the first, handwritten, was dated 24 January 1962 and has already been quoted. Its main argument was in favour of sending my father to Ireland, impossible to implement and swiftly dropped. She had sold the pass on this anyway by giving him £10. This ensured his rent, allowing him to begin the process of finding a job.

Her second letter to me, dated 7 February, expressed first her shock that he was not with me in Dublin. This staggered her, she said, but then she reported on an immediate meeting with him near her office in Fenchurch Street, 'a stormy quarter of an hour over a cup of coffee in Lyons'. He reported that Biddie was back at her job in the school. 'Nothing more was forthcoming, so the history of that episode is a mystery.'

She gave a long and detailed account in her letter of how his life worked, the impossibility of him successfully holding a job where he had to manage his money. When he needed to drink, he drank, could not pay the rent, and, but for her, ended up in a mess. He needed the residential job where, perhaps in part unwittingly, his employer was a kind of guardian. Repeatedly, sections of his life were lived out in this way, *The Lady* providing what seems to have been an inexhaustible supply of places where his undoubted talent and energy were welcome. This was a truly remarkable 'lifeline' for him over many years. Founded in 1885, and in its early days covering fashion with fine colour plates as illustration, the monthly was a rather greyer affair when he subscribed to it. I doubt he ever read an article. His sole interest was in the lively and extensive personal advertisements for employment, gentlefolk looking for staff who were expected to conform to a certain ethos of respect, hard work and deference. It worked at this level for him, as the many jobs described in this account of his life show.

Having given this account of his peripatetic progress over many years, with her helping him on innumerable occasions, Irene came to the point of present circumstances, the discussion over coffee in the Lyons café.

> After telling him in no uncertain terms what I thought of him for losing his job for the reason that he did, I got up and went. He came too, and I had a few more things to say to him on the pavement. He said he had enough money to get to Hugh's place by bus, so I left him to it, and went back to No. 22 seething with rage. Yesterday I thought, like you, that I couldn't leave him with nothing at all. I rang him up and said that when he got the first reply from *The Lady*, he could telephone me so that I could arrange about a ticket if he wished to go for an interview, and that in the meantime I would let him have 10/- a day by post.

Sadly, those letters, unlike so many others long since thrown away, were kept because they recorded a time when he became engulfed in crisis. Emotional turmoil seemed to surround us all. Worse was to follow.

My father went every day that week to see my brother Hugh,

who was working in Islington and sleeping on a camp bed in a single room there. Hugh had a job in an off-licence, and from there father telephoned Biddie. I think they were still deeply in love. But it is clear that both of them recognised that the situation was hopeless. Father wrote in his diary on 17 February, 'Finished with Biddie.' In a rare expression of self-examination, he wrote the following words across two diary pages:

> So you can see what I have lost at 63 always at the bottom of my heart knowing the loss was inevitable and the hell I have gone through if the world had been different and my age 33 what wonderful happiness would have come of it. During the short time together I was slowly changing and moulding myself but it was too late in life.

He drew a line across the page under those words. He had been reading Hesketh Pearson's *Charles II* and he wrote on again:

> The unity of all life to which human beings aspire can only be felt by two people in love, and a happy married life is the sole human condition that can impart a sense of permanence to an impermanent state – It was a condition for which Charles might have sacrificed all his mistresses and become a monogamist; but he was never deeply in love with anyone and his procession of concubines was his vain attempt to find someone who could appease his yearning for what he had never known.

On 25 February he wrote to Barbara, still working as a teacher in Nantes, France: 'I am in London until I find another job, have advertised and have three interviews this week – if you are coming back to London anyhow (I thought it was March), come back as soon as possible. The only thing is that I may have a job in the country but it won't be far out.'

PART THREE

She marked this letter 'Yes', writing back promptly not once but three times in the following week. On 4 March he wrote to her again, saying he had got a job in Worthing. Three days later he wrote to say, 'Have just been talking to Marg and she wants you back as much as I do.' And he ended it, 'Please come back darling.'

Was that the end of things with Biddie? Had he indeed 'finished' with her? Not at all. The year 1962, which I look back on as 'the crisis year', was gathering pace in an extraordinary way. The early letters to Barbara turned into a rich year of correspondence. There were thirteen letters in all, as there had been in 1961. But also, on 24 March, he rang Biddie in the evening at the school and on 2 April he received letters from Biddie *and* Barbara, both of which he answered promptly that day.

He wrote in his diary the only other entry that had reflective content, a set of seven precepts with the heading 'To Others'. 'Don't talk unnecessarily, don't reminisce, don't become nostalgic, don't philosophise, don't say "Why don't you do that?", don't air your troubles, don't boast of what you have done.' They could almost be modelled on the precepts composed by Jonathan Swift, in 1699, under the title 'When I come to be old'.

He resumed his correspondence with Barbara as though nothing at all had happened. He told her he had taken the job in Worthing. The person who employed him, Mrs Roberts, was a classic example of those people who succumbed to his mixture of practical knowledge, aptitude and charm. The job was not well paid. 'Mrs Roberts is very nice – is quite attractive and about 62 and I think would like to get married again. I don't quite know how the job will go but if there is no increase in money I shall have to find something better – '

The good news was that Barbara was giving up her job in Nantes and coming home. The bad news, expressed in his next, undated letter to her, at the end of March, was that the Worthing job was not satisfactory. 'Mrs Roberts does not know what she really wants and I cannot see that there is anything in it for me especially as there is no social or home life. I live and eat by myself and she does the same.' He ended the letter, 'Come home soon my love. I am waiting for you.'

Mrs Roberts must have sensed that he was dissatisfied since there was a sudden burst of helpful activity. Curtains were made for his room, she was charming to him, 'going to get this and that', so that he felt guilty about writing more letters to others whom he had already approached or met or by whom he had been interviewed.

He went anyway, moving to Box Lane House in Boxmoor, Hertfordshire, a tiny village on the outskirts of Hemel Hempstead beside Boxmoor railway station. The line was the main route to the north-west, running from Euston to Crewe and on to Holyhead and the ferry to Ireland. Barbara came home just after he had moved and returned to her Chelsea flat. He saw her on 21 April. He had his divorce, granted on 12 March, though not made final and absolute until 21 June. But it must have heartened both of them into an immediate rekindling of their earlier plans since he told her in his letter after that meeting, 'I will try to find out about the decree nisi.' A further letter followed midweek, enclosing a railway timetable for Boxmoor trains. He promised another Saturday visit, telling her: 'Am longing to see you again and hope I shall make you happy when we are married – Am working hard today in the sun and feel fit and full of life and also feel today that I may live to 100! By that time you may get bored with me!?'

Our second child, Hugo, was born on 3 May, and letters

were exchanged though none survive. My father was not a worry to us at that time. We knew enough of the job at Boxmoor to be relieved and then relaxed about him. We watched over Hugo with concern, anxiety, tenderness and an overwhelming love. This was not unmixed with the deepest feelings of sadness at the earlier loss of Emma against which this new event was inevitably set.

Father saw Barbara on 19 May, a Saturday, which was usual since only then could he get away; after her name he wrote the initials 'T.H.N.M.' He did sometimes write cryptic messages in his diary; more followed later that year. I have not deciphered fully what this one means, but I suspect the last two letters represent 'No Marriage'. The tone of the letter reinforces this view, since it changes towards a gentler, sadder recognition that all was not well and would not be well. Even the parting line says so:

> Keep on at Barkers [the Kensington store where she had got a job] as long as you can and I will do the same here and don't worry sweetheart, things will sort themselves out. Let me know which is the best day to phone you. I did enjoy my dinner last night – in fact I think we both did with all our worries and many thanks for the shirt, it is a nice one and I am wearing it now. It's going to be a nice day and I am going to do a lot of work. Goodbye for now. My love, George.

There were no letters after that for ten months and no further mention of her name in his diary for that year. The idea of marriage with Barbara, whether or not it was ever entirely serious, was no longer being entertained and would soon be ruled out more firmly by other events. Before that, however, a final wild fling was to attend the great climacteric as it ran its course towards his birthday on 7 November. The Greek term

He That Is Down Need Fear No Fall

means ladder, and the Greeks conceived of it, just as they defined happiness, in terms of a process concluding only in death. Ladders are there to be climbed. But I sometimes think of my father's ladder of life as one that he descended. It seems at times a descent into an abyss. More than once he had demonstrated the frantic nature of his quest and the despair expressed, early on in that year, of having lost at sixty-three the wonderful happiness he might have gained had he been thirty-three. Yet his vitality and determination restored to him once more the strength of Orion, the power of Zeus, the love of Apollo.

PART FOUR

An End to Affairs

XIII

HE MET BIDDIE once again for the day on 31 May 1962. It was a Thursday. He started to record telephone calls to her from then on. He saw her a fortnight later; Thursday must have been her day off. His diary pages in later years were peppered with money amounts spent on his increasingly obsessive betting on horses. Tiny amounts, it has to be said, but set beside the names of countless racehorses of the period. In 1962, however, in the meticulous way he had, he recorded relatively extravagant expenditures on phoning her from Boxmoor. It was her birthday on 26 June. He told her that five days before the event his divorce had become final and absolute. He phoned her on the Sunday; she phoned him the next day and told him her husband was divorcing her. He went to stay with her the first weekend in July.

I had not heard much of him during the summer. In August he and Biddie, with the children, had taken a flat in Frinton-on-Sea in Essex, and in early September he wrote to me to tell me how good it had been there, bathing in the sea every day, with wonderful sunshine. 'It has done me a lot of good and now we are both very busy answering adverts – advertising to get a job together – it is not easy because of the three children but it will be done and we hope for an interview this week.' He was still in Boxmoor; his employers had gone away to France for the month of September. They had told him to take things easy. Nevertheless, he had a host of jobs to do in the garden and the house and wrote to me that he would give them his thorough attention as he had always done. 'Am still a swan here as I have done my job.'

On previous occasions he had been burdened by divorce proceedings, over his first marriage, and then with the rancorous and protracted legal actions between Leslie Alison and himself. Now it was Biddie's turn. She said she would alter her name by deed poll until her own divorce came through. Irene had written to wish him good luck and was moving from London into a bungalow somewhere in the south-east of England. My brother Hugh had gone to sea again. Guy had visited us in Dublin, where he was giving a lecture at the Royal Dublin Society. He was still working in Canada, so this was a brief visit.

Despite the positive tone in my father's letter and the confidence he felt in Biddie's love for him, their life together was clearly overshadowed by problems of what lay in the future. He said in the letter that the rain was pouring down. He had to go out and get more stamps. 'Have answered 21 advertisements and of these four replies, three of which are negative and one possible for interview on Saturday and so you see it is not easy when there are children – most of them say not suitable for children.'

Biddie had advertised as early as March 1962, at a time when he was working in Worthing. 'Secretary, housekeeping, nursing, driver, seeks post, preferably with self-contained accommodation for three children as part salary.' He taped the personal column advertisement from the *Daily Telegraph* into a page of his diary. I found it there nearly half a century later, as I tried to piece together the difficulties they had been facing.

My heart went out to him. We were spending our last summer at Belcamp. Hugo was five months old, a vigorous baby, on whom we lavished our doting if nervous love. I continued working as a sub-editor on *The Irish Times*. And at this stage I was on late night duty, riding home on a motorised scooter so that Mavis could have the car. I was also trying to write a novel. I was editing *The Dubliner*, a literary magazine, and writing feature pieces for the paper.

I determined that I would go over and see my father in England. Guy was there, just before heading back to Canada. Hugh and his family were in Corby; Marion was in London, and Lena in Brighton. I also wanted to see my Aunt Dorothy. So I made a visit. Not many of the details remain with me.

The illusion of safety surrounded George and Biddie and an aura of happiness pervaded them and the children. I was happy with them and for them. I was there on a Sunday and we all went to church, the three children behaving well, my father singing the hymns, contentment breathing like a zephyr over us all. Though I said nothing about it, I was reminded of an earlier time when I had been with three other children, Barbara's two nieces and her nephew, and had experienced the same feeling of contentment. How I longed for it to last now; mostly, I must confess, for his sake. How I doubted that it would. I was not so sure that if it worked out for him, it would necessarily be right for Biddie or the children. Their difficulties, it seemed to me, were enormous.

For whatever reason, the return of his employers led to his departure. 'Finished Boxmoor' was his single diary entry for 29 September. The following pages, through October and November and into December, are almost completely blank, just two addresses that he moved to, the names of the roads only, no mention of what town he was in.

I wrote to Biddie towards the end of October and received a sweet and well-reasoned reply. It seemed to signify that their hopes for a life together with her three children had foundered. I include the full text of the letter. She gives, I am ashamed to say, a warmer picture of her love, compassion and understanding than perhaps the letter does in what it reveals of my own treatment of him. If I could remember more of the detail, I would give that too, but I cannot recall the nature of my censure nor the reasons that gave rise to it. She was involved in the crisis following his departure from Boxmoor; I was viewing it from far off.

> I gave your letter to your father yesterday, and he will be writing to you. I thought I would let you know that he is working – gardening five days a week divided between two gardens near Bishop's Stortford. He has found quite pleasant accommodation in Stortford, and since things have been more settled, has gradually improved in health, and seems quite well now. He is hoping eventually to find work that is easier.
>
> He spends the day with us on Sundays, and we see him once or twice during the week. We took the children to a visiting circus one afternoon, which caused enormous excitement!
>
> Don't be too hard on him, Bruce. Wish him well in the belief that the next 'crisis' will never happen. No one can judge how circumstances may have affected the progress of someone else's life. The good and positive side of him has given me more help, comfort and happiness than any 'responsible' or outwardly successful person.

They had moments of great happiness together and loved each other passionately. I wonder quite what I mean when I say 'nothing came of it'. Nothing did come of it, in the sense in

PART FOUR

which people look upon the building and the making of life as something that will go on and grow in strength and depth. He was right in the despair he expressed, the failure that he recorded at the beginning of 1962, and it is a wonder to me still that he recovered from that and for a few brief months enjoyed happiness and fulfilment, however illusory they may have been in the end.

He spent Christmas with Biddie and was with her into the new year. And then, at some stage in the late winter, they decided to part. While still at an address in Bishop's Stortford, in Hertfordshire, he went up to London. There he had a meeting with Barbara on Sunday, 24 March. He wrote to her the following day, not one letter but two.

'Darling Barbara,' he wrote in the first, 'I did so enjoy yesterday and you were very sweet – we will meet again soon. I got back safely and now have to rush off to beastly work. Feel a bit worried – life is so complicated.' She had come up to town for the day. She was in Hampshire, not in London, but was returning again, possibly at the weekend, and his second letter was an offer to meet her train at Waterloo. He said he was tired and sick of work, and bored too.

It would be ten years before they corresponded again!

My father lived for a further thirteen years, until the summer of 1975. His story, during those years, is no less bizarre than the events so far recounted.

XIV

On 18 April 1963, he wrote to me from Oxford:

> Marjory and I were married yesterday at St Giles Registry and are staying at the above address until Wednesday the 24th April when we go to Bideford. Have taken a furnished cottage until about 1st June by when we hope to have got an unfurnished cottage on the Clovelly Estate – Marjory is very wonderful and we are very much in love with each other. Now about details – we only met a few weeks ago and decided to marry as soon as possible and then live in Devon far from the madding crowd – Biddie met her as we went down to the vicarage and is very pleased – I enclose a snap – Marjory is more my age – 5' 2" and lovely feet – we will come over and see you as soon as practicable and I will write again as soon as we get to Bideford with the new address. We both send our love to you both.

Marjory was a small, West-Country woman with relatives living near to Taunton. She would have been in her early sixties when she met George. She was of a phlegmatic, even resigned, disposition, and it was soon put to the test. I think the visit to us must have disturbed him greatly. He had written to me with further news of the cottage in Clovelly, which he had decorated and where they intended to live. He told me of Guy's intended return from Canada the following year and thanked me for a photograph we had sent of Hugo. Their cottage was on an estate that had belonged to the Asquiths; he joked that 'their powers are still feudal and I believe they can still hang people'. He and Marjory had seen 'the high poohbahs and they are all out to make us comfortable'.

There was a note towards the end, in parenthesis as it were: 'Biddie has sent on my odd bits of stuff and we have a letter occasionally – *No one* in the world will *ever* replace her but it was impossible and I think I am quite lucky. Chips wrote and said something about Providence always seems to help me.'

On receipt of his letter – a total surprise – we sent them our love and invited them over. I wrote and told Irene of their marriage and she sent her love. They eventually came to stay in mid-July.

The visit went off well enough. Far from being 'very much in love,' they bickered constantly in a way that seemed to be motivated by rivalry rather than affection. She did have pretty feet, something my father always admired in women, and nice skin. Her hands were soft and caring – she had been a nurse – but her face was truculent and there was a pouting expression around her mouth. Humorously, and not so humorously, she complained about him quite a bit and from time to time I saw in his eyes the flash or smoulder of anger, quickly suppressed for our benefit. The truth was they hardly knew each other. This was a marriage of convenience and she said as much to us. He was of the same view but did not say it. I was relieved that they had decided to live in her part of England where she had relations. She would need their support, I felt. He was on best behaviour with us and with her but I noted in him certain changes. In appearance he had changed. He was heavier, slightly stooped. From time to time he made himself stand firm and upright, as I had always known him, proud of his seamanlike carriage and handsome appearance. But these were momentary physical gestures of recall. The man as he was saw life differently, and resignation about himself was part of this. It showed most of all in his face. He had at this time grown a goatee beard. His hair was now white and there was little enough of it on the top of his scalp, though he was not bald. In his eyes, when caught unawares, there was the expression of anger and also of fear. With me on my own he talked sometimes of past losses, the most significant of which, at the time, was Biddie. To him Marjory signalled the end of all that, the end of love as he had known it, the end of any possible search for the kind of happiness he had dreamed of finding in all these years during which I had grown up under his shadow.

We must also have talked of Barbara and of Irene, of Kingham and my childhood; and of course he spoke often of the family since all five children had moved back, bringing in and out of his chequered life their own on-the-whole more stable, more focused existences. He dwelt on this aspect in respect of us and was wise and caring in his advice. Hugo was just over a year old. We were still in the same house, the former dairy of Belcamp beside the Griffith family who owned it. Though only six miles from the city centre, the house lay among forty-acre fields in quite remote countryside, a mile or so off the Malahide Road. In his practical way he helped us make up our minds about what we might do, but I felt that this threw into sharper contrast his own limited and confined horizons. And it emphasised what was apparent to us anyway: the tenuous points of contact intellectually, socially even, between my father and Marjory. How they had come to marry was a mystery. Where it would lead them was a source of puzzlement at best, possibly of concern as well. We drove to various places, saw friends, sat out in the sun; and then they returned to Devon.

He engaged immediately after that in a major drinking bout.

PART FOUR

It was of classic proportions, such as I had known when much younger. Marjory at first tried to conceal the magnitude of it, writing us a letter of warm thanks and telling us just that he had been far from well, so that she had not had a minute to spare. He scribbled off the briefest of notes saying he would write in a few days' time when he felt better. She then wrote a more truthful account, of how he had drunk steadily since leaving us, spending everything he had and trying to get credit at the local pub. 'Yesterday I felt I could stand it no longer and told him (not meaning it) to get out, whereupon he drank himself into a stupor, I got the Rector ("a very nice sensible man of the world") to come and help me, he got him round sat with him for ages and sent me to my neighbours to rest a bit – George promised to *try* and today is quite contrite and very sick and very sorry and of course penniless.'

She wondered if her own health would stand up to it. He needed treatment, but wouldn't hear of it. She wondered if I would write and persuade Chips to visit and give her support. She was fearful of George, said he would 'slay' her if he knew she was writing about his drinking bout to any of us.

I replied as best I could, wrote to Chips without expectation of him doing anything and gave her some account of the pattern and frequency of my father's drinking and his powers of recovery as I had known it from childhood. Marjory had given me an address next door to write to, lest my father should see the letter. She was a determined woman and in her plain and ordinary way she appeared to love him. She was a nurse, practical and quite resigned to the tasks he imposed on her. Her comfort and security in old age were in part in his hands and she responded well to him and to his energy and charm when he displayed them. I later had occasion to say to him that he should be kinder to her. This was provoked more by his recovery than his drinking. She wrote again to say: 'George has sobered up at last. I am afraid I upset him very much by threatening to turn him out.'

He was suffering from asthma a good deal and was unable to garden. They both had very little money. He needed a job. But then, at the end of that letter, she wrote in a sweet way, which I found both sad and reassuring, since it demonstrated grit and determination: 'I'll manage somehow, and I shall not really turn him out, don't worry – but I do wish he would be a bit nicer to me unless he is drunk he seems positively to dislike me and heaven knows I've done all I can to make him happy. However don't worry I'm tough and we'll make out. Sorry I bothered you. All the best to you both. Forgive writing it's difficult to write without G. seeing me!'

The drinking episode concluded in mid-August 1963 when he wrote: 'Have had a bad break with the drink, but naturally I get my nerves cracked and there is not enough to do around here – It's all very difficult and hard to find the answer.' And that was that.

The last scenes of all in this melancholy history are dominated by Irene. She was then living on Upper Richmond Road, in Putney. Her attempts to find a place in south-east England having failed, she turned her attention to the West Country, offered my father and Marjory shared accommodation with herself and, as she put it, 'took the plunge', buying a small terraced house in Taunton, a short walk from the railway station. After some work had been done on it, under George's supervision, they all moved in. It was an astonishing development, yet it was one that I saw as an improvement on Marjory and George fending for themselves. Despite her expressions of loyalty and love, indeed of her being tough as well, I felt there was not enough to bind them permanently together. The very fact that he was not as nice or as kind as she desired pointed to this. With the presiding security offered by Irene, this undoubtedly changed. He needed two women to look after him. And bizarre as it all was, becoming even more so with time, it represented to me a satisfactory change that had the benefit of permanence written into their strange agreement.

Irene rationalised what I thought of as an extraordinary, yet not entirely foolish, decision. 'I never had the slightest intention of spending the rest of my life knocking about in bed-sitters!' she wrote, having spent all her life so doing. 'I am not keen on living alone,' she said, having lived that way for nearly the whole of her working life since she had known George. 'Now I do realise that once more I am being, as it were, a port in a storm (which is all I have ever been). They and I will live our separate lives, although they will overlap to some extent of course. I am certainly not going to give up the right to do what I like when I like, and shall be there or go away on visits as I please. It will be in one sense a sort of *ménage à trois*, I suppose, but I am having a tenancy agreement drawn up by my solicitor and shall put everything on a cut-and-dried business-like basis. Your father will do the garden. He will also do the odd jobs, bit of decorating, etc.'

Her long letter, a testament of sorts, dealt with family news, which was as well known to her as to any of us. She also commiserated with me over a visit I had made to Father and Marjory, describing it as 'not as successful as it might have been'. And then she made this comment: 'I have no illusions whatever, I can assure you, that your father's feelings will undergo the slightest change towards me and I really don't care. Between ourselves, I am rather looking forward to making a little use of *him* for a change!'

And so it came to pass that my father, with the woman he had finally chosen to marry after his second divorce, settled down. He was to share a house owned by another woman who, at that time, had loved him constantly and exclusively for twenty years and would go on doing so unwaveringly for another ten. She did so while at the same time accepting that she had only ever been a port in a storm. With ups and downs, and some breaking out on his part, that was how the last decade of his life was shaped. It was constructed for him and managed by women. And it was to end in that *ménage à trois*.

Barbara disappeared from his life for ten years, but was not forgotten. Nor had she gone for ever. They made contact at the very end of 1972. He wrote to her to say, after a telephone conversation, 'it was so lovely to hear your voice again and I'll try to see you in '73 somehow – very likely during the Chelsea Flower Show – every day I think of you, and tunes such as 'Clair de Lune' accentuate the nostalgia.'

True to his word, he went to London for the Chelsea Flower Show the following June, stayed a week with Guy and spent a happy time with Barbara, each of them indulging the other's illusions. They corresponded to the end of the year. In a September letter he put 'XXX' and in brackets beside it '(M did not see these) – Love and kisses from me darling – George.' He came to see us in our house in Glenageary – an old house with an acre of garden that he loved – and told Barbara about this. I sent him and Marjory a Christmas hamper, which is mentioned in a letter which Father wrote to Barbara on 28 December, in which he said 'Of course I shall always love you and at times think we may end our days together.'

He showed signs of failing in 1974 and wrote to her in April of 'a rather rotten relapse', but then recovered and was childishly pleased that he felt important with all the phone calls and visits. Hugh, Guy and I all visited him in turn. Barbara was hard up and he sent her a cheque. 'It should be much more as I owe you a lot for the years gone by, and you were always generous to me – I hate to think of you being hard up – Am myself, but always have been and now it does not worry me much.'

So recovered was he, after the relapse, that we all thought a visit to Dublin might be possible. I was busy at the time, doing a lot of travelling for my paper, a tour of Canada, ten days in Japan, writing articles all the time. These I sent to him, and he pasted them into a huge scrapbook he had begun to keep. In it he even started writing a memoir, beginning with his birth and childhood in Calcutta.

I had by then moved to the *Irish Independent* as political commentator, but when parliament recessed I did travel pieces. I used to send him the articles. They gave him a good sense of my life and he passed them on to Barbara, together with his views of me, of how I wrote well but was rather snobbish. 'He's a great snob, my Brucie! He has not got much time to talk to his father on the phone – I think he is getting a bit swell-headed and is inclined to "brush off" aged father – not as fit as he should be – it makes me more determined to get well.'

He did not get well nor did he travel any more. Barbara sent him photographs of herself and him, and of her sister's three children, Georgiana, Charmian and Ulick, with some news of their lives. He replied, 'It is tragic to think of all those days gone and of course the mistakes we made and cannot do much about now – I seem to have made mistakes all my life.'

I visited him several times during his difficult last summer of 1975. On one occasion my eldest brother Hugh and I were briefly there together. He had been staying and I had just arrived. Many years later he reminded me of this and told me of our walking to Taunton Station together. I was in tears, unable to accept that our father was dying. Looking back on the occasion, Hugh remembered his sense of disappointment that he had not been able to help Father. He had guessed at Father's fear of the unknown and the possible spiritual need as his health broke down. But Hugh felt also that he had made a mess of his last visit. This was partly because of the presence of Marjory. Hugh did not get on with her and this made their last encounter difficult.

He felt that Father was searching for help but didn't want to ask, possibly did not know how to ask. Hugh was naturally vocal about Father's 'badness', as well as seeing his need for help. Whatever he felt he should have said, or even done, he did nothing. Something obtruded, he said. Father was critical of him at the time, irritated by his daily attendance at Mass. There was the added problem of our half-brother, Chips, an Anglican minister, who might have tended better to Father's needs. In the event this did not happen either.

In mid-August, while I was with him, I wrote to Barbara. Marjory and I took it in turns sitting with him through the night. Hugh had visited him the previous week and Guy was flying back from Africa. 'The main problem,' I wrote, 'is sustaining Marjory in the face of his demands, but above all in the face of fatigue. He will not recover. He is impatient – childishly so, as he always was – and the most merciful thing would be an early release. But he is also enormously strong and there are some days when I think he will last forever. Your letter was a great joy to him, and it would be the kindest thing if you could write again soon with news of the family. His memory – like mine – is vivid and very much alive, of the Christmases we all spent in St Leonards and of the summer time with those who are still so firmly fixed in my mind as children: Georgiana, Charmian and Ulick.'

In his earlier letters she had not been aware of how ill he was. Now she wrote in a different, sweeter, more loving way, of what she called her 'Italian garden', with its shabby but nice-coloured flagstones, 'London Pride' and 'what I call semper vivum.' 'The names of the other plants I forget. Bruce says how vivid your memory is – mine is hopeless.' She filled her letter, as I had suggested, with news of Marg, Roberta, and the Loring children, Georgiana, Charmian and Ulick. I think I read the letter to him. He lay in bed and remembered.

That was the end of him being nursed at home. For everybody's sake, he went into Cheddon Road Hospital, on the outskirts of Taunton, on 22 August, a Friday. He died on Monday, 1 September 1975, at 9.30 in the morning. Marjory had been called much earlier and had sat with him for two hours, but he had been in a deep sleep since the previous day and did not wake. He was cremated at the Taunton crematorium two days later. Guy and I were there and Hugh arrived later the same day. Our father's ashes were buried in the grounds.

I wrote to tell Barbara of his death and she replied, thanking me for my letters and saying how glad she was that his last years had been filled with serenity. I had told her of tranquil days and sweet recollections, of his memories of the past and of his strangely powerful recall of our lives together; his with me, ours with her. I omitted references that might have conveyed a different story. But she knew well enough what his life had really been like. She had shared in it for many years. I had said in my letter what a tempestuous life it had been. She replied: 'He had the gift to calm one, and minimise one's troubles. He could be so gentle. I send you much sympathy. You will miss him. He adored you all, you especially.'

Marjory left the house in Taunton and went to live locally with her family. Irene stayed on in the house, where I regularly visited her. She survived for some years afterwards, during which time Marjory died. When Irene was too old to be on her own, she moved into sheltered housing. I continued to visit her. Her circumstances worked well for a time, but then she fell and broke her hip. She was indifferent about her own recovery. The surgeon thought she would not last very long, but I encouraged her. Then I brought her from Somerset to Dublin and we looked after her. She was in a nursing home, very demanding, devouring crossword puzzles and chocolate and occasionally talking about my father. She was clear-headed to the end, with her affairs in impeccable order. Having no Christian faith, she wanted the most modest of funerals. She was cremated and her ashes scattered in our garden. Then, last of all, Barbara died and I came into possession of the letters and put them together with the other documents on which I have drawn for what I can only think of as this love story.

Love stories never end. The love carries within itself a boundless store of rich feelings and they contain the seeds of immortality. The living spirit of love, like a great ocean, flows on. In the case of George and of Barbara, and of those times about which I write, I still feel its force, flowing from him, hitting me like the waves of the sea, pounding on the rocks that surround me, his essence and vitality and energy all still living, as though he also were living. I want others to understand and share in the events and their narrative. It is an unhappy story. He was an unhappy, frustrated man. Yet together with the events and his responses to them, George somehow expresses the line from the Bunyan poem, 'He that is down needs fear no fall' which in the book's title, I am forced to change to the future imperative to meet his matchless immortality, where I assert, as I do, that he will never die, and that his love is spread across the universe and is a mark of his eternal survival, that I suppose in the end I am speaking only for myself. Others in the family who were close to him see him differently. I therefore cannot claim for anyone else the same experience, the same conclusion, nor even that George is the same person. He is as much a creation of my love as he is of his own.